"Texas isn't another planet, Mother. It's part of the United States."

"Don't be condescending, Michelle. And before you accuse me of being snobbish, you have to admit that your sister's daughter would have many more opportunities here in Boston with me."

"Maybe, but she's with her father."

"That may be the only advantage—if, in fact, there is an advantage to living in that backward border town," the older woman said crisply.

"So what exactly do you expect me to do?"

"I want you to see what you can learn about Jacob Evans. Most people have some little secret they don't want exposed. Something that'll make your ex-brother-in-law see that his daughter—my granddaughter—would be better off living with me."

"Mother, that's blackmail. I won't be party to—"

Mrs. Davis stood up and began to arrange the china on the silver tea tray. "I want custody of the girl— whatever the cost."

ABOUT THE AUTHOR

Texas authors Margaret Masten and Saundra Pool, who make up the writing team of Maggie Simpson, are very familiar with the area in which they've set *The Trouble with Texans,* their third Harlequin Superromance. Saundra and her husband have gone downriver on a raft exactly where Jake Evans runs his expeditions in this story. Margaret and her husband have walked some of the river and driven down the highway separating Texas and Mexico. Both couples delight in the contrast between the desert and the green-ribboned oasis along the Rio Grande.

Books by Maggie Simpson

HARLEQUIN SUPERROMANCE
577—BABY BONUS
608—BRINGING UP FATHER

Don't miss any of our special offers. Write to us at the following address for information on our newest releases.

Harlequin Reader Service
U.S.: 3010 Walden Ave., P.O. Box 1325, Buffalo, NY 14269
Canadian: P.O. Box 609, Fort Erie, Ont. L2A 5X3

Maggie Simpson

THE TROUBLE WITH TEXANS

Harlequin Books

TORONTO • NEW YORK • LONDON
AMSTERDAM • PARIS • SYDNEY • HAMBURG
STOCKHOLM • ATHENS • TOKYO • MILAN
MADRID • WARSAW • BUDAPEST • AUCKLAND

ISBN 0-373-70705-3

THE TROUBLE WITH TEXANS

THE TROUBLE WITH TEXANS

PROLOGUE

Sotol Junction, Texas
March 8

PALOMA TARANGO WATCHED as Mike Cochran hunched over the table and shuffled the dominoes. The clicking of the Lucite rectangles as they banged against each other drowned out the rhythmic whir of the overhead paddle fan. Normally, a good game of dominoes relaxed Paloma, but tonight she was worried about more pressing business.

"We got any applications for the teachin' job?" Mike asked, picking out his playing pieces.

She selected seven dominoes and carefully set them on their edges in a curved line. "No, not one. But we only sent out requests last Friday."

Bill Wiley pursed his lips and studied the others as though they were in a high-stakes poker game. "We've gotta find someone pretty soon. It'd be a cryin' shame to bus our kids to Alpine. I knew that last teacher we hired was flighty, but for her to up and quit with only a couple of months to go, why, we oughta have her stripped of her teaching certificate."

"But Bill," Paloma explained for the dozenth time, "she couldn't help it that her husband was transferred to Wyoming. I'm just grateful she agreed to wait until spring break to leave. That gives us a little over two weeks to find a teacher." Paloma tried to sound optimistic, but constantly having to attract a new teacher to the isolated area had begun to wear on her nerves. Not many people found Sotol Junction on the Texas-Mexico border as appealing as Paloma had. For most, it was a place to visit and move on.

"Two weeks. Big deal," Mike said. "She could've waited two months. It was the ethical thing to do." He emphasized his point by swatting a fly that had landed on the corner of the card table. "The school's about all we got left and I sure don't relish the thought of the state closing it down because we don't have a certified teacher."

Prof Broselow played the double six, moved his marker for twenty points, then rocked back in his folding chair and propped one arm on the other while he stroked his goatee. "I think she did right. A woman's place is with her husband." He grinned at Paloma.

She returned his smile with a withering look which he missed as the other three school-board members entered the boardroom. Actually, she liked his gentle taunts and had enjoyed sparring with him since he'd retired to Sotol Junction three years earlier.

She turned her dominoes facedown. "No cheating," she warned the others. Rising from her chair, she nodded to each man as they took a seat at the long oak table. "Hello, Juan, Ramon, Jake."

"Evening." Jake Evans returned her nod while Ramon and Juan carefully laid their hats brim up along the counter beside a pot of percolating coffee. "Are you winning, Paloma?" he asked.

"Of course. Don't I always?" Paloma liked Jake Evans, too, and well understood his reasons for changing his life-style when he'd moved to Sotol Junction. She suspected he'd never worn his hair in a ponytail when he was a stockbroker, but now his black hair was pulled back in a "girly" style that was a clear irritant to Bill Wiley who'd been born in Brewster County and thought he should be running it.

"We let the little lady beat us occasionally." Prof readjusted his glasses. "It makes her feel important."

"Well, right now the little lady is too concerned about other things to waste time arguing with you. Let's see what we can get done about hiring a new teacher." Paloma banged her hand on the table. "I call this meeting to order."

CHAPTER ONE

Boston, Massachusetts
March 10

"SOTOL JUNCTION?" Without taking her eyes off her mother's face, Michelle Davis leaned forward and set her plate on the antique coffee table with enough force to rattle the delicate china cup. "You want me to go to Sotol Junction? In Texas?"

"Yes, dear." Elizabeth sounded as if she was merely asking Michelle to help with a local charity ball.

"I can't just quit my job. It's the middle of March." But even as she said the words, Michelle felt intrigued by the idea. Television images of drugstore cowboys and cowgirls swinging to country music flashed before her eyes, superimposed on the urban sprawl of Houston, the only place in Texas she'd ever visited.

"Of course you can. You could ask for a leave of absence. Finding a teacher to fill in for you at St. Mary's shouldn't be difficult. Besides, I'm only asking for two months of your time. And this is about *family*." Elizabeth gently emphasized the word.

Michelle had been raised on "family." Her mother was very conscious of the Davis's position in Boston society, and she wielded a lot of power to maintain it. Her biggest disappointments had been Michelle's choice of occupation and her eldest daughter Dee-Dee's choice of husband, Jacob Evans. Now it was driving Elizabeth crazy that Jacob had custody of her only granddaughter, Brooke.

Michelle sighed and asked the obvious question, "Why do you think I need to go to Texas? Jacob can take care of Brooke without our interference."

Elizabeth stirred her tea without making a sound, a feat Michelle had never quite mastered. "I'm not so sure. Jacob refuses to allow Brooke to spend the summer here with me."

"He probably doesn't want to be separated from her for that long. I'm sure he'll agree to the usual two weeks. He's always been more than generous about holidays and vacations." Elizabeth acted as though she hadn't heard Michelle, something she often did if the conversation wasn't going her way.

"Mother, you've never been happy about Jacob having custody of Brooke, but he's had her since he and DeeDee were divorced. It really was better for Brooke to live with her father and have a stable home rather than traipse around Europe with DeeDee and her new husband, or worse, be sent to a boarding school. And now that DeeDee is—is gone, nothing has really changed."

"I know. But at least, when DeeDee was alive—" Elizabeth swallowed and straightened her shoulders

"—Brooke spent some time with her and saw a bit more of life than is offered in Sotol Junction."

"Texas isn't another planet. It *is* a part of the United States, you know."

"Don't be condescending, Michelle. Of course it isn't the end of the world. But before you accuse me of being snobbish, you have to admit that many opportunities are denied her there."

"True, but she's with her father." Michelle thought about the students in the boarding school where she taught. They took horseback-riding lessons, music lessons, attended celebrity lectures and had all kinds of opportunities, but they didn't have a parent to comfort them at night. Brooke did.

"I can think of no other advantage, if *that's* an advantage, to living in that backward border town," Elizabeth said crisply. "When I spoke to Brooke on the phone this morning, she gave me some startling news. Her school's teacher has resigned and if a new teacher isn't found immediately, Brooke may have to be bused to Alpine an hour and a half away. I just can't stand the thought of the child making the trip twice a day when it can easily be avoided."

"So...you want me to quit my job immediately and go down there to teach in a one-room schoolhouse?" Michelle asked incredulously.

Elizabeth frowned. "I simply want you to take a leave of absence. Besides, it isn't as though you need that job."

Her mother's comment irritated Michelle, but again she had to admit the suggestion was strangely appealing. St. Mary's School for Girls prided itself on its staid and proper curriculum for its staid and proper young ladies. Nothing exciting had happened since Sarah Worthington ran away with her boyfriend three years ago, and Mr. J. C. Worthington III had threatened to withdraw his contribution to the building fund. The headmistress still referred to the incident as "a dark time in St. Mary's history."

Michelle was not an impulsive person. She always thought through every move she made, weighing all the consequences. Every now and then, she wondered what it would be like to be more like her sister DeeDee had been and do something just for adventure. But DeeDee's adventures had had a way of misfiring, and Michelle had learned from observing her as they grew up that it was better to play things safe. "No, Mother, I can't . . ."

"Think of your sister. You owe it to her to do what you can for her little girl."

Michelle and DeeDee had never been close. DeeDee had been several years older and more interested in the social side of being a Davis. Michelle was quieter, more reserved. She'd been interested in the volunteer and philanthropic efforts of their family. Until her father's death five years earlier, she and he had worked together for several good causes.

Michelle knew her mother was trying to manipulate her, as usual. It might be time for a change, to escape Elizabeth's control, to experience other parts of the States. And the Southwest did have a certain raw appeal. Then, too, there was nothing really to keep her in Boston. Her relationship with Brent Paxton was going nowhere. They'd dated for eighteen months, but if he called and begged off at the last minute, she was only mildly annoyed at the inconvenience. Perhaps putting some miles between them could help her make sense of her ambivalent feelings. She looked at her mother. "Two months. That's all?"

"I believe so, except . . ."

"Except?"

"You know how I feel about Brooke's situation, and I'd be remiss if I didn't do something." Elizabeth Davis smoothed her skirt and sighed deeply before leaning toward her daughter.

"Do what?" Michelle asked.

"I'm . . . I'm not sure that Brooke is being properly cared for. I mean, well, before—before DeeDee's accident, Brooke was supervised when traveling with her mother in the summer." Her voice caught and she looked down at the carpet for a moment. Though almost two years had passed since a private plane crash had taken the life of her daughter and new son-in-law, Elizabeth still would not use the word *death* when speaking of DeeDee. "But now, the situation is quite different. From what I can tell, Brooke is often unsupervised when she's not in school. She's not quite nine years old, and on her own for hours on end. It would be much better for her to live here. With me."

"What does that have to do with my teaching in Sotol Junction?"

"While you're there, I want you to see what you can learn about Jacob Evans. Almost everyone has some little secret they don't want exposed."

"Mother, that's blackmail. I won't be a party to..."

Elizabeth stood up and began to arrange the china on the silver tea tray. "I want custody of Brooke—whatever the cost."

Sotol Junction, Texas
March 15

"I SAY WE'RE MAKING a big mistake if we hire her." Jake Evans tossed the application onto the table and got up to pour himself another cup of coffee. Only the creaks of the worn but highly polished pine floor reacting to his weight broke the silence. His ex-sister-in-law. Why the hell did she want the job? Since Sotol Junction needed a teacher desperately, he'd have to make a good case to get the other members of the Brewster County school board to agree with him not to consider the application.

He studied Paloma Tarango, the board president, who was in her early fifties, but who looked every bit of sixty after spending years in the sun. He liked her. After all, she'd had a hand in seeing that the small community had accepted him four years earlier. He tried to read her thoughts in her weathered face, but failed.

He scanned his fellow board members. To his left was Mike Cochran, his partner in Junction Outfitters. Across from Mike sat Ramon Abalos, a very influential local rancher, then Prof Broselow, Bill Wiley and Juan Lopez completed the circle. They were a confident group used to taking their own easy time making a decision, but hell, they needed a teacher. Now.

Mike leaned forward to pick up the packet Jake had tossed on the table. "Even if we didn't have to hire a teacher, just look at this application. I've never seen anything like it." He flipped about halfway through the portfolio that had been sent express mail. "Look at the projects the woman has developed. I think she would be good for our kids. Besides, we have to hire a teacher tonight, no more postponements. We've simply run out of time." Mike emphasized his last words.

Ramon picked up the few remaining applications. "Paloma and I called about most of these applicants." Slapping down the forms one at a time, he said, "This one has been in four different schools in four years, which tells me a lot. This one had constant trouble with parents at the last school where she taught." He hesitated as he looked at an attachment to the next application, "This fella's had some trouble with the law," he said before slapping it down on the growing pile. "And these last three were just spit out of college. Our kids deserve an experienced teacher." He eyed Jake. "You know how much trouble we've had finding someone who was willing to teach six grade levels in a one-room school this far from a city.''

Jake nodded. "Yeah, I do. And that's exactly my point. There must be something wrong with Ms. Davis for her to want this job.''

"It's unlike you to be so against someone without reason.'' Paloma leaned forward and idly rubbed the eraser of her pencil against the well-worn oak. "According to her references, she's not only highly qualified, but resourceful. When I called the school where she teaches, the headmistress said Ms. Davis wants to get out of the city for a while. Apparently, she said she is a bit of a do-gooder and thinks this would be a good place to do good.'' All the board members laughed except Jake.

Paloma continued, "Why are you so opposed to her when you've not voiced the same reservations about the other applicants?''

Jake leaned back in his chair and crossed his arms. He had to tell them. "She used to be my sister-in-law. And if Michelle Davis is anything like her sister, the Texas-Mexico border is no place for her.''

"Ah.'' Mike nodded in apparent understanding. "That paints a slightly different picture. Does that mean you have some inside information we need to know?''

"No, I've only met her a few times. Haven't seen her since Brooke was born. It's just that she's a city girl from the East. Pampered. I think we need a teacher with a different background.'' His memory of his bride's kid sister had faded. But he knew the type—a socialite more interested in shopping than in helping kids. She'd probably become a teacher as a lark.

''I see what you mean. A Yankee just might have trouble fittin' in down here.'' Bill patted his palm on the table for effect.

Jake knew he had to latch on to every bit of support he could get. ''You're right. And after she gets a load of this place...'' He conjured up all the negatives he could think of. ''The scorpions, the remoteness, the scorching heat, she'll be gone. And we'll be stuck without a teacher again.''

''Jake, we all respect your opinion and definitely understand your reservations, but we're in a bind,'' Paloma said. ''We have to do what we think is best for our children. That means personal feelings shouldn't influence our decision.''

''I've voiced my opinion,'' he said. ''You folks do what you have to do.'' He listened as the others discussed the pros and cons of hiring an Easterner, and of Brooke's having her aunt for a teacher.

Finally, Ramon said, ''I need to get home. I've got a mare that could foal any time. I make a motion we take a vote to hire Michelle Davis, even if she wants to go back East thirty minutes after school's out for the summer. That'll give us a little time to find someone else for next fall.''

The others nodded.

"A motion has been made by Ramon Abalos that we hire Ms. Michelle Davis," Paloma said. "Do I hear a second?"

Mike said, "Second." Turning to Jake, he lowered his voice, "Sorry to upset you, buddy, but she's our best choice."

"Okay," Paloma said, looking at Jake, "if there's no further discussion, all in favor, raise your hand."

Jake watched five people indicate approval, but he couldn't make himself go along with them. Michelle was up to something other than "doing good." He was sure of it. He'd bet anything Elizabeth had put her up to this.

"Opposed?"

"Well, I think I'm gonna put my money on Jake this round, folks," Bill Wiley said and raised his right hand. "I mean, I've got a kid in that school that I have to think about."

Jake shrugged, then, he, too, raised his right hand in objection.

"Let the record show that Jake Evans and Bill Wiley oppose the hiring of Michelle Davis for the position of elementary-school teacher," Paloma said. "Now we've got a game of dominoes to finish."

March 20

THE WEST TEXAS landscape didn't improve as Michelle neared Sotol Junction. It was all so brown! Only a few scraggly cacti and spots of purple wildflowers softened the rocky hills bordering both sides of the highway. Ancient, rugged mountains jutted from the desert floor in the distance. The great monochromatic blanket stretched to the horizon in every direction, making her slightly nauseated. The nearest thing to it she'd experienced was sailing in the Atlantic. The same feeling of insignificance washed over her. It was hard to believe this place was on the same planet as Boston with its surrounding hills and woods, much less in the same country.

Already she missed the lush green trees of New England. Why had she agreed to come here? Even after mailing her application, she hadn't been certain she would accept the job if it was offered to her. That was, until Jacob had called her mother and suggested Michelle refuse the position. There had to be a reason he didn't want her in Sotol Junction, and the most logical one was that she would find out Brooke was being neglected. Her first allegiance was to her family, and if Brooke needed her, Michelle would go anywhere in the world—and that included Sotol Junction.

Besides, the idea of teaching in a one-room school was exciting. She could bring new experiences and ideas to these underprivileged children. She could really make a difference to their lives.

Ms. Delmonico, the headmistress at St. Mary's, had agreed that it would be the opportunity of a lifetime, and she'd promised not to hire a permanent replacement. Knowing she had a job waiting for her back

East reassured Michelle as she drove down the lonely highway that stretched for miles in front of her.

Heat waves glinted across the asphalt creating a mirage of water, only to flash farther up the road as she approached them. Considering she hadn't met another vehicle for twenty miles, she decided she'd certainly hate to have car trouble in such a desolate place. She took a sip of the now-tepid soda she'd purchased more than an hour ago. It tasted terrible. She fiddled with the radio for a while, but snapped it off after five futile minutes of trying to find a station broadcasting in English.

Rounding one of the foothills, she was surprised to find she had arrived. At least, that's what the sign said: Sotol Junction. Population: 63

On one side of the road, several adobe dwellings blended with the land. On the other side was a stretch of two-story buildings that looked like a Western movie set. A tour bus filled with senior citizens pulled out of the dirt parking lot revealing a string of cars with out-of-state license plates lined up in front of a rustic boardwalk. Michelle pulled into a vacant spot and waited for the dust to settle before opening the door.

The instructions she'd received had said to meet Paloma Tarango, the president of the school board, at her pottery gallery in the shopping strip. Trying to erase the signs of hours driving, Michelle slipped on a pair of pumps, touched up her makeup and smoothed the tan linen skirt and white blouse she'd chosen to wear that morning. Satisfied she'd pass muster, Michelle strolled along the boardwalk looking at the string of shops, but when she found the art gallery, she also found a note tacked on the door: *"Be right back."*

Michelle sighed. She'd pushed hard to complete the drive from Boston in three days so she'd have the weekend to prepare for school on Monday. She hadn't bargained on having to search for this woman named Paloma.

She decided to start her hunt at one end of the boardwalk and work her way down. The first store was an old-fashioned drugstore with a high ceiling and tourist paraphernalia piled on shelves. A balding man with wire-framed glasses and a neatly trimmed goatee looked up from a domino game. "May I help you?" he asked in a well-modulated voice.

"Yes. Do you know where I can find Paloma Tarango? Her business was closed a few minutes ago."

"Sometimes she closes up to go visit someone in another store. Just walk down the boardwalk. She'll be there somewhere. Say, by any chance, are you Michelle Davis, our new teacher?"

"Yes, I'm Michelle Davis."

"Well, little lady, we've been waiting for you all day. I'm Prof Broselow, the proprietor of this drugstore, retired history professor and a member of the school board that hired you. Pleased to make your acquaintance." He stood and offered her his hand.

"Hello. I'm glad to be here, Mr. Broselow."

"Prof. Call me Prof." He turned and gestured toward the other man at the table. "This is Bill Wiley."

Michelle had never seen such long, skinny legs unfold before the man named Bill stood up. The man had to be six-six, and she'd swear four feet of that was legs.

"Ma'am." He removed his hat and sized her up. "I've got a son who's gonna be in your class."

Michelle wondered if the boy looked like his father. "I'll look forward to meeting him, Mr. Wiley."

After a short conversation with the two men, Michelle walked past Paloma's locked door to the next place of business, the general store. Everything she could imagine was crammed onto shelves stacked to the ceiling. The aisles were narrow, only allowing one person at a time to pass through. If Paloma was in there, Michelle didn't see her. Coming outside again, she noticed the sun had dipped behind the mountains. If she wanted to get settled in before dark, she would have to find her hostess soon.

Trying not to lose her patience, Michelle stopped and looked through the next window into the tiny post office. It was empty; so was the restaurant. Only one store left. Junction Outfitters. According to her mother, this was Jacob's business.

Jacob. A man she hadn't seen in the eight years since Brooke was born. Even then, the two days she'd been in Houston with her mother and sister, Jacob had spent most of his time at work. Her lingering impressions of him were of a tall man wearing starched white shirts and expensive dark suits. A bit stuffy. Self-important. She wondered what he looked like now. He would be in his mid-thirties. Twenty pounds heavier? Balding?

She reached for the door handle, then stopped. No doubt, he would have questions to ask her, questions she would prefer to wait until tomorrow, when she was rested, to answer. Yet, her desire to get settled in was stronger than her reluctance to talk to Jacob. Taking a deep breath and squaring her shoulders, she opened the door and stepped inside. When the door chime rang, two women seated at a small table stopped their conversation and looked up. The younger of the women, a petite blonde, set down a cup of coffee. "May I help you?" she asked in a wavering voice.

Michelle wondered what caused her white, drawn face and red eyes. "Yes, I'm looking for Paloma Tarango."

The older woman rose to her feet, her denim skirt stopping just short of the floor. A mustard-colored suede vest topped a plaid shirt, a silver concho belt cinched the shirt at her waist. Her thick, black hair was laced with silver strands.

The woman stepped forward and offered her hand. In a rich voice, she said, "That would be me. You must be Michelle Davis. I'm sorry I wasn't at the store when you arrived, but when Cynthia needed me, I came right over," Paloma explained.

Michelle felt she'd just met a friend. "Yes, I'm Michelle Davis."

"And this is Cynthia Cochran."

The blond woman stepped forward wiping her palms on her shorts before she extended her hand. "Welcome to Sotol Junction, Michelle. I'm sure you're tired after that long drive."

"Yes, I'm ready to get moved in, but I'd like to see Brooke first."

"She and my daughter Katy are out messing around somewhere. They'll be in shortly," Cynthia said, glancing out the window. "Paloma and I . . . with the help of the girls . . . did our best to get the house in shape for you."

"Thank you for all your trouble. I can't wait to see it. I'm really looking forward to a nice bath and a soft bed."

Paloma said, "I think we have everything ready. The telephone and TV were hooked up this morning."

Before Michelle could reply, Cynthia returned from her post by the window. "I know you're anxious to get there," she said, "but something's come up. Our driver, Greg, should get back soon with Mike—he's my husband—and Jake and the other river runners. One of them was bitten by a rattlesnake on the river today."

Oh, Lord, Michelle thought, her attention riveted. Ever since someone had thrown a garden snake at her one year at summer camp, Michelle had been terrified of snakes. Even now, she refused to go into the reptile house at the zoo. Still, she tried her best not to let the women see how the news affected her. "A snake?"

"Yes," Paloma answered. "But we don't know who it was or how badly he's hurt. Another group of river runners passed them and relayed a message for an ambulance to come to the mouth of the canyon."

"You don't know if the person's okay? Can't you contact them or something?" Michelle asked.

Cynthia shook her head. "No, we put our rafts in the river about a quarter of a mile from here and pick them up twelve miles down the river. We can't reach them during that time."

Michelle was surprised. "You don't have radios or cellular phones?"

"No, not in the rafts. They won't work in the canyon. If a group gets into trouble, they have to float out and use the emergency phone at the mouth of the canyon."

"Don't people die from snakebites?" Michelle was sorry for her words the minute she said them. Cynthia gasped and put her hand over her mouth.

"Very seldom." Paloma placed her arm around Cynthia, and sent a pleading look to Michelle. "All of our guides are trained Emergency Medical Technicians and carry medical supplies."

"Is there anything I can do to help?" Michelle asked.

"No, thanks. We just have to wait." Cynthia tried to smile. At the sound of running footsteps along the boardwalk, she whispered, "That's Katy and Brooke. Don't say anything in front of them."

Two little girls, with hair sticking out of ponytails and dirt smudging their shorts, barged in the front door. "Aunt Michelle! Aunt Michelle!" Brooke flung herself at Michelle. "I heard you were here."

Michelle hugged her niece and tucked loose strands of Brooke's hair behind her ears, all the while noting that the child had apparently been running around town unsupervised while Jacob was out on the river possibly dying from a snakebite. Elizabeth had been right to be concerned, she decided.

"Have you seen your house yet? Me and Katy fixed it up for you. There's even an extra bedroom. For me and Katy to spend the night with you." The little girls giggled.

"That'll be great." Michelle pulled her close. She'd made the right decision to come here. She and Brooke would have a good time for two months. Just then, the sound of tires crunching on the caliche road outside the store diverted everyone's attention.

"There's the van. Thank God," Cynthia yelled as she rushed past Michelle and out the door.

"Aunt Michelle, I've gotta go clean up before Daddy sees me like this," Brooke squealed. "He told me to stay away from the river, and if he sees the mud, I'll be in trouble, bi-i-ig time. See you later." With that, she hurried to the rear of the store.

From behind the plate-glass window of Junction Outfitters, Michelle watched as people piled out of the van. Cynthia and Paloma had disappeared in the crowd gathered around the vehicle. A man gestured toward the north and patted Cynthia on the shoulder before she and Katy hurried to a Jeep and sped off.

Dread crept through Michelle's body. She hung back, reluctant to go outside. She wondered who had been bitten. Was it a tourist, or Cynthia's husband, Mike? Or Jacob? As she clutched the doorjamb she searched the crowd looking for a middle-aged yuppie who could be Brooke's father.

One man caught her attention. He was tall, well over six feet. Cutoff jeans and a tank top revealed well-muscled arms and legs hardened by hours of rowing. His skin was a deep bronze and his raven hair was tied back in a ponytail. Michelle couldn't see his face clearly in the fading sunlight, but deepening shadows accentuated the angles of his body as he moved through the small crowd still clustered in front of the store. When he turned his head, the light glinted off a tiny gold earring in his left ear.

A modern-day river pirate! Who was he? Probably a tourist. But there was something about him that affected her. She looked away and rubbed her arms to prevent the shudder that threatened to envelope her.

Again, she searched the group for Jacob. Where could he be? she wondered. A loud clomping sound interrupted her thoughts.

Running up the boardwalk, Brooke was yelling, "Daddy! Daddy!"

Michelle stepped outside into the heat at the same time the pirate turned. A big smile lit his handsome face as he picked up the little girl and swung her into his arms.

Jacob!

CHAPTER TWO

AFTER KISSING and hugging her father, Brooke slid out of his arms and tugged him toward the boardwalk. "Guess what, Daddy. Aunt Michelle's here."

Michelle took a deep breath as the man walked toward her. The smile was gone, replaced by a frown and tense facial muscles. If she could have seen into his eyes in the dim light, she knew they would have held displeasure.

He stopped in front of Michelle and looked at her hard. "Why did you come here?"

She released the breath she'd been holding. She'd expected him to be hostile about her arrival, but she hadn't thought his opposition would be so direct. "I'm here to teach. You didn't think your phone call to Mother would dissuade me from coming, did you?"

"Not really, but it was worth a try. Knowing your family, I should have realized you would consider it a challenge." The shadows along the boardwalk hid one side of his face, but Michelle didn't need to see all his features to feel the barely controlled animosity he was trying to hide from his daughter who was still clutching his hand and peering at the two adults with puzzlement.

He was right. It *was* a challenge. "I know you don't want..."

"Let's continue this conversation later," he interrupted, nodding almost imperceptibly toward Brooke.

"Of course." His sensitivity to his daughter didn't fit with the image she'd formed of her sister's ex-husband who, according to DeeDee, had been so insensitive to his wife's needs. Michelle couldn't say she was eager to continue their conversation, but knew it was inevitable. Her gaze never wavered from his as she changed the subject. "How is the person who was bitten by the snake?"

"We don't know. The ambulance took Mike to Alpine for stabilization before he's airlifted to Lubbock for treatment. It'll be tomorrow before we know much of anything."

"You said Mike? Isn't that Cynthia's husband?"

"Yes."

Paloma, who had been standing nearby, looking anxious, asked, "What kind of snake was it? Not a Mojave...?"

"No. A Western diamondback. It appeared to be a shallow bite. At least, that's what we're hoping."

"Thank goodness. We were so worried," Paloma said.

"What's a Mojave and how is its bite worse than a diamondback's?" Michelle asked.

"It's a type of rattler," Jake answered, "but a bite from a Mojave can cause respiratory failure within a few hours. If you're in the canyon, that's fatal. The diamondback's venom gives us a little more time. Mike's going to be out of circulation for a while. Cynthia's promised to call in as soon as she knows something specific. Now, ladies, if you'll excuse me, I've got some work to do."

Paloma brushed a strand of hair away from her face and nodded. "I know you do, Jake, but could I speak to you for a minute?"

"Sure." He turned to Michelle. "Would you excuse us?" Without waiting for an answer, he led Paloma through the group of vacationers and stopped in front of her gallery.

Jake had known Michelle was expected today, but he'd hoped she'd be safely in her house before he got off the river. He'd planned to avoid her as much as possible. She was a problem he didn't need at this point. Not that she wasn't an attractive problem. The self-conscious teenager he remembered had grown into a beauty, but beauty or not, he didn't trust her motives for coming to Sotol. And he hadn't counted on her arriving in the middle of a disaster. His best friend and partner could have died on the river today.

"Jake." Paloma repeated his name when he didn't respond. "Jake?"

"Uh . . . sorry. What were you saying?"

"I know you're concerned about Mike . . . and about Michelle being here, but I've got a feeling Michelle will do well, so don't worry about her," Paloma reassured him. "And Mike, he's tough. Now, I need a favor. I want to catch Cynthia before she leaves her house. She shouldn't drive herself to Alpine. I'd planned to take care of Michelle before you got back, but with all the excitement..." Her voice trailed off almost apologetically.

"And...?" He felt a sense of impending doom.

"Would you mind showing Michelle to her house? It's on your way home," she said before he could interrupt. She dug a set of keys from the pocket of her skirt and held them up to Jake.

He looked over Paloma's shoulder at Michelle, who was talking to Brooke. "Can't Greg take her? I need to close the store and get things ready for tomorrow. I promised Mike I wouldn't cancel any of the scheduled trips."

"Yes, Greg could, but she's *your* sister-in-law." She patted his arm and continued, "I'm sure the two of you have a lot of catching up to do."

Jake wasn't in the mood to catch up. He wasn't in the mood to display artificial manners, either. He was tired and upset. All he wanted to do was get ready for tomorrow, then go home with Brooke and plop down on the sofa. Grab a beer—anything to ease the muscles slowly tightening across his upper back. He ached from the effort of struggling against the current to get Mike help as fast as possible. He didn't want another battle—especially with Michelle Davis—at least not until morning.

Paloma's eyes bored into him. "Damn!" he swore under his breath. "You know how I feel about her being here." Paloma's gaze never wavered. "Okay," he said, taking the keys to the teacher's house. "I'll see that she's taken care of."

He decided he wouldn't stay long at the house. Deliver her there, maybe unlock the door if she couldn't get the lock to work and say good-night. She probably wasn't anxious to talk with him any more than he wanted to talk with her, so there was no danger that she'd invite him in. Hell, she had work to do, too, like unloading her belongings. The thought of moving boxes elicited a groan from his aching body.

BROOKE WAS CHATTERING like a magpie, but Michelle was too tired to really concentrate on what she was saying. Then, too, she was partially focused on Jacob and Paloma, wondering what they were talking about.

When they started her way, Michelle unconsciously straightened her shoulders, expecting bad news of some sort.

"Michelle—" Paloma gestured with her hands "—I'm afraid I can't take you to your house right now." She explained about going to the hospital with Cynthia and Katy. "Jake has agreed to show you where it is."

"It's not a problem. Of course you have to go." Michelle smiled, though her heart felt as if it had sunk to her stomach. She glanced at the churlish look on

Jacob's face. "I appreciate your kindness, Jacob, but if you'll just tell me where the house is, I can find my own way. You must have a million other things to do, considering what's happened."

"They can wait," Jacob said.

Paloma added, "Jake is more than happy to help you get settled in." She said good-night to everyone, then got in her car and disappeared down the road Cynthia had taken a few minutes earlier.

Without glancing up at his face, Michelle knew that Jacob would be happy to send her back to Boston, not help her settle in.

He palmed the keys he'd been dangling and shoved them in the front pocket of his cutoffs. "I've got a few things to do here before I can leave."

Michelle watched him disappear behind the van before she sat down beside Brooke on the boardwalk. She patted her niece's knee, and said, "I know you're worried about Katy's dad, but he'll be fine."

Brooke nodded in agreement. "I know he will, Daddy says he's a real tough guy. He says it takes real tough people to live in Sotol Junction. Are you tough, Aunt Michelle?"

"I think so." Michelle didn't know for sure because she'd never had to be "tough."

Sitting on the wooden steps, they waited while Jacob and Greg cleaned out the van. Michelle's attention was divided between the small girl at her side and the man unloading the vehicle. In place of the soft-looking, pale man Michelle remembered, was a chiseled athlete whose lithe, lean body reminded her of a cross-country runner.

Carrying the last armload of equipment up the steps, Jacob paused and glanced over at his daughter. "Angel, would you get the door?"

Brooke jumped up, opened the door and followed her father into Junction Outfitters.

Michelle leaned back against a support post, wrapped her arms around her chest and enjoyed the stillness. She could hear Jacob's rich baritone. It floated around her into the twilight filtering over the tiny village. What was it about the man that she found so unsettling? Since his arrival less than an hour ago, she had been aware of his every move, every sound, every nuance. Even now as she heard the door swing open behind her, she felt his presence. She rose to her feet.

Motioning toward an old pickup truck parked by the side of the building, he said, "All set. Just follow me."

Brooke asked, "Daddy, can I ride with Aunt Michelle? Please?"

"I don't think..." Jacob began before glancing down at his daughter. Then he said, "Sure. Go ahead."

Michelle took her niece's hand and led her toward her white sports car. She watched Jacob climb into the dusty pickup he'd pointed out a moment before. It was hard to distinguish its color from that of the surrounding road and buildings. She couldn't picture

DeeDee getting into such a rig. It was as unlike the green Jaguar her sister had driven while married to Jacob as it could get. Of course, DeeDee had always been concerned about appearances.

In the fading sunlight, Michelle followed Jacob down a winding caliche road bordered by dilapidated fences and flat-topped houses. Not more than a hundred yards down a meandering path, the brake lights in front of her flashed and the pickup swerved to the left. What was he doing? Michelle slowed down—but not in time.

In the middle of the road, something white flashed in her path. Michelle slammed on the brakes a split second before she felt and heard a sickening thud against the car's right fender. "What on earth . . . ?" A sudden fear clutched at her heart. She reached over to her niece. "Brooke, are you all right?"

"Yeah, let's see what you hit." Brooke practically bubbled with excitement as she unbuckled her seat belt and scrambled out the passenger door.

Up ahead, Michelle saw Jacob's pickup turn and head back toward them. She had to get out now, but wasn't sure her legs would hold her. She fought the dread that enveloped her when she swung open her door. What had she hit? As she rounded the front bumper, Brooke fell in beside her.

"It's a *cabritto*," Brooke said.

On the ground lay a small black-and-white goat. Michelle felt sick as she dropped to her knees to check the animal. Mercifully it was dead. Had it been someone's pet or had she killed someone's means of support? Either way, she'd just made a fine impression, she was sure. For twelve years she'd driven the congested streets of Boston without hitting anything, and now, on a lonely road in the middle of nowhere, she'd killed a goat. What a way to begin her new job!

Jacob pulled up and got out. Michelle could just imagine his thoughts about her driving. He might not let Brooke ride with her again. "I didn't see it in time." She started to explain.

"There was no way you could have," he agreed. "Are you both okay?"

"I'm fine," Brooke said. "Aunt Michelle made me buckle up."

"That's good." He turned toward the sound of barking dogs in a nearby yard.

Michelle watched a middle-aged man come out on the porch of a nearby house. The man looked around and scolded the dogs. *"Qué pasa, perros?"*

Michelle had learned enough Spanish in college to know he'd asked what was going on. Then the man noticed the vehicles in the road, and he started toward them, buttoning his shirt as he walked.

Brooke whispered to Michelle, "Here comes Eduardo. It's his goat."

Michelle asked, "What should I do?"

"Let me handle it." Jacob stepped forward to meet the man. He shook his hand. "There's been an accident, Eduardo. Ms. Davis, the new teacher, is sorry she hit your goat."

"Ay! Mi cabritto." The man said sorrowfully while shaking his head, even though he didn't approach the goat or even give it more than a casual glance.

Michelle said, "I'm sorry... I didn't see him... I'll pay you for him. How much do you want?"

The man seemed to mull it over. "For my son, this *cabritto* was like a pet. They grow up together. For it to die like this will break my Pablo's heart."

Michelle felt even worse. "I..."

"No money can replace it, but maybe...maybe two hundred dollars for my little *cabritto* will help." The man's voice was downright pitiful.

Jacob muffled a cough.

"I'll go get my purse." Michelle started to walk away, when she felt Jacob's fingers on her arm. She stopped and looked up at him.

He turned to Eduardo and said, "I know how much this goat means to you, Eduardo, but you've only had him a couple of weeks. He didn't grow up with Pablo, your nephew. You must be thinking of another goat. This goat is only worth twenty-five dollars. See how small he is."

The man shook his head. "But he was so smart. One-fifty."

Jacob counteroffered, "Forty. You know this goat stands in the road all the time. Someone was bound to hit him."

"He was a fine goat. One hundred dollars."

"Sixty."

"You're robbing me, Jake. I take seventy only because you're a fine *amigo.*"

Jacob reached for his wallet, but Michelle stopped him. "I hit the goat. I'll pay for it."

"No. I—"

"No. This is my doing."

Eduardo watched them with a smile on his face as they argued.

Finally, Jacob said, "Okay, you pay."

Michelle pulled her purse from the front seat and got out some money, which she pressed into the man's hand. "I'm so sorry I killed your goat."

"De nada." He shrugged and started for the house.

"Hey, wait," Michelle called out. "What about the goat?"

"It's yours now. You paid for it," Jacob said with a smile.

"But I don't know what to do with him." What did one do with a dead goat? Bury him? She didn't have a shovel. She couldn't haul him in the trunk of her car. She looked at Jacob for help.

He shrugged his shoulders, seeming to enjoy her discomfort.

"I know, Aunt Michelle," Brooke exclaimed. "Give the goat back to Eduardo."

"What would he do with a dead goat?"

"Barbecue it," Brooke piped back.

"Oh, my Lord. You've got to be kidding." Michelle swallowed the nausea that picture conjured up.

"No, she's not," Jacob offered. "Barbecuing a goat is a big social event around here."

"Ugh," Michelle muttered, but she also realized she was not in Boston, and that she should not snub local customs. She turned and hurried after the retreating man. "Eduardo, wait!"

The man stopped, one foot resting on a concrete-block step leading up to his porch. *"Sí, señorita?"*

"I don't have any use for the goat. Would you like to have it?"

Eduardo's face lit up. "Ah, *señorita*. You are a fine lady. Most generous. Eduardo will take your goat. It will make a fine barbecue. *Sí,* tomorrow night, I'll have *una fiesta grande.* You will come? No?"

"How kind, but I don't know if I'll..." Michelle was at a loss for words. How could she refuse the invitation? On the other hand, she couldn't imagine eating something she'd killed with a vehicle.

"She'd be happy to come," Jacob said, walking up with the goat balanced over his outstretched arms. "Where do you want me to put the main course?" he asked Eduardo.

"Lay it here, on the porch. I will get the hole ready. You're invited too, Jake. That rice and chili dish you make, it would be nice with the goat."

Jacob put the goat down as he looked up at Eduardo. "I thought it was your fiesta."

"I provide the goat."

Jacob grinned. "Count me in. Now, we need to go and get Ms. Davis settled."

"Good night," Michelle told Eduardo over her shoulder as they walked back to their vehicles, amazed at how the man altered his accent and how his English came and went as he pleased. "What did he mean, 'get the hole ready'?"

"He'll dig a hole, then build a fire in it. When it's burned down to hot coals, he'll put in the goat, dressed out, of course. Much like a Hawaiian luau."

Michelle got into her car and followed Jacob's pickup with caution. She was grateful to him for getting her out of a mess, but she still had to come to terms with the idea of eating the goat. She thought about it as she drove down what could only be described as a wide alley full of potholes and barking dogs. When Jacob eased to a stop in front of a small flat-top house, she followed suit and breathed a sigh of relief. She had arrived.

When she heard Jacob rap on the car window, she got out and joined him.

"Let's get this unloaded," he said.

Careful not to bump against him, Michelle unlocked the trunk, more eager than Jacob to get the task over. Although she'd experienced a brief burst of adrenaline when she'd hit the goat, she was weary again. "Let's just take in a couple of suitcases," she said. "I can get the rest in the morning."

"I'm here now. Let's get the car unloaded and be done with it."

"You don't have to help."

"I know I don't." Without looking at her, Jacob lifted a large box and carried it toward the house.

Brooke tugged at Michelle's hand. "Come on, Aunt Michelle. You've got to close your eyes when you go inside. Me and Katy made you a surprise."

"Katy and I." Michelle absentmindedly corrected Brooke's grammar as she watched Jacob push open a small gate with his knee and walk up the narrow rock path to the porch. Why should the man make her nervous? He'd taken her to her new house—at Paloma's request; he'd gotten her out of a jam with Eduardo—probably more for Brooke's sake than for her own; and now he was going to unload her boxes—out of a sense of duty. She'd rather he just left her alone. Eventually, she knew, they needed to have a talk. Tomorrow.

When she joined him on the porch, Jacob handed Michelle the key. It was still warm from being held in his hand, she noticed as she inserted it into a rusty latch that guarded the dark oak planks of a door heavy enough to keep out even the most determined intruders. The key turned easily and the door swung open welcoming Michelle to her new home.

"Daddy fixed the door so it would work." Flipping on the light, Brooke hurried into the house, her tennis shoes thumping on the tile floor as she ran through the house illuminating it room by room.

Michelle was confused. She knew Jacob didn't want her in Sotol Junction, yet he'd fixed the lock on her door. And even though she'd sensed his hesitation in letting Brooke ride with her, he'd nevertheless allowed it. It was as if he wanted to keep their private feud just that—private.

Jacob stepped back so Michelle could maneuver her belongings through the doorway. Her first impression of the living room was that it was Spartan but comfortable. Small windows, recessed in the thick white walls, formed narrow ledges. Woven wool rugs softened the terra-cotta floor, and to the side, near a small corner fireplace, lay a stack of wood. Michelle couldn't imagine ever needing to build a fire in this part of the country, but she'd read it could get cold at night. Occasionally in the winter, the temperature even dropped to freezing.

A brown-and-ivory-striped sofa and chair sat in the middle of the floor separated by a well-used coffee table that would be perfect for her to prop her feet on after a long day. Michelle smiled. In the center of the coffee table was a pitcher filled with wildflowers, yellow, pale lavender and a deeper purple. Brooke returned to the living room and stood at attention beside the table.

"Is this your surprise?" Michelle asked, setting down her boxes and going to the table.

Brooke nodded. "Me and Katy picked them ourselves. And Paloma gave us the jar to put them in. She made it."

Michelle smiled at her niece, then knelt and studied the fragile flowers and the gray-blue pitcher. "The flowers are wonderful. Thank you so much." She stroked the rings left by the potter's fingers as the clay had turned on the wheel. "Paloma does beautiful work."

Jacob came to stand beside her filling the narrow space between the table and the sofa. "Yes, she's recognized worldwide, though you'd never know it from her."

Brooke added, "She's the Dove."

"The Dove?" If Michelle turned even slightly, she would feel the hair on Jacob's leg brush against her bare shoulder.

"Yes," he explained, his voice had become softer and filled with the warmth he evidently felt for the woman. "*Paloma*—the Dove. Her mark is on the bottom."

Michelle stood up, and wanting to put distance between them, stepped away from him. "What a coincidence. I've seen some of her work in a little gallery in Rockport. I had no idea what her real name was or that she lived here."

"That's the way she likes it. It's not that she shuns fame, she just doesn't seek it. Enjoying her craft and knowing that it gives people pleasure is what's important to her. This way she has enough time to enjoy life."

Michelle suspected he wasn't just talking about Paloma Tarango but about himself, as well. After all, he'd given up a lot of things other people deemed important—money, prestige and his marriage—to come to this remote part of Texas.

"Thank you again for the flowers, Brooke." She gave her niece a big hug. "You and Katy were very thoughtful. Now you'll have to teach me the names of the flowers. I don't know much about desert plants."

"Daddy has a book all about 'em. He'll let you borrow it. Won't you, Daddy?"

Michelle didn't know what to say. She'd wasn't sure Jacob would want to lend her anything, but if he thought Brooke had put him in an untenable situation, he hid it well.

"You're welcome to borrow it," Jake said. "I'll get the rest of your things."

"Thank you." Michelle was grateful for his help.

Ten minutes later, Brooke threaded her way past the boxes in the bedroom and came to stand by Michelle. "You sure have a lot of clothes. And shoes."

"I wasn't sure what I would need, so I ordered a wide assortment of things from L. L. Bean and Patagonia."

Jake leaned against the doorjamb and surveyed the baggage. Though he appeared to agree with his daughter about the volume of clothes, he didn't say a word. Michelle got the impression that he didn't much care what she did or how many clothes she had as long as she didn't interfere with him and Brooke.

Jake looked at his watch. "It's after eight. I've got to get Brooke home and fed. I have a few things to do before tomorrow begins at five o'clock."

"Five a.m.? Why so early?"

"There's a lot to be done before the rafts are ready to leave at eight. And with Mike gone . . ." He left the obvious unsaid.

"Isn't there something I could do to help out?"

"Not unless you can make guacamole for my trip tomorrow."

"Sorry. I've eaten it, but don't have a clue how to make it." Michelle had only cooked a few times in her life, preferring to eat out or heat things in the microwave.

Brooke said, "Daddy's guacamole is good."

"You cook?" she asked him.

Jake nodded. "You sound surprised."

"I'm surprised that anyone cooks for a rafting trip. I guess I assumed that everyone would bring a sack lunch."

"On the day trips, we serve mostly cold foods. But on the overnight ones, we cook gourmet meals. Tomorrow, all I have to prepare is the guacamole. The rest is just a matter of getting things together and putting them into ice chests."

"Where does Brooke stay while you're at work?"

"That depends. Sometimes she stays with Cynthia, or I get a young girl named Victoria to come to the house and stay with her." He added, his voice firm, daring her to challenge him, "I'm not neglecting her."

"I wasn't suggesting . . ."

"Daddy, could I spend the night with Aunt Michelle?"

"No. Your aunt just got here. She's tired."

"Please." Brooke gave her father a pitiful look. "I haven't seen her in a long time."

"She needs to unpack before she has visitors. Then we'll see." Jake smiled at his daughter.

Michelle was relieved that he sounded as if he would allow Brooke to stay another time. She put her arm around Brooke. "As soon as I get my things put away, I can make you a decent bed and then we'll talk about your spending the night."

"Can I come tomorrow and help?"

Michelle looked at Jake. She would enjoy Brooke's company but she didn't want to undermine his authority. His face was inscrutable. "Do you mind?" she asked. "Since Cynthia is gone."

"I guess not." His voice sounded begrudging.

That wasn't a yes, but it would do.

He said, "Do you want me to drop Brooke off on my way to work, say, around six?"

"That would be fine." Michelle would have liked to stay in bed until midmorning, but an early start was a good idea. She had a lot to do. She had tomorrow and Sunday to get ready for a school that she'd never set foot in.

"Oh, by the way." Jake paused at the door and turned around. "Shake out your shoes before you put them on in the morning. Scorpions sometimes crawl in them at night."

CHAPTER THREE

MICHELLE CURSED JACOB. Aloud. He must have known she wouldn't be able to relax when he'd told her about the scorpions. An involuntary shiver moved up her spine as she glanced around at the corners of the floor, afraid she'd spy one of the ugly creatures lurking there.

Seeing nothing, she exhaled slowly and leaned against the door to assess her new home. Its rustic design was such a contrast to her town house in Back Bay. Back Bay . . . Boston . . . Mother! In all of the excitement, she'd forgotten about calling her mother.

She glanced at her watch. Five minutes until ten. Almost eleven o'clock in New England. Elizabeth would be unhappy at being called at this late hour, but not nearly as unhappy as if Michelle didn't call. Paloma had said the telephone was hooked up, so Michelle hurried to look for it.

She found it on an end table next to the sofa. Punching in the numbers, she curled against one of the arms and waited. On the fourth ring, Elizabeth answered. "Hello."

"Mother . . ."

"Michelle? Is that you? Are you okay? I've been so worried waiting for your call. It's almost midnight, you know. What took you so long?"

Michelle interrupted the stream of questions. "Of course it's me, Mother. And it's almost eleven, not midnight." She shook her head at her mother's propensity to exaggerate, then she began explaining all the things that had happened to her on the journey. "Then when I finally arrived," she went on, "Jacob's partner, Mike, had been bitten by a snake."

Elizabeth gasped. "Oh, how dreadful. Things like that are precisely why I worry about Brooke." Without asking about Mike's well-being, she pointedly asked, "How is Brooke?"

"She's doing fine. She looks wonderful and seems like a happy—"

"Michelle," Elizabeth interrupted, "you know looks can be deceiving."

"I know that, Mother, but it's obvious she's healthy and that Jacob loves her." Michelle recalled the unrestrained joy father and daughter shared when he'd come in from the rafting trip.

"But, of course, that's what he wants you to think," Elizabeth chided. "Do you think he would behave like a negligent parent the first day you arrived?"

"No, but even though it's also obvious he doesn't like my being here, he's been very cordial. He helped me carry in my luggage and boxes."

"Hmmph. Well, it's nice to know he hasn't forgotten all his manners. Given his situation, I'm sure there's little occasion to display them. Besides, he probably just wants to ingratiate himself with you."

Michelle took a deep breath and tried to hide her growing frustration. "I don't think so, because when I killed the goat, he—"

"You killed a goat?" Elizabeth's voice was incredulous. "Michelle, whatever have you been doing? A snake? A goat? Do animals just run around everywhere?"

Michelle thought for a moment. "Something like that."

"I told you that was no place to rear my granddaughter. In two months I want you and Brooke back here."

"Mother, I don't think Jacob is going to agree without a fight."

"I'm leaving it up to you to make sure he doesn't have a choice."

"Mother, I told you that I don't want any part—"

"He's a manipulative, coldhearted person, who cares only for himself or he would never have moved to that godforsaken place."

"Mother, I don't think that's true." She wasn't sure what she was basing her own observation on, but the man she'd spent the past two hours with didn't seem to be the same man her mother was describing.

"You don't know. Remember how easily DeeDee was fooled by him." Elizabeth let her words soak in, then her voice became softer. "By the way, Brent called today and asked about you."

Michelle felt guilty that she hadn't thought of Brent in the last three days. "That's nice. Tell him hello for me." That was all she could think of to say. Suddenly, the tiresomeness of the whole conversation was overwhelming. "Mother, I need to get some sleep. It's been a long day."

"Of course, dear. Give me your number, and I'll call you tomorrow when you're more rested."

After repeating the number scribbled on a yellow note stuck to the phone, Michelle said goodbye.

Replacing the receiver, Michelle felt haunted by her mother's words. Initially, Jacob had indeed given her the cold shoulder, but in no way had he been manipulative. Was she really so naive that a good-looking man could so easily fool her? No. She'd been around plenty of handsome men in her life, and had never been taken in by their smooth talk. And Jacob certainly hadn't tried to smooth talk her.

Quite the opposite.

Later, soaking in the hot water and bubbles, she fretted over her decision to come here. She thought about her mother's plot...and Jacob...and the goat...and Mike. The litany seemed endless.

She sighed and settled into the bubbles, listening to the silence. There was something about Sotol Junction that was unsettling. In the city, noise was a constant. At any hour of the day or night, she'd been able to hear cars, people, sirens. Here, in Sotol Junction there was none of that. Turning off the water, she strained to hear something, anything. Dead silence. It was creepy.

Michelle wrapped a large towel around her body and, barefoot, hurried back to her small bedroom. When she remembered Jacob's warning, she slipped on some scuffs, turned around and carefully walked to the kitchen in search of a broom. If a scorpion did make an appearance during the night, she planned to be armed. Satisfied that the bed covers were tucked up off the floor so nothing could climb into bed with her, she turned off the light on the nightstand, but she couldn't keep from thinking about snakes and scorpions. Finally, she switched the knobby brown lamp back on, picked up her slippers and put them on the foot of the bed.

Just in case.

JAKE STIFLED A YAWN. In the east, a faint pink glow signaled the start of a new day. A day he hoped would be better than the previous one. He'd called the hospital in Lubbock this morning, and Cynthia had assured him Mike would be okay, though he would be in ICU for a couple of days. Jake would have gone to visit his partner, but he knew Mike would prefer him to stay and keep the business going.

Today, at least, Jake didn't have to dread Michelle's arrival. He only had to worry about getting along with her now that she was here.

At 5:50 a.m. when he rounded a bend in the road a couple of blocks from her house—if one could call the haphazard division of property in Sotol Junction a block—he was surprised to see the lights flickering through the windows. He should be ashamed to have come ten minutes early hoping to catch her unprepared, but he wasn't. Of course, she'd be on her best behavior for a while. Still, he didn't care how perfect it was, he wasn't going to be taken in. She was here for no good purpose.

He glanced at his daughter who was yawning, even though she swore she wasn't sleepy. He hated to leave Brooke with her aunt, knowing Michelle would pump the child for information. He knew he was overreacting. What could Michelle learn from Brooke? That the girl was happy, well-cared for and had a loving relationship with her father. Michelle might as well find that out right now.

Jake thought about the boxes and luggage he'd seen the previous night. A couple of containers had been labeled School. Michelle had asked Jake to leave them in the car, assuring him she and Brooke would take them to the school today. He'd been surprised that Michelle had bothered to make any preparations. DeeDee would have assumed someone else would attend to all the details.

He felt guilty remembering DeeDee in such a light. After all, he'd loved her once, or thought he had. She'd been the perfect wife for an up-and-coming stockbroker. Then, when he'd decided he didn't want to be a stockbroker, DeeDee had come apart. She'd refused to even discuss a change in their life-style, which had been featured often in Houston's society pages. It wasn't that she was a bad person. Neither of them were. It was just that they were so different. While DeeDee needed luxury and position, he yearned for the outdoors and freedom. When it was obvious they couldn't reach a compromise, they'd separated.

The marriage hadn't been a total waste, he reflected, looking at Brooke. The pleasure she gave him overshadowed any pain caused by his divorce. He reached over and gently shook his daughter's shoulder. "Wake up, Angel," he said as he eased the pickup close to the gate set in the rock fence surrounding the teacher's house.

"I'm wide-awake, Daddy," Brooke said, and to prove the point, she scrambled out of the pickup. Before she was halfway through the yard, the front door opened, framing Michelle in a halo of light. Jake grabbed a book on wildflowers he'd brought from home, slammed the pickup door and followed his daughter.

"Good morning," Michelle greeted them from the porch.

"Good morning," Jake said, wishing he could take his eyes off her. But when she knelt and hugged Brooke, he was startled by the resemblance between aunt and niece. The same shade of golden-blond hair swung in response to their movements. Both had slightly upturned noses that gave them a mischievous look. And even the early hour couldn't camouflage their twinkling blue eyes.

Suddenly he felt uneasy. He would have preferred to deny the two belonged together, but with the evidence of their relationship staring him in the face, it was hard to do. He shook his head and asked, "Did you get a good night's sleep?"

"Short is a better description," Michelle answered with a smile. "Would you like a cup of coffee? I found a can in the kitchen along with some food and a fruit basket."

"Leave it to Paloma to make sure no one starves, but I really don't have the time," Jake said, holding out the book in his hand. "I brought you the guide on desert wildflowers."

"Thank you." She took the book, glanced at its cover and clutched it to her chest.

Jake cleared his throat, strangely conscious of her gesture. "You're welcome," he muttered. Feeling extraordinarily uncomfortable with his sister-in-law, he hugged Brooke and turned to leave.

"Wait," Michelle said. "Did you hear how Mike is doing?"

"I talked to Cynthia a little while ago." Jake took a step up on the porch.

"Tell me about it while I pour you a cup for the road."

"You talked me into it." He'd allowed himself a few extra minutes in case there were any unexpected problems because of Mike's absence, so it wouldn't hurt to take a few of them now. "This morning Mike was a lot better. He's over the nausea, but last night the doctors had to do a little surgery to relieve the swelling in his foot."

Michelle grimaced. "I didn't get to meet Mike, but Cynthia and Katy seem like such nice people."

"They are." As Jake followed her to the kitchen—Brooke skipping along beside him—he watched the swaying of the ponytail that made Michelle look sixteen. Nothing else about her looked sixteen. The khaki-colored shorts she was wearing—though loose and almost knee-length—hugged curves he knew would mold against a man. Her crisp white shirt was unbuttoned to right above the valley formed by her small breasts. Yesterday he'd been too upset about Mike to appreciate how attractive she was. *Be careful,* he warned himself silently. *This is DeeDee's sister.* No matter how beautiful she was, he had no intention of getting involved with his ex-sister-in-law. In any way. At any level.

Regardless of Brooke—or maybe because of Brooke—he wanted Michelle Davis out of Sotol Junction. And if there was anything he could do to hasten her departure, he'd do it. He'd missed a golden opportunity last night when she'd run over the goat. Just why in hell had he bailed her out with Eduardo? He couldn't afford to make another mistake like that. The sooner she left, the sooner they'd be able to hire another teacher for the coming year.

CHAPTER FOUR

"THERE IT IS." Brooke pointed to a small adobe building surrounded by packed dirt. Next to the doorway, a lone yucca sprouted from the foundation, guarding the entrance with its spikes. The bright sun spotlighted every crack in the mud plaster, every unpainted board framing the small windows. Fifty yards behind the building Michelle could see the yawning canyon that hid the Rio Grande. When she turned off the car engine, she could hear the water rushing and tumbling over rocks. Who would build a school so close to a river? Didn't the community care about the safety of its children?

Michelle lugged a box up the steps, tried balancing it on her knee while she fumbled with the key ring, but finally had to set it down. Locating the right key, she inserted it into the metal lock. As she pushed open the door, a blast of cool air rushed out to greet her. She was amazed at how well adobe buildings stayed cool in the desert. Brooke placed the hamburgers they'd picked up at the drug store on the teacher's desk and pulled up a couple of chairs. "Lunch is ready," she announced with a flourish.

After they finished eating, Brooke helped her unpack the boxes while she explained how things were "supposed" to be done. Michelle was impressed with the efforts the community had made to keep up with educational trends. Only the outside of the building looked as if it were transplanted from another century.

Inside, she saw a laser-disk system for science, CD-ROMs for the computers and a long-distance learning system that she had no idea how to use. The magazines and books were up-to-date. The desks were new. For some reason, she'd envisioned a potbellied stove and old desks carved with the initials of these students' grandparents. The wooden floor creaked, but it was clean and shiny. She'd been pleased to learn a woman came in every afternoon after school to clean.

Two hours later, they were back at Michelle's house. "Why don't we rest for a while?"

"I'm not tired." Brooke insisted.

"We can watch TV." She knew Brooke had to be exhausted.

"Okay." Brooke curled on the sofa and watched satellite television until she drifted off to sleep.

Michelle sat in the chair opposite the sofa and admired her niece, whose face was framed by wisps of loose blond curls. How could a child look so innocent and yet be so knowing? She had been a big help all day. Michelle would have had a hard time getting things ready before Monday without her.

Michelle leaned her head back on the chair, and, repositioning her feet on the coffee table, she closed her eyes, oblivious to the fly buzzing around the room. Her head bobbed to one side as she lapsed into sleep.

A thunderous crash awoke her. Michelle leaped from the chair. "What on earth was that?"

Brooke stirred. "Uh?"

"That noise. What was it?"

"I don't know." She sat up and stretched. "Let's go look."

"No. You stay here." Pushing Brooke behind her, Michelle rushed to the screen door to investigate. In the center of the small yard, a brown burro nibbled on purple and white petunias spilling out of an overturned clay pot—the source of the crashing noise. Other flowers lay trampled under the burro's hooves.

The entire yard consisted of sporadic tufts of Bermuda grass growing under several cacti and a mesquite tree just beginning to bud out. The only plants that required much water were in pots on the porch. Five flat rocks in a meandering pattern led the way to a two-foot wall of white flagstone surrounding the house—a wall that was apparently ineffective because the burro seemed at home standing inside the fence munching on the few precious flowers.

"Get away from there, donkey!" Michelle yelled from behind the door. The donkey didn't move. Wondering how on earth she was going to get the animal to leave, she ran to the kitchen and got the broom.

"You stay here, Brooke," she said, stepping out on the porch. "Shoo, shoo. Go away." She edged toward the gate holding the broom between herself and the mangy animal, hoping it wouldn't turn on her.

With a look of total disinterest, the burro watched her ease the gate open. Then Michelle circled the animal, shaking the broom at him. He moved a few feet and took a bite of grass. She followed him. "Shoo, I said."

The burro moved slightly and took another bite, this time it was of flowers again. Michelle approached his side and gave him a gentle nudge with the broom. He backed up, knocking over another pot.

From the porch, Brooke burst out laughing. "His name is Burrito."

"You know this beast?" Michelle wiped away the sweat running into the corner of her eyes. Damn! It was hot in this place.

"Sure. He belongs to Pablo."

Michelle licked her lips. "Well, call Pablo and tell him to come get his . . . his . . . animal out of my yard before it destroys everything."

"Pablo doesn't have a telephone." Brooke jumped off the porch and walked over to Burrito.

Michelle groaned in frustration. "What do we do?" she asked.

"In a little while, Pablo will come hunting for him." Brooke patted the burro's dusty coat. It responded by twitching its ears.

"You mean we just let this animal stay here until someone comes?"

"Sure. He won't hurt anything."

"Nothing but flowers." Pointing at what was left of the purple and white petunias and the red geraniums, she said, "He's already destroyed two pots of them."

"We can replant them, and they'll grow right back."

Michelle stared at her matter-of-fact niece. Brooke was right, of course, but Michelle wasn't sure she could get used to the laid-back attitude everyone here displayed. People were bitten by snakes; goats and burros ran loose in the roads and yards; stores closed whenever the owners felt like it, and no one seemed to care.

Michelle wondered how she could teach the children about responsible behavior. Everything was so different out here.

"Here comes Pablo now." Brooke pointed her finger down the road.

Michelle looked up to see a young boy, thirteen or fourteen maybe, ambling up to the fence as if there was no reason to hurry.

"Miss?" The boy's slow speech was heavily accented. Unkempt black hair hung over the collar of his faded cotton shirt. Old twill pants two sizes too large hung over his thick-soled leather sandals. From his fingers dangled a delicate horsehair bridle.

Michelle pushed a damp curl off her forehead. "Is this animal yours?"

"Sí." His dark eyes held a hint of intelligent arrogance. "You want me to get him?"

"Yes, please."

Pablo walked up to the burro and stroked its neck and muzzle, at the same time slipping on the bridle. "You the new teacher?"

"Yes. I'm Ms. Davis. Do you go to school here?" Michelle thought he was probably old enough to go to Alpine since the school in Sotol Junction ended at sixth grade.

"Sometimes." He started to lead the burro through the gate. "When I feel like it."

"When you feel like it?" Michelle asked. The lean boy kept walking, not acknowledging she'd said anything. She looked at Brooke and Brooke shrugged.

Just then, Jake pulled his pickup behind the house, planning to load up Michelle's empty boxes and put them in the storage room at the rear of Junction Outfitters. She'd need them when she was ready to leave Sotol Junction. Hearing a commotion, he walked around the side of the house in time to see Pablo leading Burrito out of the yard and down the dusty road. Jake leaned against a porch support and watched Michelle slinging soil back into a pot while Brooke picked up the petunias.

"That animal made a mess! Why would anyone want to keep one?"

"You can ride them. It's fun," Brooke told her. "And they keep snakes away."

Jake noticed Michelle blanch before she surveyed the yard. "Snakes?" she asked, jumping up.

He could hear the fear in her voice. She'd hidden it well last night. He cleared his throat a couple of times before she saw him.

"They don't den here in the village," he explained as he joined her and Brooke.

Michelle's knuckles were white as she clutched a terra-cotta pot. "Oh, great."

He changed the subject. "Looks like you had a visitor."

She knelt back down. "Some visitor. Just how do people keep donkeys out of their yards around here?" She patted the soil around the petunias she'd stuck back in the pot, then wiped her forehead with the sleeve of her white shirt.

"Oh, there's a way, but I doubt you'd be interested."

"Try me. I don't want him back in here. He may be a pussycat, but he makes me nervous. Now, what do I do?" The late-afternoon sun shone in her eyes, causing her to squint.

"Well, you can plant ocotillo along the wall. In a few years, it'll grow into a tall fence of spiny stems that will even keep out the rattlesnakes." He wished he'd watched his tongue when he saw her stricken look return.

"I thought you said there weren't any snakes here in town."

"I said, they don't *live* in town." Jake knew he could frighten Michelle—possibly into returning to Boston—but he didn't want to look bad in front of Brooke. Besides, Ms. Davis would find enough reasons to leave without his help.

Michelle gave him a disgusted look. "You're really funny."

"I'm sorry. Occasionally a snake does show up around here, so you do need to be careful. But it's really nothing to worry about."

"Oh, sure." Michelle didn't look reassured as she stood up and dusted her hands off.

He asked, "How was your day?"

"Fine. We got moved into the school. Brooke was very helpful." She smiled at her niece. "What about yours?" Her voice was controlled and polite now, hiding any of the emotion and fear she had shown moments before.

"Great. No problems on or off the river." He took the clay pot she was struggling with and set it back on the porch. "I see you met Pablo as well as Burrito."

"Yes, I did." She leaned against a cedar porch support. "What's going on here? Do the kids just go to school when they feel like it?"

"No," Jake answered, "except maybe Pablo. He lives with his great-uncle Eduardo on this side of the river so he can go to school in the United States. He goes home on weekends and sometimes he stays a few extra days if his family needs him to help with the crops or the cattle."

"Eduardo—as in who owned the goat I killed?"

Jake nodded his head.

"And Pablo is Mexican, not American?"

"Yeah."

"Then why doesn't he go to school in Mexico?"

"I think he'd have to walk about eight miles into Ojinaga."

"Why can't he ride a bus?" she asked, undeterred by his answer.

"Do you have a problem teaching Mexican children?" Sensing her disapproval, he didn't bother to tell her that there was no bus, that the children either walked or didn't attend school. If she had a problem teaching Mexican children, it would give him an excuse to get rid of her.

"Not in the least. I'm asking about something totally different—namely, citizenship."

"Apparently, you don't know anything about border states. We educate everybody—American or Mexican. It's not just a legal obligation, but a real need—for the whole community."

"You don't have to preach to me, Jacob. I admit I don't understand why he doesn't go to school in his own country. But if he does come to school here, then why doesn't he stay put? He shouldn't go back and forth across the border as he pleases."

"To answer your first question, there may not be a school available, or maybe there's a school building, but no teacher. Even the lucky ones who get to go to primary school often can't go to secondary school because of tuition costs. Few families can afford it, something you probably don't understand. As for your second question, the border is so accessible, lots of folks cross back and forth. When the river is low they walk across it, when it's high, they row across. Almost everyone has relatives that live on the other side—parents, brothers, cousins. Mexican families are very close, so they help each other out by boarding nieces and nephews to let them get at least a few years of schooling."

Despite her admiration for people who willingly took on the responsibility of extended families, Michelle realized she'd have her work cut out trying to convince people that a few years of schooling wasn't enough. "I hope I'll be able to make them see that education is really important. It's a way out of poverty."

Reformer. She's going to have a rude awakening, Jake thought. Of course, he agreed with her about the importance of education, but he also knew she would alienate more people than she would help if she set about trying to change traditions she didn't understand. But he'd let her find that out on her own.

CHAPTER FIVE

THE BARBECUE WAS unlike anything Michelle had ever seen. Bright cotton cloths covered several wooden planks which had been placed across sawhorses to serve as tables. Two floodlights—one hooked to the roof and another hanging from a tree—lit the hard-packed dirt around Eduardo's house, forming an isolated pocket of artificial brightness in the vast desert. It made Michelle feel insignificant and alone even though Jacob and Brooke were guiding her through the clusters of people.

A huge array of dishes were crammed together on the center table, but Michelle recognized few of the fragrant foods. She'd eaten Mexican cuisine several times, but she didn't see a single enchilada or a taco on the table.

"CAN YOU FIND a place for me to set this down?" Jake asked, nudging Michelle with his elbow.

"Oh, sorry." Scooting a plate aside, Michelle made way for the rice dish he was holding. Then she searched the crowd filling the yard, wondering where they'd all come from. Everyone who lived in a twenty-mile radius must have come to Eduardo's fiesta. But she didn't see her niece. "Where's Brooke?"

"She's gone to play with the other kids," he said, taking Michelle's arm. "They're probably around back playing tag or something. Don't worry. She'll be fine."

Michelle tried to ignore Jacob's grasp as he guided her through the crowd, but it wasn't easy. His touch was disconcerting, so she was relieved when they reached the cooking pit, and he released her.

Eduardo was supervising the removal of the goat; the men, who had wielded the shovels, were now leaning on them watching other men unwrap the meat. When Eduardo spotted Jake and Michelle, he hurried over to shake their hands. "Señorita Davis, I'm so happy you come to my party."

"I wouldn't have missed it." Actually, she would have been happy to miss it but Jacob had pointed out that she would offend Eduardo and the local people if she didn't come.

"Eduardo, where do you want us to put this?" a voice yelled, Michelle was glad Eduardo turned and missed Jacob's look of disbelief at her comment. She raised her chin and glared at him, daring him to contradict her.

He seemed to find her little white lie humorous because he grinned, shook his head and followed Eduardo to help carve the goat.

Michelle was left standing alone under a large willow tree, staring at his back. The noise of more people arriving finally drew her attention away from him. The men greeted one another with a slap on the back, and the women hugged each other. The sounds of English and Spanish were woven into a single language that everyone except Michelle seemed to understand. She felt like an outsider. Even Jacob had abandoned her.

She fingered the bole of the tree, totally unaware of its rough texture. At home, she would have mingled with people, but here she had no idea what to talk about. She realized even her long, red-striped dress was out of place.

Besides, she really needed to be at the schoolhouse getting ready for Monday. She didn't intend to feel like an outsider there. She was considering slipping away when Paloma appeared at her side. Relief at seeing a familiar face flooded through her.

They talked awhile, and Paloma introduced her to several of the residents. Michelle was impressed by the quiet authority Paloma seemed to wield. She blended in with the people, yet remained apart. Neither Anglo nor Hispanic. Neither local nor an outsider. But clearly, highly respected by all.

Alone with Paloma once again, Michelle noticed a goatskin hanging across a wire strung across the porch. Nodding in its direction, Michelle began, "That skin, is that ah..."

"Yes, from the very same animal you had the misfortune to hit. Would you like to go up and see how Eduardo cleaned it up?"

"I'd rather not. Why's he displaying it?"

"Oh, he's letting it cure. It will make a good throw rug this winter." In response to Michelle's raised eyebrow, she continued, "It's very practical and warm."

"I didn't realize that. Tell me about Eduardo. It seems strange that he'd have this gathering. I mean, I haven't seen a wife to help him."

Paloma glanced at Eduardo's slight figure as it shifted from one place to another, directing the activities. "He's a lonely man. His wife died last summer, and they had no children. Parties help cover his loneliness."

"Oh." Michelle nodded in understanding.

"Did you get settled in?" Paloma asked.

"Yes. And thank you for getting the house ready for me. You and Cynthia went to a great deal of trouble. Incidentally, have you heard from her?"

"I talked with her this afternoon. She said Mike isn't in as much pain now, and the doctors don't think he'll have much permanent damage. He's lucky. If the bite had been deeper he might not have made it."

"I'm so glad to hear he's okay. I can imagine how relieved Cynthia must be."

"Momentarily, she's relieved, but I'm a little worried about her. Although Cynthia's generally upbeat, she's never been a very strong person. She moved here to make Mike happy. You know, the line about a wife's place is at her husband's side. But I'm afraid this little incident may make her try to convince him to leave."

"I can understand how she feels. After all, Mike could have died." Little incident, indeed! Cynthia had almost lost the man she loved.

"Accidents happen wherever one lives. Safety can't be guaranteed, so one must try to be happy in the meantime."

Michelle wasn't convinced but she said nothing.

Paloma continued, "I don't know what would become of Junction Outfitters if Mike leaves. I just don't know if Jake can find the..." She left the sentence unfinished as she shook her head.

Michelle wondered if Paloma was referring to Jacob not having enough time, ability or money to run the business alone. She was debating violating the rules of good manners by asking more questions, when she heard the tinkling of a bell.

"Goat's ready!" Eduardo called, laying aside the triangle he'd been striking. "It was cooked in honor of our new teacher, Señorita Davis." Eduardo twisted through the people and bowed his head respectfully before her. His hand outstretched toward the table, he said. "Here, *señorita,* you come to the front of the line."

Heat rushed through her body as Michelle felt every eye turn toward her. She searched the crowd for Jacob. He was standing slightly apart, his arms folded, watching her. She knew he wasn't going to come to her assistance. Offering a weak smile, she had no choice but to follow Eduardo.

"You go first. Try our fine food." Eduardo shoved a plate toward her as she stood, self-consciously aware of how different she must appear to be to all these people. "You won't find anything like it in Boston."

Of that, she had no doubt. "Thank you." Michelle prayed she could avoid the goat and only eat Jacob's rice dish and the Pecos cantaloupe everyone bragged about. No such luck.

"*Señorita*, for you." Eduardo dumped a large strip of barbecued meat on her plate. "And get one of those jalapeños." He pointed to a bowl heaped with peppers.

"Are they hot?"

"Ah, no, very mild. *Bueno*. Good. Good." Eduardo rolled his eyes heavenward and licked his lips.

"Hot is relative," Paloma warned in a low voice behind her. "But if you don't take one, you'll be failing a rite of passage."

Aware several people were watching her, Michelle chose one of the smaller peppers and, not wanting to offend any of the cooks, proceeded through the line, taking small portions of several of the dishes. With her plate filled with more food than she could possibly eat, Michelle looked behind her. She noticed that the men had formed lines on either side of the table, while the women hung back and watched their men joust for food.

She sat on a bench in front of a plank table and observed as the women lined up next. The children came running up and joined the end of the lines. When Paloma sat down beside her, Michelle asked, "Why weren't the children first?"

"Custom." Paloma turned toward Michelle and spoke so others who were gathering at the table couldn't hear. "Michelle, I know what you're thinking. But it really is okay for the children to eat last. Plenty of food is saved for them, and it gives the adults time to eat before having to attend to the children."

Despite the explanation, Michelle couldn't help thinking that women and children were second-class citizens here. Another challenge, she thought. She did notice that Jacob found things to do around the cooking pit until he was the last to go through the line. She wondered if he found it hard to give up customs he'd grown up with. Had he deliberately gone through the line last, or had he merely been distracted?

Michelle watched as Jacob surveyed the crowd looking for a place to sit. His expression turned to a frown when he realized the only spot was one vacated by a man who had been sitting beside Michelle. As he approached, she scooted over on the bench so he could slide in without touching her. He nodded his thanks, then began visiting with a man named Ramon sitting across the table. His dismissal hurt, though it shouldn't have. Jacob's opinion of her wasn't a factor in her decision to remain in Sotol Junction.

While the conversation went on around her, she saw that many of the guests had chosen not to sit at the tables, squatting with seeming ease and balancing their plates on one knee as they ate.

Michelle sipped some iced tea and looked around until she spotted Brooke sitting in a circle of children under a willow. Squeals of laughter interrupted their eating.

Having put off the inevitable until the point of rudeness, Michelle scooped up some rice and a tiny bite of goat, hoping the rice would camouflage the meat. *Hmm,* she thought. *Not bad.* She tried another bite without the rice and was pleasantly surprised. *Not bad,* she thought once more.

Maybe the jalapeño would be okay, too.

She carefully picked up the slender green vegetable everyone was eating like candy and took a tentative nibble. It wasn't too hot at all, a bit sweet with a mild acidic flavor, so she took another bite.

Then it happened.

A burning sensation spread quickly, causing every nerve in her mouth to explode in a numbing fire. She caught her breath. She couldn't talk. Her mouth dropped open allowing cool air to rush in, but if anything, it only intensified the pain. She began gasping, her eyes and nose began running and her ears were assaulted with loud ringing.

Jacob laughed and handed her a glass of water. "Don't swallow. Just hold the cold water in your mouth."

It didn't help much. Finally able to breathe, but still in agony, Michelle listened while Paloma and Ramon sympathized and told her about the first time they'd bitten into a jalapeño.

Eduardo came by and patted her on the back. "I give up the peppers for Lent. The saints know how much I love them, too. Soon, *señorita*, you'll get to like them as much as Eduardo does."

Not in this lifetime, she wouldn't! Holding a piece of ice on her tongue, she wondered why no one had told her those stories before she'd taken a bite. Finally, her respiratory system returned to normal, although her tongue felt as if it was permanently singed. She tried to appear as though nothing had happened, but what she really wanted to do was go home.

After several others shared their war stories about jalapeño peppers, people went back to their private conversations and Jacob leaned close to Michelle and whispered, "Congratulations. You passed."

She was beyond caring. If she had to commit acts of self-torture to be accepted here, maybe she should go back to Boston where people were more civilized. She glanced at Jacob, figuring he'd like that. But his expression was one of sympathy and something else. Approval? She must have imagined it—Jacob would never have approved of her.

Juan Lopez, a quiet man who she knew was on the school board, took a big gulp of iced tea, wiped the moisture off his black mustache, and leaned forward. "Hey, Jake, you gonna help us with the *candelilla* this year?"

Jake glanced down at his plate and took a deep breath. "Juan, you know I'll do what I can." He held up his hand as though he were pushing away something distasteful. "Up to a point."

"That's all we ask." Juan nodded his satisfaction and got up to refill his plate.

Michelle sensed something clandestine in the tone of voice the two men had used. She frowned and turned toward Jacob. "What's *candelilla?*" She stumbled over the word.

"It's just a plant that grows around here." He seemed hesitant to say more.

"What do you have to do with it?"

Jake looked up and down the table at the people engrossed in conversation. He lowered his voice. "Since I go up and down the Rio Grande all the time, I get a chance to see a lot of country. If I find a place where there's a lot of *candelilla* growing, I tell Juan and the others. It makes their job easier."

"When they find the plant, what do they do with it?"

"They make wax from it."

"So, what's wrong with that, and why are you talking so softly?"

"I'd just as soon everyone not know. Okay?"

"Why not?"

"You ask a lot of questions." Jacob slid off the bench and walked away from her.

Michelle watched him dump his paper plate in a barrel and join a group of men who were gathering at the side of the yard to play horseshoes. Jacob was by far the best looking man there. Not that his looks mattered to her. But it would be easier to ignore him if he wasn't so attractive.

Was it illegal to harvest *candelilla?* she wondered. Why would Jacob not discuss it? She hesitated to ask Paloma, but filed this tidbit of information away for further investigation. Her mother might be correct in assuming Jacob had something to hide.

JAKE WAS WONDERING the same thing about Michelle. As he gripped the horseshoe and took measure of the stake twenty feet away, he wondered why his ex-sister-in-law had really come to Sotol Junction. For adventure, for teaching, for doing good or for snooping. He glanced over to where she was now sitting on a blanket under a willow tree and felt guilty about leaving her alone. Michelle wouldn't know that there was enough old colonial Mexican culture left here to discourage an unmarried man and woman from publicly showing friendship. Not that he and Michelle were friends by a long shot, but he could damage Michelle's reputation, her honor, if he paid her the kind of attention he'd like to. He was more intrigued by her than he wanted to admit.

He stepped back and let another person take his turn. As horseshoes were pitched amid loud taunts about babies being able to play better, Jake overheard whispers about the prosperity of this year's *candelilla* harvest. It had been one of the few sources of extra revenue for border residents even before Texas became a state. But the United States government prohibited its harvest from public lands. He didn't like being involved, but when he'd moved to Sotol Junction, he'd resolved to accept the people for who they were. He'd learned they were a hot-blooded but fun-loving people.

Across the expanse of light sprinkled with flying insects, he saw Michelle still sitting on a blanket but now with Brooke's head in her lap. He wondered what Michelle thought of the party. Was she denigrating it because of the crude furniture, the informality, the gender segregation? He suspected Michelle found the whole thing very strange.

Michelle did find it strange. Only Paloma—and the three men the woman was playing dominoes with seemed oblivious to the demarcation as strong as the Mason-Dixon line had been a hundred years earlier. Men on one side, women on the other.

Michelle picked out Jacob's hearty laugh from among yells and boisterous talk on the men's side of the imaginary line. Undoubtedly, he was having a good time. She hated that he'd ignored her most of the evening, but she hadn't come to Sotol Junction to socialize with him. Still, his behavior stung and she had never felt so lonely. Even though everyone had been friendly and nice, she missed Boston.

Yet, there was a certain peacefulness here. The buzz of cicadas in the trees down by the river mixed with the laughter coming from the men playing horseshoes.

Michelle had almost drifted off to sleep when she felt a hand on her shoulder. She was startled to see

Jacob kneeling beside her. Shadows formed by the floodlight shining through the willow tree danced across his face making it look almost harsh, reminding her of the first time she'd seen him on the boardwalk. In her half-awake state, she flinched, wondering if he did it on purpose—this standing in shadows. If he did, it was effective. She wouldn't want to cross him.

"Sorry, I didn't mean to frighten you." In a hushed tone, he gently asked, "Are you ready to go?"

She nodded. "I think Brooke is past ready."

He lifted his sleeping daughter into his arms and led the way to where their host was bidding the last of the guests good-night.

Eduardo laughed. "I'm sorry I have no more goats. Señorita Davis says she's driving this way tomorrow. We could have another barbecue."

Jacob was still chuckling when he placed Brooke in the front seat of the pickup. "Michelle, your driving is now local legend."

"Ha-ha." She had to laugh at herself as she settled Brooke's head on her lap. "Of course, it could be worse."

"How?" Jacob started the engine and pulled onto the road.

"I could have killed the burro, too." Michelle studied Jacob's face in the glow from the lights of the instrument panel. Her mother would be appalled at his long hair and the earring. Barbaric, she would say.

When he smiled, he was the handsomest man she'd ever seen. That thought didn't make her happy. She didn't want to think about Jacob Evans at all. She wanted to concentrate on Brooke and the other students at the school where she would begin teaching the day after tomorrow.

Or was it tomorrow already? Michelle glanced at her watch. Twelve-thirty. In a little more than thirty-two hours she would have a roomful of students, all of different ages and at different levels.

A thought crossed her mind. "Lots of children were there tonight, but I didn't see Pablo." Paloma had explained to her how Pablo had come to live with his great-uncle after Eduardo's wife had died. It was a good arrangement for both of them. The boy was able to go to school, and the older man had company.

"He went home for a couple of days."

"Then he won't be here for school Monday. How far away do his parents live?"

"Probably twenty miles from here. Pablo rode the donkey to see them."

"He rode the donkey? Alone?"

"Sure. Why not?" Jacob pulled into her driveway and came around to help Michelle get out of the pickup without waking Brooke.

After getting Brooke settled on the seat, Michelle quietly closed the door and turned to Jacob. "I'll tell you why not. Pablo's too young to travel that far alone. Why didn't his parents come get him?"

"If they could afford a car, they could get him to school in Mexico. Besides, he's not too young. The kids around here are pretty independent."

"There's a difference between being independent and being unsupervised." She thought of Brooke and Katy playing yesterday. Anything could have happened to them.

"Unsupervised here is a lot different than unsupervised in a city." Jacob's voice took on a steely edge.

"Sure. Here they are only threatened by snakes, scorpions and maybe even drowning." She realized she was pushing Jacob, something she hadn't meant to do. Still, she was concerned about the children.

"Well, it sure as hell beats being in a city with muggers, knives, smog and traffic. "

"I'll withhold judgment on that." The conversation she had wanted to have was getting away from her. She had planned to be cool and matter-of-fact, but a seemingly innocent question had exploded in her face.

"It's a good thing, because I think you're saying Brooke would be better off in Boston." Jacob raised an eyebrow in question and held Michelle with a level gaze.

"That's not what I was saying, although Boston does have its merits." Although she'd told her mother Jacob would not give up without a fight, Michelle had hoped she could convince him to see things her way. Instead, she was face-to-face with the most masculine force she'd encountered in her life. Her skin was hot, not from the desert temperature, not from a jalapeño pepper, but from Jacob's burning glare.

"Let me get one thing straight. Don't interfere with me or my daughter. Don't try to get her to go back to Boston with you. You were hired as a teacher, not a social worker. I recommend you stick to your job and leave Brooke and me alone. Is that clear?"

"Don't you dare threaten me, Jacob Evans. Brooke is my concern, too. She's my niece. I want what's best for her."

"Being with her father is what's best for her."

CHAPTER SIX

"MY DAD SAID your aunt can't be much of a teacher or she wouldn't have come here." Austin Wiley gave his red hair a swipe and threw back his shoulders as though he were the official leader of the cluster of children gathered on the concrete porch of the small schoolhouse.

"She is, too, Austin!" Brooke planted two feet firmly in front of the boy, put her hands on her hips and stared him in the eye. "You'll see."

"You better not be mean to her, Austin," Katy threatened.

"Yeah, Katy'll beat you up again," Manuel's small voice uttered in glee.

"That was a pure accident when I wasn't looking. You wanna take me on?" Austin challenged Manuel.

"No, I don't wanna fight you," the boy said.

"Then keep your mouth shut." Seemingly confident he had everyone's respect, he turned his attention to Brooke. "My dad says she's a *Yankee.*" Austin's voice interjected the word into the conversation as if it were one of the dirtiest epithets he could think of.

"Yeah!" John, a boy about Austin's size, confirmed in his most adult manner. "We don't want no Yankees. They think they're better than ever'body."

Katy sidled up to Brooke to present a united front against Austin and his friends. "Ms. Davis isn't like that. She's nice."

Michelle stood inside the entryway listening to the exchange, grateful for the support from Brooke and Katy. She knew she was a good teacher; all she had to do was prove it to these students and their parents. She felt up to the task, having spent most of yesterday getting things ready for class and surveying the building.

It housed two large rooms—the combination business office and boardroom separated from the large classroom by two rest rooms and a storage closet.

She'd also been pleased to learn that the last teacher had not totally abandoned these students. Mrs. Blevins had left her old lesson plans so Michelle had an idea at what level each student was working. Still, preparing for several grade levels had been a challenge. But she was ready. Even for the little boys who disliked Yankees.

Deciding it would be wise to pretend that she'd just walked up and hadn't heard any of their conversation, Michelle stepped through the doorway, crossed her arms and cleared her throat. "Good morning, children."

Startled, the children spun around and saw her. "Uh, good morning," a few of the students said before looking down. Obviously they were embarrassed at being caught talking about her.

Michelle slowly looked at all the children casually clad in jeans and T-shirts. The snaps on one of the little boy's jeans gapped open, too tight to close around his chubby little body. The tongue of his running shoes stuck straight up, unrestricted by shoelaces. Yet, when the child flashed her a gap-toothed grin, Michelle felt her heart melt. "Hello," she said, kneeling beside him. "What's your name?"

The boy continued smiling, his black eyes glistening like freshly mined coal.

"His name's Javier," Brooke told her aunt. "He just started school after Christmas and he doesn't speak much English. We have to translate for him."

"You said his name is Javier." She knew how important a name was to a person, so Michelle intended to get names right the first time. She gave the boy a reassuring pat on the shoulder. As she stood up, she heard a couple of boys, probably ten or eleven years old, say something in Spanish before bursting into laughter. Michelle fervently wished she knew more Spanish.

The little red-haired boy who had been doing most of the talking walked away in open defiance. His expression dared her to say or do anything. Michelle felt a sinking feeling in the pit of her stomach as she studied the children. This job wasn't going to be easy.

"Well, let's come in and get acquainted. I'm Miss Davis. I'll appreciate it if you sit where you did for Mrs. Blevins."

Brooke and Katy, clearly eager to be first, hurried through the door while the others moved at their own speed. Soon, fourteen desks squeaked under the weight of wiggling students, while two desks at the front remained conspicuously empty. One must belong to Pablo who was still in Mexico and the other obviously belonged to the red-haired boy pecking his fingernails against the chalkboard, flexing his fingers as though he was about to scratch it at any minute.

Michelle quelled her involuntary shiver, determined not to lose the opening play so easily.

"I've looked over the names of the students and you must be Austin. What an important name. Were you named for the city?" Michelle asked, hoping to break the boy's resistance.

"Nope." Austin rolled his eyes and blew out his breath. "Don't you know nothing about Texas history?" A few of the children twittered.

Michelle stared at the boy, trying not to lose her temper. "I know some Texas history. Why do you ask?"

"'Cause you asked a dumb question. I was named after Stephen F. Austin and every fourth-grader who knows anything knows who he was."

"I'm sure they do." Michelle resolved to learn who Stephen F. Austin was before class the next day. "Now, I want to know a little about each one of you."

By ten o'clock, Michelle had sorted the children into various groups. The first-grade class comprised three students: Javier, who knew no English; Francisco, who knew a little English; and Claudia, who was one of the most beautiful children Michelle had ever seen. Tomas and John were the two second-graders. Brooke, Katy and a shy little girl named Rosa, Javier's cousin, were in the third grade. Only one student, Manuel, the boy who'd briefly stood up to Austin, was in the fourth grade. Austin, Antonio, another boy named John, and Lydia, who Michelle learned was Paloma's niece, made up the fifth grade. Pablo, who was not in school today, was the only sixth-grader.

By midmorning, Michelle decided that the word *difficult* was an understatement. The job was going to be impossible if she couldn't find a common ground for herself and her students. Even though the children had specified desks, no one seemed compelled to sit in them. Austin and John had dumped all their belongings on the floor and were digging through them to find their math books. Finding his, John shoved the rest of his books into the desk, leaving a folder half hanging out, and walked over to look out the window.

Rather than having another set-to with Austin, who was smoothing out a rumpled paper, she addressed the other boy. "John?"

"John," she repeated a little louder. This time both the fifth-grader and a second-grader looked up. She'd forgotten there were two Johns in the class.

"Huh? You want som'um?" the second-grader asked.

"No. You may continue with your handwriting. I'm talking to this John." She addressed the fifth grader. "How about if I call you John the Second, like a king, so we won't get mixed up anymore?"

After John the Second gave his approval and went to work, Michelle looked at Antonio. "Would you get your paper and pencils and return to your seat?" She tapped the desk top.

"I didn't bring no paper and pencil, miss."

"Then I'll lend you some paper and a pencil. Just come have a seat and quit wandering around the room."

Reluctantly Antonio inched toward his while Michelle watched him. A moment later, she felt a tug on her denim skirt. When she looked down, the six-year-old boy with the big, black eyes pleaded, "Miss?"

"Yes, Javier, what do you need?"

The little boy stared up at her, not answering.

"Brooke, can you tell me what Javier needs?"

Brooke left her group, which was visiting rather than working anyway, and walked over to Michelle. "Well, he needed to go to the rest room, but," she said, wrinkling her nose, "I think it's too late."

Michelle looked down to see a puddle gathering at the little boy's feet. She couldn't believe this was happening.

Michelle felt herself losing patience with the whole group. Even Brooke and Katy had gotten tired of sitting and trying to pay attention when the rest of the students were running around and talking. They were behaving no better than Austin and Antonio.

"Oh," Michelle looked around the classroom. "Where's Antonio?" He hadn't stayed at his desk for five minutes.

A mass of black hair peaked from under a table. "Here, miss. I found a pencil."

She breathed a sigh of relief. What would she have done if he had disappeared? She couldn't have left the other children and go look for him. In Boston, she'd never really appreciated the support staff that had been available at St. Mary's. There had been teachers' assistants, counselors, a custodial staff and the headmaster. If there was any problem in the classroom or with a student, there had been someone to help. Here, she was everything, including daytime janitor, she thought, looking ruefully at the floor.

Finally, with Javier cleaned up and some semblance of order restored, she had the children seated in straight rows so she could begin the math lesson. First, she gave an assignment to the five fourth- and fifth-graders, then she formed a group of first-through third-graders. No sooner had she opened a book than Austin's hand went up.

"What page are we supposed to do, Miss?" Austin stood up and started toward her.

"Miss Davis," she corrected. "The page number is on the board." She brushed away a damp curl that had come loose from the clip at her neck and used her eyes to direct him back to his desk. "Now, please get started."

Pulling up a chair, she grouped the younger students around her and began to explain their lessons. They fidgeted but looked at her with adoring eyes. Michelle returned their smiles. She was going to make it.

"It's hot in here." Katy said.

"Yes, it is getting a little warm. Let's open the door so we can get a breeze."

Five kids jumped up and scrambled toward the door before she could stop them.

She glanced at the big old-fashioned wall clock and saw it was eleven. Only half the day was gone, and she still hadn't accomplished much. For the first time in her life, she questioned her ability as a teacher. Didn't most children want to please the teacher, to do well? Some of the kids had finished their math assignment in ten minutes while others didn't have their names on the paper after twenty minutes. She would just have to keep trying to reach them.

Michelle went from student to student helping them with their work, talking to each one softly. Relief flooded through her to find that her approach seemed to work. She directed the students who'd finished their assignment to do silent reading or to use the math flash cards until everyone was finished.

It worked up to a point, but when she stopped to give instructions to a single student, some kids took it as an excuse to wander around the room talking and occasionally tripping or shoving each other. Michelle tried to tune out the noise as she bent over Austin.

"Austin, you know how to add, but your answers are wrong because your columns aren't straight. Let me show you." She erased a problem and was demonstrating the correct way to align columns when she heard the children begin shushing each other. Without turning around she knew that they had a visitor, someone the students respected.

As Michelle straightened, the children in her line of vision were all staring toward the rear of the classroom and the open door. Then they glanced at her as if gauging how she was going to react.

Slowly, she turned to face Jacob. Only a few feet separated them. He was leaning against the doorjamb with his arms crossed and a look of disbelief marring his handsome face. The muscles in his jaws rippled almost imperceptibly as she stepped toward him.

"Hello, Mr. Evans." She tried to use her schoolteacher voice with just the right amount of formality. After the way they'd parted Saturday night, there didn't seem to be much point in pretending she was glad to see him, even under good circumstances. And these weren't good circumstances. "May I help you?" Her voice quivered slightly, betraying the frustration

and embarrassment she felt at him finding her classroom in chaos the first day.

His expression barely altered as he searched the
room for his daughter. "I thought I'd come by and
bring Brooke's lunch. She forgot it in the excitement
this morning."

Brooke ran across the room and took the paper bag.
"Thanks, Daddy. Do you want to stay and eat with
us? Please, please, please, please."

"Brooke," Michelle said in horror, "I'm sure your
dad doesn't have time. Why don't you put your lunch
in the refrigerator and go back to your desk."

Brooke looked from her aunt to her father before
hurrying away to the adjoining room as if she'd sensed
the tension between the two adults.

"I'm not in any big rush." He looked over the
classroom, then said in a voice loud enough to carry
to the far corner of the room, "Is anyone here giving
you any trouble?"

"No. We're just getting acquainted." Michelle tried
not to let her annoyance show. Just who did Jacob
Evans think he was? She didn't need his help. And she
certainly didn't need him thinking she was incompe-
tent.

Oblivious to Michelle's stony glare—or perhaps
choosing to ignore it, he continued, "Well, if any of
them ever cause any trouble, you just let me know."
His gaze moved from one student to the next, as if
coming to an understanding with each, then he turned
and strode to his pickup.

JAKE DREW a big red circle around the total at the bottom of the ledger, dropped the pen and shoved his swivel chair away from the desk. Damn! It didn't matter how many times he added or manipulated the figures, they told the same story. Junction Outfitters wouldn't make the needed income if they had to hire someone to replace Mike for the months he needed to recuperate.

As it was, they'd been operating on a narrow margin trying to build the business, support two families and put aside enough for the slow season. Thanks to Jake's previous income, he and Brooke could weather the rough spots easier than Mike and his family. Mike had no savings to fall back on for his family's livelihood.

Jake debated about taking some money out of his savings and putting it in the business, but he knew it would make Mike feel bad not to be carrying his part of the financial load. Mike, conscious of the discrepancy of finances, had been adamant about sharing equally when they'd formed their partnership. To suggest otherwise now would wound his friend's pride, something Jake was loath to do. Deep in thought, he missed the soft footsteps.

"Hello, Jake," Paloma called from the doorway. "I brought you a cup of coffee." She held up two ceramic mugs and flashed him a wide smile.

He jumped up from the chair, walked through the outer office and opened the screen door. "Hello, Paloma, come on in. Let's go to my office." He shook some of the stiffness out of his shoulders and followed her to the back. "Have a chair."

Paloma settled herself across the desk from Jake, smoothed her long denim skirt and sipped from her cup. Her dark eyes softened as they studied him. "You look worried, Jake. Is it Mike or something else?"

Jake grinned. Paloma ordinarily asked few questions, letting others tell her what they wished her to know. Today, she came straight to the point. He wondered why. "Not that I know of. Why? Have you heard anything?"

"Nothing since yesterday." Her silver bracelets clinked softly as she lifted her cup to take another sip. "How are you managing without him?"

"I'll get by." Jake carefully closed the ledger. "I'll have to turn down a little business and cut out the wildflower excursions until I can find some extra help. Right now, with it being the middle of the season, most of the guides around here have full-time jobs. And I don't want to hire someone I don't know anything about."

Paloma nodded in agreement. "I understand. Maybe that college student who worked for you last year could drive down from Sul Ross to help on the weekends. What was his name?"

"Wesley. I've already thought about him, but this is his senior year, and he may not want to mess up the last semester."

"I see." Paloma scanned the room before her gaze once again settled on Jake. "I wonder how things are going at school. I started to drop in, but I didn't want Michelle to think I was spying on her."

Jake took a deep breath. "Well, I did spy at lunch, and it didn't look too good. It reminded me of an ant bed after a rain."

Paloma frowned. "I hate to hear that. But this is her first day, I'm sure she'll get it figured out eventually."

"Well, I don't want to say I told you so, but Michelle doesn't have a clue about how to handle our kind of kids."

AFTER THE LAST student left for the day, Michelle crossed her arms on the desk and slowly lowered her head to rest on them. Her anger at Jacob's interference had long worn off. She was simply too tired to expend energy on any emotion. Every muscle in her body ached. Especially her feet. Other than at lunch and for a few brief minutes, she couldn't remember having sat down all day.

How was she going to reach these kids? They were such a ragtag group, separated by age, race and gender, and limited by experiences. Only Brooke and Katy had traveled much beyond Alpine, sixty miles away. For the rest, the scope of their small world was widened only by school and the rare satellite TV. For the first time, Michelle realized how much she'd taken for granted in Boston, and how much more effort it was going to take to teach students who saw little need for an education. This was no *Little House on the Prairie* job.

Then, too, she had to deal with Jacob. She groaned, remembering his appearance in the classroom. She'd been mortified that he thought he needed to interfere. Then, at the end of the day when he'd picked up Brooke, he'd ignored her.

Oh, well, she thought as she reluctantly lifted her head, and tried to slip her swollen feet back in her shoes. Only thirty-nine school days to go.

THURSDAY AFTER SCHOOL, Michelle refused to let Katy and Brooke walk the quarter of a mile to Junction Outfitters as Jacob had requested in a note that morning. She drove them instead. He'd written that he would be on the river until about six, but the girls could stay with Victoria.

With difficulty, Michelle had kept her mouth shut about Jacob hiring a sixteen-year-old girl to be his receptionist. The teenager needed to be in school, not working. However, Michelle knew Jacob needed Victoria's help while Cynthia was with Mike and would resent any comment Michelle had to make.

After delivering the girls, Michelle dropped by the post office to pick up her mail and was headed back to her car when she noticed Paloma's gallery was open. She pushed open the door and looked around. If she had to describe the room in one word, *peaceful* would be the word. It was cool and calm. Cases of exquisite pottery lined the white walls. The pine floor was polished to a sheen. And somehow, Paloma had managed to fend off the cloaking dust that seemed to settle on everything outside the gallery.

"Hello? Is anyone here?" Michelle called.

A few seconds later, Paloma appeared in a rear doorway. "Michelle, I'm glad you stopped by."

"I hope I didn't interrupt anything."

"Not at all. Come on back, and I'll show you what I'm working on." Paloma led the way into a large studio cluttered with packing crates, tables and benches laden with tools. "I just took these pots out of the kiln. They're for a shop in Santa Fe."

Michelle nodded and studied the delicate geometric etching on the smaller pot. "Jacob told me who you are."

Paloma lifted an eyebrow as she inspected the bottom of one of the pots. "And who did he say I was?"

"The Dove. I had no idea. I've seen your work in several shops back East. One of my friends who collects your work says it's authentic southwestern art."

Paloma cocked her head to one side, then slowly shook it. "It's no more authentic than most southwestern art that's actually made here rather than in Taiwan. It's just that I'm one of the lucky artisans. I do what I love and am recognized for it. Few artists are so fortunate. Most do what they must."

"Why do you stay here when you could live and work anywhere?" Michelle was curious about Paloma's choice, when places like Santa Fe would have more to offer and would be much more convenient.

Paloma motioned Michelle to a chair, then sat on a stool and seemed to think about the question before answering. "My family is here. My husband died before we had children, and I've never found another man I wanted to marry, but I have nieces and nephews. I am *Tía* to many children here. For us Hispanics, the family is important, above all else. I am nothing without my family."

Michelle smiled at the similarity between Paloma's and her mother's statements about family.

Paloma continued, "I see you know what I mean. That is why you are here. No?"

"Yes. I wanted to be near Brooke, to make certain she was okay."

"Then you understand why I won't move to Santa Fe or Dallas or some such place." She stood up and made a sweeping arm gesture. "Besides, here I do as I please. There, art critics would be telling me how to make pots, and retailers would be telling me how fast to make them."

Michelle watched her carefully wrap a pot and pack it in shredded paper.

"When I was young, I lived in Dallas for five years." Paloma said the words softly. "I rebelled against my family and went away to study art."

"And became successful."

"Success is measured differently in Dallas. I was alone. That is not success in our culture. I would have slowly killed my parents and ultimately myself if I had stayed."

"So, you came back."

"Yes. This is home. I'm my own person within my family, and that is important to me. But more important, I feel needed here." She taped the box closed and led the way back into the front display area. "I help support the local economy with this shop, I help with my nieces and nephews, and I serve on the school board."

"Paloma..." Michelle hesitated, not wanting to offend this woman.

"Yes?" Paloma encouraged her to continue.

"Why is doing well in school not very important to many of the students?"

"What makes you think that?" Paloma countered.

"Things are not going as well as I'd hoped. The children won't work by themselves, and I just don't seem to be able to juggle all the different levels. The children are adorable—no, that's not true. The young ones are. But those older boys, I simply don't know how to relate to them. They resist everything I try."

"Hormones. Children enter adolescence quite early in hot climates. And with your being a woman..." Paloma shook her head.

"What does my being a woman have to do with teaching?"

"The males around here, no matter their age, are macho, they don't like to take orders from females."

"That's archaic." Michelle recalled the fiesta at Eduardo's where the men ignored the women. Apparently, women's rights were nonexistent in the border area.

"That's the way it is. To succeed, you must learn to work around it."

"Then that's why I can't get the boys to do their homework. It's like it wasn't even assigned."

Paloma nodded. "That and the fact that many children have to work when they get home. It takes everyone's efforts to feed a family here. When a boy is fifteen, he is expected to find a job and help support the family."

"But those children will never get a decent-paying job without an education."

Paloma assumed a thoughtful look before she answered. "Basics are important to most of the families. But, after sixth grade, the students are bused to Alpine. That can be nearly a two-hour ride each way. Every day. Even my nieces and nephews—who, with my encouragement, will finish school—can't participate in extracurricular activities because of the distance involved. With three to four hours taken from their day by the bus ride, and the added pressure they get from home to quit school, most kids drop out."

"How did *you* manage?"

"My father was different. He believed in an education, even for his girls." She smiled. "Though I think he regretted his progressive thinking when I went to Dallas. Not everyone embraces all of the old ways. Some people are trying to change things. But it's a slow process, and not all change is for the better."

The crunching sound of vehicles in the parking lot outside interrupted the conversation. "I see the river runners are back," Michelle said as she watched the mud-splattered Junction Outfitters van pull up next to her car.

She wished she'd left sooner; now, after successfully avoiding Jacob for three days, she'd have to be polite and speak to him.

"I don't know how much longer Jake is going to be able to keep up this pace with neither Mike nor Cynthia to help," Paloma said. "He's going to kill himself. For the past two nights, he's been here till after one o'clock."

"What did he do with Brooke?"

"She probably slept on the sofa in his office until he was ready to go home."

"No wonder she was so tired in school today. After lunch, she fell asleep reading." Why hadn't Jacob said something to her? She'd have taken care of Brooke.

"I'm sure this is only temporary, and as soon as Jake finds a replacement for Mike, he'll see that Brooke gets plenty of sleep."

Michelle started to say something else, but a young couple came into the store, and Paloma's attention turned to them.

"Thanks again. I'd better go." Michelle headed toward Junction Outfitters. If Jacob was going to work until after midnight, she'd take Brooke home with her. Someone had to look after the poor little girl.

CHAPTER SEVEN

MICHELLE CASUALLY thumbed through the T-shirts and caps in the outer office of Junction Outfitters while Jacob and Greg finished unloading the van. Michelle watched Jacob and couldn't help comparing him to the longshoremen she'd seen in Boston. Except this man exuded more masculinity, and something about him took her breath away. She tried not to stare when he strolled inside.

Taking his time acknowledging her, he twisted the kinks out of his back, then turned toward her. "You need to see me? Or were you wanting to buy a T-shirt?" He stopped a couple of feet in front of her and looked at her with a sardonic smile. "Somehow, I can't see you sending one with our logo to your mom for Mother's Day."

The image of her mother in a Junction Outfitters T-shirt was absurd, but Jacob's jab was insulting. With effort, Michelle softened her glare and schooled her expression. Showing him how angry he could make her with offhand statements would defeat her objective—Brooke's welfare. "No. I don't think that would be a good idea. Mother's tastes are a little more conservative." Michelle turned to walk away from the rack of tourist merchandise and from him. But she couldn't resist a parting shot over her shoulder. "Do you treat all of your customers this way, or do you like being nasty to me in particular?"

"I like being nasty to you." He stepped closer, cutting off any escape from the heat of his body. The faint scent of sweat filled the narrow space, causing Michelle's pulse to beat rapidly. "You're the one who decided to come here," he said. "I didn't invite you."

"Something you've reminded me of several times." She turned around, and, masking her growing attraction with anger, thrust her face toward his. "I'm here whether you like it or not, and the longer I'm here, the more I can see I was justified in coming."

He leaned forward until their noses were only inches apart. His green eyes blazed into her blue eyes. "And just what is that supposed to mean?"

"Brooke." While she was concerned about Brooke's late hours and her being allowed to explore every hillock and gully in the area, Michelle had meant to give him an opportunity to explain himself, and she would have if he hadn't immediately declared war.

Jacob raised an eyebrow, hooked his right thumb in a pocket of his khaki shorts and assumed a defensive stance with his long legs spread slightly apart. "What about Brooke? I saw her outside just a minute ago. She said everything was fine today."

Michelle noticed Victoria had stopped writing and was tilting her head as though she was listening to them. Not wanting to broadcast her grievances against

Jacob to the whole town, Michelle asked, "Do you mind if we go into your office?"

Jacob hesitated before nodding agreement.

Michelle led the way around a corner and into a tiny office. When Jacob pushed the door shut, she was aware that she'd made a mistake. If she'd felt crowded in the other room, now she felt trapped, not so much by Jacob as by her growing awareness of him. There was barely enough space to maneuver around a large oak desk into a gap between a metal folding chair and a small leather sofa. Trying to keep anxiety from showing on her face, she took a deep breath. "I don't know if it's a problem or not, but Brooke fell asleep at school today." *Go easy,* Michelle told herself. *Don't start another argument. You can't win. Not here on his turf.*

"Yeah." Jacob nodded his head as though he knew all about it. "And . . . ?"

Bullheaded man! He was determined to make her the heavy. Any decent father would have offered some explanation. Any decent father would have kept his chest covered in these circumstances. Yet, here he stood with his shirt unbuttoned with no embarrassment. Michelle studied the clutter on his desk so she wouldn't be caught staring at the sheen of his bronze skin, skin which molded his rippling muscles.

Michelle licked her lips and stepped back from him. She needed to put some distance between them. Feeling pressure against her calf when she moved away from him, Michelle glanced down at the sofa which took up one entire wall in the room. "I understand Brooke stayed here with you last night and didn't get home till after midnight."

"Yes, she did. In fact, she helped me after she'd done her homework."

The man was offering no defense, just statement of fact. A series of questions flooded Michelle's mind. *Couldn't you have gotten her to sleep earlier? Couldn't you have taken some of your work home with you so she could have gone to sleep in her own bed? Couldn't you have called me to come get her? Don't you care at all about your daughter?*

"Well, she didn't get all her homework done." Her voice sounded accusing despite her weak efforts to tone it down. "She must have enjoyed helping you too much."

"Michelle . . ." As if tiring of the whole conversation, Jacob ran an open hand over the back of his neck, massaging it while he talked. "I can tell you want to eat me alive, but are too . . . well brought up to do so." The last few words were tinged with sarcasm.

When she started to speak, he shook his head and altered his tone. "No, let me explain. Until Mike is able to come back, I've got a lot of work to do every night when I get in. In the meantime, I've made arrangements for Brooke to be cared for. She's young, she's resilient. I love her, and I'm taking care of her." He met her gaze as though daring her to contradict what he'd said.

Then he stopped his massaging and lowered his arm. His shirt fell back in place, leaving only a sliver of his chest exposed, making it easier for Michelle to look at him and concentrate. But as she tried to think of an appropriate response, Jacob added, "Do you have anything else you want to discuss with me?"

"No. I just want you to know that I'll be happy to keep Brooke for you when you're in a bind. She can spend the night with me."

"I appreciate it." He turned his back on her and began shuffling the papers on his desk.

For a moment, Michelle was stunned by his sudden dismissal. Then, as she opened the door and marched toward her car, she realized she hadn't said a thing she'd meant to. But how could she? For one thing, the man had stood so close to her, with his shirt unbuttoned. Nobody could think straight under those circumstances. And then of course, she had to admit, Brooke *was* being cared for—by the whole village.

AN HOUR LATER Michelle put down the eight-page weekly paper she'd been reading and stretched to the coffee table to pick up the book about desert wildflowers that Jacob had lent her. She was curious about the desolate sotol, but what she really wanted to know about was *candelilla* and why Jacob refused to talk about it.

On page thirty of the guide, she located a picture of a cluster of grayish-green rodlike branches. If this was the celebrated plant, it certainly didn't look like much.

She read the caption underneath the picture. She learned that during the rainy season, the stem filled with milky sap, then in the dry season, this sap coated the stem as wax, which protected the plant from drought.

The book explained that *candelilla* was often pirated from Big Bend National Park because of its commercial value. It was used to make fine-furniture lacquer, chewing gum, a high-grade dental wax and candles, among other things.

The plant sounded highly valuable. Was that what Jacob was up to? Pirating? She slammed the book shut and tossed it on the coffee table.

Feeling nervous and uncomfortable about her suspicion, she went to the kitchen and poured a glass of ice water. She was adding a twist of lime, when the phone rang. Glancing at the clock on the mantel, she moaned aloud, "Mother."

She was right, immediately recognizing her mother's tense voice and clipped pattern of speech.

"Michelle, where have you been? I've been trying to reach you for the past two hours."

Feeling like a tardy schoolgirl, Michelle took a deep breath and willed herself not to apologize or make excuses. She had learned something from her conversations with Paloma, and even Jacob. At some point, people had to decide what was best for themselves. For Paloma, it had been returning to the bosom of her family, for Jacob, starting a new life in Sotol Junction.

"Michelle, can you hear me?"

"Yes, Mother, I can. How are you?"

"Not very well. I've had a touch of a headache most of the day, but after a nap, I feel a little better."

"I'm sorry to hear you're having headaches again."

"I'm sure it's just the tension of you and Brooke being so many miles away in that godforsaken place."

Michelle couldn't argue with her mother's assessment of Sotol Junction. The town had one part-time beauty operator, and a mobile medical clinic came in once a week. No videos to rent, no places to go.

"I'll be home before you know it, Mother."

"Not a moment too soon. And, to think, I'm the one who sent you there. It's just that I miss you. Where were you this afternoon?"

Michelle wasn't sure how much her mother really missed her or how much Elizabeth missed running her daughter's life. "I stopped by and visited a friend's pottery gallery."

"There's a pottery gallery in that place?"

"Yes, Mother. The woman who owns it signs her pottery as The Dove. You may have heard of her work. It's quite well known."

"I can't say that I have. And I really don't care much for pottery. Too coarse."

Michelle felt a tingling at the nape of her neck. Typical of Elizabeth to deliver a negative judgment of Paloma's art without knowing a thing about it. "The pieces I've seen are lovely, Mother."

"Michelle, there's plebeian taste, then there's classical taste." Elizabeth changed the subject. "Have you seen Jacob lately?"

"Yes. I saw him this afternoon," Michelle answered as she looked at the rough-textured vase adorning the coffee table. She liked pottery, her mother's narrow-minded assessment notwithstanding.

"And...? What have you learned?"

"He's working hard because his partner is still out."

"What is he doing with Brooke while he's so busy? He's not leaving her alone, is he?"

"No, Mother. Here, everyone helps with the children. Today, she was at school with me until four, then I took her to Jacob's office. She stayed with Victoria—that's the receptionist—for a couple of hours until he got in from the river."

The phone lines did little to conceal the frustrated sigh Elizabeth emitted. "Michelle," she said, "I don't like it—the thought of my granddaughter existing here and there, moment by moment. She needs to have a regular routine."

Michelle heard the urgency in her mother's voice. "Mother, Brooke's a happy child with a lot of friends." That was more than Michelle could say for her own childhood with its restrictive routine. She recalled her one-and-only slumber party where she'd been allowed to invite three girls to stay overnight. They'd giggled into the wee hours discussing whether a French kiss could make a girl pregnant. Elizabeth had ruled out subsequent slumber parties as being too stimulating. A wry grin crossed Michelle's face. It had been stimulating and a lot of fun. That's what Brooke had here. Constant stimulation and fun.

"I can't tell you how delighted I am to hear the child's happy. Heaven knows, there needs to be one bright spot. However, I still say she needs a routine that I suspect is nonexistent. Last night, I called Jacob's house but no one answered. Michelle—" Elizabeth paused for effect "—it was after nine o'clock on a school night."

"But, Mother, Brooke was at the office with Jacob. He had to work late last night." Michelle recognized her error immediately and tried to make amends. "She did her homework, then she slept on the sofa in his office while he worked. I talked to him this afternoon and offered to bring Brooke home with me, but he said that he was caught up now and shouldn't have to stay again." Michelle felt her little white lie was justified.

"Michelle, this is too much. Do you realize you have been defending the man ever since you got there? Has he already got you wrapped around his finger just like he had DeeDee until she finally came to her senses?"

"Good heavens, no!" Michelle denied the accusation immediately.

"I thought you were smarter than that. You were always the sensible one. Can't you see what he's doing? He cares more for that . . . that so-called business than he does for his own daughter. If he cared for her, he would see that she was fed and in her own bed every night. He'd move back to civilization.''

Her mother had a point, Michelle conceded, but her own assessment of the situation wasn't as critical as it had been before she'd talked to Jacob. He'd lessened her concerns about Brooke's well-being. Although, she sharply reminded herself, Brooke did need more rest.

Michelle had cringed at Elizabeth's jab about her being like DeeDee. That accusation was pure and utter nonsense. DeeDee had sought glitz and glamour all her life, while her own expectations were more down-to-earth. But was her mother right about her reaction to Jacob? she wondered. Was the fact that Michelle found Jacob attractive beginning to color her judgment?

IN THE EARLY Saturday-morning light, Michelle stood on her porch and watched the Junction Outfitters van haul a trailerload of inflatable rafts down to the river. She could hardly believe seven days had passed since she'd come to Sotol Junction. While it wasn't worthy of the *Guinness Book of World Records* to anyone other than herself, she'd survived a week!

Dew glistened off the sparse grass in the yard, dotting the brown terrain with jewels of green. The cool, crisp air washed over Michelle as she closed her eyes to savor its freshness. In the distance, songbirds chirped in harmony. The glorious morning beckoned her to stay outdoors. She grabbed a sweater and trotted down the road toward the break in the tamarisk and cottonwood trees where the van had vanished moments earlier.

She sat on a log well out of the way and watched Jacob and Greg ready the rafts. They moved in harmony, each man performing his task with only an occasional word to the other. Greg, shorter and a little heavier than Jacob, moved in staccato beats, jerking first one way and then another as they loaded the coolers and oars. Jacob was the antithesis. With the grace of a dancer and the strength of a fighter, Jacob lifted, unfolded and fastened the gear in the rafts. Michelle was mesmerized by his lithe body.

When he was apparently satisfied the rafts were properly packed, Jacob turned to give last-minute instructions to the eight people who'd been milling about watching the preparations. Michelle imagined they'd paid more attention to the job the man had done, while she'd been more interested in the man himself.

She strolled closer so she could hear Jacob's voice as he explained how to use the life vests. He'd obviously been studying each member of the group to pick up personality traits and potential problems, because he walked over to a hesitant young man who'd nervously watched everything Greg and Jacob had done. Jacob laid a reassuring arm across the teenager's shoulder and, in a voice too low for Michelle to hear, pointed to the raft, the water and the distant canyon.

Both the boy and Jacob broke into a chuckle at the same time Jacob patted the young rafter's back before stepping away.

Standing off to one side, two older ladies clad in gaudy wind suits giggled like fourteen-year-old girls on their first dates. Michelle found their enthusiasm contagious as she listened to their chatter and questions, and the way they remonstrated with each other. She'd bet they'd be fun on the trip.

Jacob glanced over their heads and spotted Michelle standing near the trees. He took one last look at the people clambering into the rafts before walking over to her. "What brings you out this early?"

"The morning. I've never seen a more beautiful dawn in my life." Her words surprised her. Beauty? In this place?

Jacob nodded. "I know. Sunrises and sunsets here are magnificent." As an afterthought, he added, "You don't get them like this in the city."

"Touché."

"We're headed down the river in a few minutes. Want to join us? We can make room for one more." Was he offering her an olive branch? This was the first time he'd acted as though he wanted her company.

And she really wanted to go. The thought of floating down the river with Jacob and escaping another worrisome day appealed to her. "I'd love to, but I really have to stay here and get things prepared for school Monday." She regretted reminding him of her class, and letting him know it would take her all weekend to prepare for the next week.

He shrugged. "Whatever. Maybe another time." He glanced back toward the raft.

"I'd like that." For a very brief moment, she was tempted to change her mind. Since her conversation with her mother last night, Michelle's thoughts had been filled with Jacob. What was he really like? Was he fun? Had he come here to escape responsibilities or simply to change them? She wanted to know more about this man. But entertaining such fantasies was ridiculous. Jacob was her ex-brother-in-law. Besides, she wasn't at all sure that he wasn't involved in something illegal. Although, standing face-to-face with him in the soft morning light, that possibility didn't seem likely.

"Have you heard from Mike since yesterday afternoon?" she asked after the silence between them became uncomfortable.

"Yeah. He's supposed to get out of the hospital in about a week or ten days. The muscle damage was a little worse than the doctors originally thought. But he's doing okay."

"Thank goodness. I know that has to be a relief for everyone." When Mike and Cynthia returned, maybe Jacob would have better hours. Her mother's words still rang in her ears. "Where's Brooke?"

"Victoria is staying at the house with her."

Michelle wondered why Jacob had not asked her to take care of Brooke since she'd made it clear she was available. He must want to keep his distance from her, to avoid any sense of obligation.

Jacob seemed to notice her disappointment. "If you want to relieve Victoria later, tell her I said it was all right."

"Good. Will it be okay for me to take Brooke home with me?" Michelle didn't want to spend time in Jacob's house. There was something about being in a man's house without him there that was more intimate than she wanted to get.

"Sure. I should be back by six-thirty or seven tonight, so if you and Brooke aren't at my house, I'll come by yours and pick her up."

Michelle watched Jacob rejoin the others in the raft. In a matter of minutes, they shoved off. She walked to the shore to watch the raft powered by Jacob's strong arms move toward the beckoning chasm.

Why did she find him so interesting? God knows, she didn't want to. All she really wanted to do was finish her contract, convince her mother that Brooke was fine and return to Boston.

WHILE HE PADDLED the thirteen-foot raft into the center of the slow-moving water, Jake watched Michelle's body grow smaller and smaller as she stood on the sandy bank of the Rio Grande. She put a hand up to shield her eyes from the glaring sun. Then, as she lowered it and turned to leave, he thought he saw her wave goodbye. Not that it made any difference to him. She was only his daughter's teacher, nothing more.

Then why had he asked her to join them? He didn't really want to spend any more time with her than necessary. In less than two months she would be gone. Which was a good thing because he had to admit he was attracted to her. Every time he saw her, he had to find something to do with his hands to keep himself from touching her. He'd massaged his neck and shuffled papers while he'd ached to caress her, to brush her hair away from her face, to stroke her soft cheek that flushed so easily in frustration. A man would have to be dead from the neck down not to want to.

But there was no way he was going to get involved with his ex-sister-in-law. He vowed to redouble his efforts to ignore her, although for Brooke's sake, he wouldn't be rude. But Michelle was smart enough to pick up on the fact that he wanted nothing to do with her without him having to spell it out.

Satisfied he'd talked himself out of a passing moment of lust, for that was all it was, he began his speech to the other occupants of the raft. Though he had made most of the same observations to every group, he schooled his voice and manner to project the image that this was the first time.

"To your right, you will see the river is lined with tamarisk and Bermuda grass. Both are alien to the Chihuahuan desert. It's a shame they're here because they're slowly replacing some of the native plants, such as the *lechuguilla* you can see up on the mesas there." He pointed to a low limestone uprising.

"The *lechuguilla* only grows in this desert. The tips of its succulent blades are armed with sharp spines that can easily pierce the leather of hiking boots. When Cabeza de Vaca was here in 1535, the *lechuguilla* grew so thick he and his men didn't dare walk around at night. Even though the plant can be damaging, it can also be useful. The conquistadors and Apaches used its strong fibers to make ropes."

The people held on to the sides of the raft and craned their necks looking at the changing vista. Jacob never ceased to gain pleasure watching tourists' faces brighten in awe when the bleakness of the desert was forgotten as the beauty of the deep canyon reared up before them. He, himself, was still amazed.

But today he had more on his mind than the trip. It was nearly time for the *candelilla* harvest. He wished there was another way for the locals to make a few extra dollars without poaching off the park. But *candelilla* was a weed that multiplied faster than rabbits. Uncontrolled, it was a nuisance, so maybe the law needed to be changed. Besides, he wasn't actually involved in the harvest itself. He just knew it was going on.

He was jarred back into doing his job when the raft rocked precariously as one of the women decided to get a better seat. "Whoops, better move easy or not at all," he warned.

He continued in a strong voice that could be easily heard in the almost eerie silence that fell each time he held the long oars out of the water. "On the Mexican side of the river, you can see a *candelilla* wax processing plant.''

''Where? I don't see anything but some old rusty barrels,'' one of the ladies said. ''What's *candelilla?*''

''It's a scraggly weed, not worth enough to cultivate. The Mexicans gather it in the spring and take it to the specially constructed pilas—which are fifty-gallon barrels with fires burning beneath them. You can see the barrels abandoned on that rise. Parts of the plants are dumped into the hot water, and after the wax melts and rises to the top, it's skimmed off and sold. The natives allege it's also a treatment for venereal disease. That's why its species name is *antisyphilitica.*''

The teenager snickered. ''I don't see much need of that around here. I haven't seen but one babe since I got here.''

The older women lit into their nephew for his inappropriate comments, then, satisfied he'd been properly disciplined, turned back toward Jake, as ear-to-ear grins spread across their faces.

Jake knew who that babe was. He'd seen the boy eyeing Michelle earlier on the bank. He hadn't liked it then and liked it less now.

Why did he keep trying to kid himself about having no interest in Michelle? In less than thirty minutes he'd done another about-face. He couldn't help wishing that she had come along today. He'd have liked to share information about the Big Bend with her. Somehow, he was sure she would be an eager pupil.

Maybe something exciting would happen today that he could tell her when he got back. If she took Brooke home with her, he'd have an excuse to go by her house tonight. A flush of warmth swept over him, countering the chill of the morning air.

Without looking at his watch, he knew it was about nine-thirty because they had just floated past a black-and-white layered mesa that for all the world looked like an Oreo cookie. But he didn't point out the comparison to his guests. Michelle Davis was occupying his mind, and if he couldn't shake thoughts of her, it was going to be a long day.

CHAPTER EIGHT

MICHELLE PULLED UP to Jacob's house at exactly three o'clock. It had taken her most of the day to prepare for the coming school week. She'd felt like a beginning teacher again. But finally, she thought she had things ready. Austin, John, Antonio and their compadres were in for a surprise Monday morning. That thought gave a lift to her stride as she walked up the path toward the door.

Jacob's house was larger and looked newer than her own, yet, with its low adobe walls, it had the same Mexican styling. Scattered pots of colorful flowers and a weathered swing adorned the long, front porch, giving indication that a family lived there. A warmth filled her heart as she imagined Jacob and Brooke sitting in the swing at dusk sharing the day's events. Yet, she simply couldn't visualize Jacob caring for the flowers.

The soft-spoken, proper Jacob she'd seen eight years ago might have found comfort gardening, but that Jacob was gone. A vague feeling of uneasiness gripped her about entering his house. Before she had time to consider further, she lifted the heavy brass knocker and almost immediately, the large, double wood doors were thrown open, startling her.

Brooke, flaxen hair in pigtails, emerged from the doorway. "Hi, Aunt Michelle. Victoria is glad I'm going with you, so she helped me get ready."

Victoria appeared in the shaded hallway behind Brooke, an obvious look of embarrassment on her face. "Brooke, honestly!" She turned to Michelle. "Hello, Miss Davis. When you called, I, well, see, Miguel, he asked me to go with him tonight, to Alpine. But Mr. Evans needed me, so I couldn't tell him I didn't want to work today."

Michelle smiled. "I understand, Victoria. It's Saturday and you have a date, so this is working out for all of us. You can leave as soon as you need to so you'll have plenty of time to get ready. I'll see to Brooke until Mr. Evans comes home."

"Thanks." Victoria wasted no time lingering for other polite exchanges. She grabbed her purse and excused herself, all the time thanking Michelle for understanding.

Brooke bounded across the small terra-cotta-tiled entry. "I've got some stuff to show you, Aunt Michelle. Come on."

Michelle followed Brooke into the living room and stopped in amazement. Silhouetted in the long windows were the craggy, barren mountains that separated Texas from Old Mexico. The vista was an extension of the room's warm, southwestern decor which contained none of the commercial tackiness of the current fad. It had a timelessness that would be as lovely in thirty years as it was now. For a split second, Michelle pictured herself spending time here, then the vision vanished.

As she stepped forward, she noticed that other rooms branched off this area. Whoever had decorated the house had intended it to be a home for a family. Michelle sensed Jacob had done it himself. She could almost feel his presence though he was miles away on the river.

Brooke's voice interrupted her thoughts. "Let me show you the rest of the house." She grabbed her aunt's hand and said, "My room first."

In little-girl excitement, Brooke talked nonstop as they inspected her bedroom "—*and* bathroom—" and the guest bedroom before they made it to the large country kitchen. Brooke came to an abrupt stop, then twirled around. "Daddy really does like the kitchen."

It was a working kitchen with lots of counter space. "It's nice."

"Daddy's teaching me how to cook. He's always teasing me that I've got to cook for him when he gets old."

Michelle remembered the big dish Jacob had cooked for the barbecue. She'd thought it was just a quirk, until now when she noticed the rows of green herbs lining the double window ledges. Jacob Evans and his talents were surprising her more all the time.

The last room Brooke led her to was the master bedroom. Knowing she was an intruder, Michelle hung back near the doorway and surveyed the masculine domain. She tried to keep from staring, but her eyes were drawn to the queen-size wrought-iron bed that faced a large window and a small corner fireplace. A woolen Mexican blanket, its ivory and black stripes threaded with a subdued red, was tossed haphazardly across the bed as if its occupant had left hastily. It was easy to picture a fire in the fireplace on a chilly night with Jacob sprawled across the bed, his body glistening in the flickering light. She felt a tug on her hand and gave a guilty start.

"Come on," Brooke said. "Let's go get some ice cream, then we can stop at Paloma's to see if Katy wants to play. Would that be okay? For Katy to come to your house with us?"

"Good idea," Michelle agreed, still amazed that Brooke's chatter was constant, like a windup toy that never wound down. She should have thought of inviting Katy herself. Paloma had been taking care of the girl while Cynthia was with Mike in Lubbock. Since Saturdays were busy shopping days, Paloma would probably appreciate having time to attend to her customers without worrying about Katy.

And Michelle did want to get out of Jacob's house as soon as possible. Ice cream—or anything that could keep her mind off Jacob—would be fine.

BY SEVEN, Michelle was a bundle of nerves. Jacob would be arriving soon, and she knew that without any move on his part, her feelings about him had undergone a subtle change since morning. Now she was faced with the knowledge that she found him more than a little attractive.

The situation might have been easier if he had been a total stranger rather than her ex-brother-in-law. That complication never left her mind. Nor did Elizabeth's crusade. Michelle knew how inappropriate—not to mention inconvenient—her feelings for him were. She was simply going to have to be more resolute about staying away from Jacob. And that was fighting a losing battle.

The sound of his pickup crunching on the rocks in front of the house drew her to the porch. As he came up the walk, Michelle's heart skipped a beat, but she was determined that she would make just enough conversation to be polite, then bid him and Brooke good-night. "Hello. How was your day?"

"It was better than usual." Jacob walked up onto the narrow porch. "You missed a great time. You should've come."

Meeting his gaze, Michelle felt her resolve crumbling. "I wish I could have, but duty called." She moved back and opened the door for Jacob. "Come on in. Brooke and Katy are playing in the backyard. Those kids never run out of energy."

"She didn't give you any trouble, did she?" he asked as he stepped around her and entered the house.

"Oh, no. Brooke has wonderful manners. Would you like something to drink?" Michelle could have kicked herself. She hadn't meant to ask that. She'd meant for Jacob to be on his way.

"A tall glass of iced tea would hit the spot."

"I understand. I seldom drank iced tea until I came out here. Now, I always keep a pitcher in the fridge." Just one of the many things about her life she'd changed since she'd been here. Iced tea for Perrier, and long evenings alone planning classes for five different grades rather than having a social life. But not everything had been difficult to give up—she didn't miss wearing pumps and panty hose one bit.

"It's the climate. If you don't want to dry up and blow away, you have to drink an awful lot of liquid." Settling his tall frame into one of the wooden chairs in the kitchen, he ran his hand over the back of his neck.

"I've noticed," she said, putting ice into two tall glasses and filling them with tea. As she held one out to him, her thoughts returned to his earlier invitation. "Jake, did you mean it when you said I could go with you another time?" She groaned inwardly, not having meant to ask that, either. And she certainly hadn't meant to call him Jake. She knew everyone else did, but somehow the more formal Jacob added distance to their relationship. Oh well, it was too late to take it back now.

He took the glass. "Sure, I meant it." He drank half the tea, hesitated a moment, then finished draining the glass. "Lord, I was thirsty." Michelle handed him the pitcher, and he poured himself another glass. "The best time to enjoy the river would be after the spring season, in May when most of the tourists have left. Then it's not as crowded. If we work it right, we could be the only raft on the river. That's when you really get a sense of how awesome nature can be. I'm planning to take an overnighter about that time with a couple of guys from Houston. We're trying to work out something for the company I used to work for. They're interested in a type of corporate retreat. You may want to go then."

Michelle had intended to be back in Boston the end of May, but maybe she would stay a few extra days to float the river with *Jake*. "That sounds wonderful." What had she just agreed to? Spending the night in the middle of the desert with a man who, only hours before, she'd vowed to stay away from.

"We can work out all the details later." Jake sipped from his second glass of tea and drummed his fingers on the tabletop. "Now, if I had any energy left, I'd gather up my kid and head home."

"She'll come inside in a few minutes." Michelle doubted Brooke knew her father had arrived, or she'd have hurled her body inside immediately. From what Brooke had said about her daddy, one would think Jake Evans was next to God.

Michelle didn't have cause to regard him quite so highly, but it wouldn't hurt to spend just a few more minutes alone with him before she called Brooke in. Maybe it was time to get to know her niece's father a little better. After all, they both had Brooke's interests at heart.

"Let's go to the living room where it's a little cooler," Michelle said, leading the way. She tucked one foot under her when she sat in a corner of the love seat. "Do you realize today is the first time we've talked without getting into a fight?" she asked.

A wry smile softened his face as he took a seat beside her on the small sofa. "The day isn't over yet. Do you think we'll make it?"

"Maybe. If you don't say much." She smiled back at him. It was amazing how different his face looked when he relaxed. How could she have ever thought him cold and sardonic? she wondered.

"Maybe it's not me. You just overreact." He raised an eyebrow.

Her corresponding eyebrow raised in reaction. "I think we're getting on dangerous ground. But I'll tell you what. For today, you can talk all you want, and I'll control myself."

"Well, I certainly can't pass up a deal like that," he said. Apparently giving the proposition deep consideration, Jake stroked his chin as he looked at Michelle. "That takes all the sport out of antagonizing you."

"Can't spar without an opponent, huh?"

"Right. Tell you what. I'll control myself, too." He cracked a knuckle and grinned at the same time. "Childhood habit."

She laughed.

He laughed. "Say, do you really want to go on the river run with me, or are you just being polite?"

"I really want to go," she said.

"Good. I couldn't ever talk DeeDee into trying it—she said it was too dirty—and I guess I thought you would be the same."

Michelle shook her head. "In lots of ways DeeDee and I were very different, even though we were raised by the same parents in the same environment." Although time had blurred the reasons for her disagreements with her sister, she could still remember how she'd always felt overshadowed by DeeDee.

"I'm beginning to figure that out. For DeeDee, if something didn't involve style, it wasn't interesting. Hang the substance." Jake's tone of voice hardened as he spoke.

Coming to her sister's defense, Michelle said, "That isn't completely accurate. I knew my sister before you did, and she had a lot of character. She was...she was a wonderfully supportive sister." Even as she said the words, she knew they weren't true. DeeDee had never really cared for anyone other than herself.

"Well, she wasn't my sister. She was my wife, and definitely not supportive. Of me or Brooke." His glance challenged Michelle to deny his accusation.

"Well, we didn't make it, did we?"

"What?"

"We didn't make it through the day without fighting."

"I'm sorry, I didn't mean...it's just that Brooke is so important to me that I react..."

"So, you admit that you overreact, too."

"I react, not overreact. There's a difference. I—"

They were interrupted by the crashing sound of footsteps running up the porch and into the house. *"La Llorona! La Llorona!"* Brooke and Katy were yelling in unison as they ran into the room.

"What are they saying?" Michelle turned to Jake as they both rose to their feet.

"We heard her! Down by the river! We heard her calling!"

"Who?" Michelle asked. "Who was down at the river?"

Brooke caught her breath and explained, *"La Llorona!* The ghost woman. We heard her calling for her babies."

Katy, shaking, began to cry. "She'll get us."

"Brooke! Katy! You know there is no such thing as ghosts," Michelle said, trying to calm the girls. "No one is going to get you. You probably heard an animal or something." She put her arm around her niece's shoulders.

"There are too ghosts. Tell her, Daddy," Brooke pleaded. *"La Llorona* is real."

Jake explained, "The local people believe *La Llorona* is a woman condemned to wander the earth looking for a child to replace her own children she drowned in the river."

"But you can't believe that or allow your daughter to think such nonsense!"

"It is too real. You'll see. Come on." Brooke pulled at her hand and dragged her outside along with Jake and Katy. "Just listen."

Sure enough, from the direction of the river, Michelle heard something that sounded like a baby crying. The human sound sent shivers down her arms and she wrapped her hands tightly around them. She followed the others to the fence that surrounded the yard. This time when she heard the sound, it was closer than she'd thought. She walked along the fence until the soft cry seemed to come from near her feet. She curled her toes in retreat.

"There's a flashlight in my pickup," Jake told Brooke. "Run and get it."

When Brooke returned with the flashlight, Jake shone it at the ground and flipped over a rock with his boot tip. "This is what you heard. It just sounded like it was a long way off."

In the harsh circle of light, Michelle saw the ugliest insect she'd ever seen, and it was a full two inches long. She jumped back.

Brooke stepped forward. "Yuk. Just look at that. You can see its guts." Katy and Brooke had a yuk contest as they bent over the insect trying to burrow itself in the ground.

"What is it?" Michelle asked.

"*Niña de la tierra,* a child-of-the-earth. It's an insect that sounds like a baby crying or a woman wailing. They are often mistaken for *La Llorona* because of their cry and because they're drawn to moist places in the desert. Such as a river. You've probably been watering the flowers around here since you moved in. That's why this little fellow was attracted to your yard."

Michelle shuddered and backed farther away until she felt a porch support at her back. "Then I'm through watering," she said. If she never saw another child-of-the-earth, she wouldn't regret it. "Why didn't you tell the girls that the whole story isn't true?" she asked Jake.

"Who said it isn't true?"

"I do. It's just a big, old, ugly insect that makes a loud noise."

"That's what we heard tonight, but that may not be what you hear next time. Maybe the legend got started by a mistaken sound. Or maybe not. It's not for me or you to decide. Mexicans in Texas and New Mexico have told their children the story for hundreds of years. Paloma said it scares the hell out of the kids and keeps them from wandering too near a river at night."

"That's cruel."

"By whose standards?"

"Any civilized person's."

"You've got a lot to learn." Jake turned to leave, beckoning the girls. "I'll drop Katy off on our way home. Thanks for the tea."

Michelle stood on the porch and watched until the red lights from Jake's pickup disappeared in the night.

Yes, she might have a lot to learn, but one thing she had already learned well. She and Jake Evans couldn't get through one day without having words.

CHAPTER NINE

"HEY, BUDDY." Mike lowered himself into the metal folding chair across from Jake's desk and propped his crutches on the sofa. "How's it goin'?"

Startled, Jake turned around from the file cabinet. Flipping off the blaring music of the radio, he moved around the desk to get a better look at his old friend. He didn't like what he saw. Mike had lost a few pounds on an already-thin frame. "Well, you're still as ugly as ever. I'd hoped the hospital food would make you look a little better. Now, what the hell are you doing here?"

"Glad to see all the extra work didn't affect your sweet personality."

A wry grin crossed Jake's face. "Sorry. It's just that I talked to Paloma this morning, and she said that you'd be bedridden for a while."

Mike waved off the suggestion. "Paloma's a mother hen."

"But you really should be at home." Jake was concerned about his friend. He knew that the snake venom had dissolved part of the muscle in Mike's leg.

"I'm goin', I'm goin'." He motioned with his hand. "I just thought I'd sneak in here to see what was happenin'."

"Nothing much is happening. We have a raftload going out tomorrow and two more are scheduled for this weekend." Jake positioned his body between Mike and the ledger he'd been working on. There wasn't any point in saying anything to Mike about finances until Jake had had time to figure something out. "I've got it all covered."

"I wasn't as useless as all that. You need help and you know it. You hired somebody yet?" Mike's voice wavered slightly as if the strain of being up and about was getting to him. "'Cause if you haven't, I think I'll be fit by—"

"No way. You can't go back to work until the doctor releases you."

"That might not be for a month or more, and you know we'll have a cash-flow problem. I sure had time to think about that while I was propped up in that skinny little hospital bed."

"And here I thought you were having a beauty rest."

Mike offered Jake a weak smile and rubbed his swollen leg. "You oughta see this sucker. All shades of purple." Mike shifted slightly. "Seriously, Jake. I really did do a lot of thinkin'. Our liability insurance is coming up, and..."

"Hey, don't worry about it, Mike. We can work something out. I've been doing some thinking, too. I can loan the business a little cash just to get us through.''

''No,'' Mike said. ''I don't like it. You puttin' your savings into this.'' He waved his arm around. ''We agreed when we started not to sink any more into it than we could afford to lose.''

''And up until now, that's been okay. But we need to hire another guide, and you're going to have medical bills over insurance payments. I won't put in much. A couple of thousand. Just enough to make sure we won't have any problems.''

''I still don't like it.'' Mike's face had grown more ashen as he talked. Sitting silently for a few seconds as though to gain strength, he finally said, ''But for now, I guess I don't have much choice.''

''Mike, trust me. It'll be okay. Now, you need to get home and prop that leg up.'' Jake stood and looked toward the street. ''Let me find Cynthia to help me haul your carcass out of here.''

''Cynthia'll be right back. She dropped me off on her way to school to pick up Katy. Paloma said she's really missed us, so Cynthia thought she'd surprise her.''

''Is it already that time?'' Jake glanced at his watch and cursed to himself. ''I've got to go get Brooke. Lock the door on your way out if I'm not back.''

MICHELLE STOOD in the classroom doorway and watched the students straggle out as she visited with

Cynthia. "I know you're tired of answering the same question, but how is Mike doing?"

"Physically, he's doing okay, although it's going to be hard to keep him down," Cynthia said. "At least another month, the doctor said. Mike's literally chomping at the bit. He insisted I take him by the office on my way here." Cynthia fidgeted with the strap of her purse. "I came by to see how Katy was doing in school. We hated that she missed a couple of days, but we thought it was best for her to be with her father, and we didn't want to impose on Paloma any more than we had to."

"I'm sure Paloma enjoyed keeping her, and Katy has already caught up with her work. But I think she's been missing the two of you. Her attention hasn't been on her assignments."

"I worried about that. I called her every night to reassure her."

"She'll be fine. Children are more resilient than adults."

Cynthia looked at the ground, Michelle could tell she was upset.

"What's wrong?"

"Nothing. I'm just tired." Cynthia brushed a tear out of her eye and looked up.

"Are you sure? Is there anything I can do to help?"

"No, it's just I don't know how much longer I can take this place." A look of total despair settled across Cynthia's face. "I've got to get out of here or I'm going to go crazy."

"What about Mike and the business?" Michelle stepped aside as Antonio hurried back in the building.

"I forgot my pencil," he said, brushing past her.

Cynthia hugged her arms as if she were chilled in the hot afternoon sun. She shook her head. "I don't know. But I'm thinking about going back to my folks' place in East Texas. I can put Katy in a real school."

Michelle winced, even though she didn't think Cynthia meant to insult her. She was just distressed. Almost losing her husband must have been a terrible shock. "Don't you think when Mike recovers and you rest a bit, things will get better?"

"This isn't anything new. I've been thinking about it for a long time. This accident has convinced me. I'm not going to stay here and watch my husband or my daughter die in this godforsaken place. No doctor for sixty miles. It's madness." She tilted her chin in determination just as Katy and Brooke dashed across the playground toward them. Katy asked, "Mom, can Brooke spend the night with me? Please?"

Cynthia placed her hand on her daughter's shoulder. "Not tonight, Katy. This is your daddy's first night at home and he wants to hear what you've been doing." She looked back at Michelle. "Sorry. I didn't mean to dump on you. I guess we better go pick up Mike."

"It's okay." Michelle watched Cynthia and Katy climb into their Jeep and drive off. She was sorry for the other woman. Michelle remembered what Paloma had said about Mike selling out to Jake and the bind that would put him in. It looked as if it might really happen now.

Michelle hadn't seen Jake in more than a week—ever since they'd argued about DeeDee. She wondered how he was doing. Not that he would confide in her, anyway.

She turned to go back inside, but there were still children milling around the school yard so she stopped and leaned against the doorjamb to watch them. A couple of parents usually came to pick up their children, and four students rode the small school bus to their homes on neighboring ranches. The majority walked home. Today, as all the previous days, several kids seemed reluctant to leave. They came back in the small building once or twice to get things they had left, or they needed a drink before the walk home or they just wanted to visit. She'd come to enjoy the extra few minutes she got to spend with them, getting to know them better. She wondered if they were simply trying to avoid going home. For two of them, she suspected that was true.

"Miss! Miss!" Austin's voice was unmistakable.

Michelle hurried off the porch toward the group that had formed around a large rock near a mesquite tree in the school yard. She could tell from a distance that the children were excited and anxious. Had two of them gotten into a fight? But rather than loud, angry voices, she heard whimpering as she drew closer.

Three kids stood about ten feet from a little boy sitting on top of a large rock with his knees pulled up against his chest—Javier crying and mumbling something in Spanish.

"What is it? Michelle asked as she passed the older children and headed to pick up the little boy.

"There." Austin pointed to the ground under the rock. "A snake."

At first, Michelle didn't see anything. As Javier's crying got louder, she made out the outline of a tannish yellow snake with brown diamonds on its back. She froze barely six feet away from the reptile partially hidden by the limestone rock.

The rock wasn't tall or big enough to keep the snake from striking the child. And though she didn't know much about snakes, she was certain that as soon as the snake figured out where the noise was coming from, he would strike at it. She spoke softly, her voice trembling and weak. "Be quiet, Javier. Don't cry anymore."

His sobs just got louder as he tried to stand up, his little boot kicking loose dirt down the face of the rock. Michelle watched in horror as the snake began to move. Its rattlers clicked an almost imperceptible warning as it slithered from under the rock's edge. She could see all of the reptile's four-foot length as it slowly advanced.

Michelle held one of her hands up and told Javier. "No! No! Don't move." Not taking her eyes off the snake that was now coiling at the base of the rock,

Michelle whispered over her shoulder, "Someone tell him in Spanish not to move or make a noise."

In a halting voice, Rosa explained to Javier. He seemed to understand the urgency of his cousin's words because he stifled his sobs until only muffled weeping remained.

"It don't matter, Miss," Austin told her. "Snakes are deaf. And they don't see too good, neither."

Michelle could feel the palms of her hands growing damp, and it seemed the temperature had dropped several degrees in the past few minutes. Her skin felt clammy in the slight breeze that chased a sheet of paper through the narrow space between her feet and the snake only a yard away. She'd read somewhere that a rattlesnake could strike from that distance.

Behind her, Austin went on to explain, in a quiet voice, she noticed, "They go after things that are warm and move around."

Even her muddled mind could register that the nearest warm thing to the snake was Javier's foot and that if he moved it again the snake might notice. She had to get to him but her muscles wouldn't work. She couldn't move either to help him or to save herself if the snake decided to turn on her.

"What are you going to do?" Lydia asked softly as the snake sent out a louder warning. Its tail held high, flicking back and forth faster than Michelle's eye could follow, it prepared to battle. She'd read that if you ever heard a rattlesnake, you didn't have to be told what it was. That was true. The sound was like dry beans being shaken in a paper cup.

"I don't know. Let me think a minute." Her voice cracked with fear.

She vaguely heard one of the kids whisper, "It's a *Mojave!*"

Oh, God. A Mojave. Jake had said they were deadly, paralyzing a victim in minutes. She had to do something. "Rosa, you stay where you are and talk softly to Javier to keep him calm. Austin, you run to get some help. I'll get a stick to try to draw the snake away." She just hoped her legs would support her.

"Here comes Brooke's daddy," Austin yelled. "There's a Mojave over here, Mr. Evans."

"Don't anyone move until I see what's happening." Jake's voice, filled with cool authority, commanded from somewhere a few feet behind her.

Michelle hadn't heard his pickup drive up, but the sound of his voice overwhelmed her with relief. "I've got to help Javier."

"No, let me take care of this." He took a step forward and sized up the situation. "Tomas—" Jake nodded his head in the direction of his pickup "—there's a shovel in the back of my truck. You and Brooke go get it. Move slowly."

"Sí, señor," the boy said, taking a couple of steps backward then whirling around and running.

Jake's voice was low and soothing as he tried to calm Michelle. "It'll be okay. Snakes like humans even less than we like them. If they don't feel threatened, they'll try to find a way to escape."

As he talked, Michelle could see him out of the corner of her eye moving the other children farther away from the rock and the snake. Since he'd arrived and taken over, Michelle felt the adrenaline seeping from her body. Her bones felt like mush. She was afraid she was going to faint. It seemed like hours passed before she heard Jake thank Tomas and take the shovel.

"I'm going to chop off his head," Jake said. "Just stand still." She felt him easing up beside her. He spoke to Javier in Spanish, reassuring him and explaining what he planned to do.

Michelle saw his arms raised, the shovel poised as a weapon, then she heard a swish before the shovel delved downward, separating the snake's body from its head. The rattles still sounded in death throes as the body writhed on the ground. Michelle closed her eyes to blot out the sight. She knew she'd never forget the sound as long as she lived.

Jake scooped up Javier and hugged him before handing him to his cousin. Javier clutched Rosa and began sobbing again while she patted his back in comfort.

Michelle started shaking, the relief so overwhelming she feared she was going to cry louder than Javier, but she didn't want her students to see how distraught she'd been. She looked up when she felt warm hands on her shoulders.

"Are you going to be okay?" Jake asked.

When words wouldn't come, she nodded.

He drew her into his arms and held her. "It's all right. The snake's dead and Javier's fine."

Michelle was grateful for the strong support of his arms because without them she would have fallen. She felt safe in his embrace. Minutes passed before she recovered enough to notice he was stroking her hair. It felt good and she wanted to stay where she was, but they were surrounded by curious children. She pulled back to look into Jake's eyes, their normal green darkened with emotion. She could see he had been upset by what had happened. "Thank you...I...don't know what would have happened if you hadn't come."

His arms tightened briefly before he steadied her with his hands and stepped back to put some space between them. "You would have managed."

Michelle was chilled where his body had been pressed against hers. "No, I couldn't do..." Just as she started to explain, she noticed the children had dragged the dead snake away from the rock onto clear packed dirt and were proceeding to cut it to bits with the shovel.

As she started toward them, Jake restrained her with a firm hand on her upper arm. "Let them go. It's a kind of catharsis. They were scared, too."

"Do you want these for a souvenir, Miss Davis?" Two-inch-long rattlers dangled from Austin's fingertips.

She grimaced and shook her head. "No, I don't."

Jake patted her on the shoulder. "Why don't you go inside and sit down while I help the kids dispose of the remains. When I'm done, I'll drive you home."

"Okay." She forced one foot in front of the other, slowly walking toward the school. Her legs still wouldn't move fast. She felt Brooke slide a little hand inside hers.

"Daddy said you might like some company." Her niece looked up at her with a sympathy that surpassed her years.

A somber smile crossed Michelle face. "He's right, sweetheart." Jake was so thoughtful. When he'd put his arm around her in comfort, the week they'd spent avoiding one another slipped away.

THREE HOURS LATER, Paloma walked through the school's hard-packed dirt playground area and stopped near the large mesquite tree. Beneath its branches, the disheveled dirt around the small boulder was all that physically remained of the afternoon's drama.

Emotional remains were another matter. News of the incident with the snake had swept through the small community faster than a brushfire, growing a little worse with each telling. She'd heard at least four different versions herself.

Unlocking the heavy oak door, she entered the schoolhouse to prepare for that evening's board meeting. In a matter of minutes, she heard a vehicle stop in front. Through the window, she watched Jake get out and reach into the pickup bed, withdrawing a brand-new hoe. He ran his thumb over the edge he'd obviously sharpened and turned toward the building as other vehicles pulled up. All were early.

Paloma stepped out on the porch. Knowing this was not going to be an ordinary meeting, she wanted to greet everyone, to offer a calming influence. But as the men started to enter, she heard the squeal of tires a couple of blocks away. A pickup followed by a wake of dust sped toward the school and whipped into the driveway. Hardly waiting for his truck to come to a complete stop, Bill Wiley jumped out and slammed the door with a vengeance. He looked as though he was loaded for bear as his long strides crossed the playground.

His face red and his eyes glaring, he blurted out, "Well, folks. Let's get this show on the road. We got us some important stuff to discuss tonight, on the agenda or not on the agenda." Pushing through the others, he headed toward his chair as though defying anyone, particularly Paloma, to cross him.

When everyone was seated at the oak table, Paloma's gaze met Jake's in understanding. "The meeting is called to order. We'll follow the agenda as posted, then, under miscellaneous items, you can bring up your concerns, Bill."

The agenda, including the opening prayer, minutes, paying the bills and approving a few other items were completed in a record fifteen minutes.

"Is there any other business?" Paloma asked, looking at Bill.

"I wanna talk about that snake this afternoon and how our little Yankee lady didn't do nothing to take care of our kids." Bill stomped across the floor and spit his tobacco into a soda can. Out of habit, he said, "Excuse me," to Paloma.

"Yeah, I been thinking about that, too," Juan Lopez said. "When my little girl Rosa brought Javier home today, he was still crying." Juan shook his head, taking up the alarm. "My sister would never forgive me if anything had happened to her boy while he was living with me."

Bill nodded his head toward Jake. "You was right from the beginning, Jake. Little Miss City Girl's not the right person for this job. I'm glad I had the good sense to follow your lead."

"I understand your concern, Bill," Jake answered him. "After all, Brooke was there, too. But, in Ms. Davis's defense, we should have shown her what to do if she saw a snake. We all knew she was a city girl."

Paloma was pleased but not at all surprised with Jake's defense of Michelle. "I noticed that you brought a hoe to school, Jake."

He nodded. "Yeah. One should've been here all along."

"Hell—ah, excuse me, Paloma—anyone who's got a lick of sense would have done something, hoe or no hoe. There were sticks, rocks..." Obviously, Bill wasn't going to be shaken loose from his anger and proved it when he uttered another expletive.

"There's no need for that kind of talk, Bill," Prof Broselow interceded. "She's new to the area, and, yes, she made a mistake. One she can't afford to make again. She probably feels worse about this than anyone."

Rolling his eyes upward, Bill snorted in disgust. "You're not gonna gloss over her incompetence with saying, 'She's sorry.' She coulda done somethin' other that holler for someone to go get help. It could've taken a week of Sundays before someone got there."

"But it didn't." Jake's jaw tightened as though he was fighting down words he'd later regret.

"But it could've. And, I'll tell you another thing," Bill was really glowering now, "she's been picking on Austin." Punching his index finger on the table, he added, "And I'll not stand for it."

"Bill, I think it's time you heard some hard truths." Paloma's voice commanded respect. She wasn't going to allow this forum to turn into a roast of Michelle Davis. "According to the other children, your Austin is no angel. It's time a teacher took him on."

Bill's jaw went slack when everyone started laughing.

"But..."

"We're talking about the snake, not classroom discipline." Both eyebrows raised, Paloma presented a formidable opponent.

Jake intervened. "This afternoon, Ms. Davis saw me kill a snake, probably the first time she's ever seen it done. I can guarantee you that she knows what to do now. And a brand-new hoe is stowed on the porch. I also suggest that we arrange for her to take a class in CPR."

"Good idea," Ramon Abalos agreed. "She's here another six weeks. Now, I move this meeting adjourned and we get out the dominoes."

"I second the motion," Prof said. "And I don't intend for my recreation to get tangled up in any seriousness, so anyone who makes mention of a snake is going to be thrown out."

A chorus of voices "thirding" that motion circled the room.

CHAPTER TEN

MICHELLE SAT beside Brooke on the sofa and stared at the small portable television set next to the empty fireplace. Staring was all she was doing because she had been unable to focus on anything since the frightening scene in the school yard that afternoon. She was thankful Jake had allowed Brooke to stay with her for a few hours. She didn't want to be alone with her thoughts this evening.

She wished she'd behaved differently this afternoon. She should have been able to think clearly and rescue Javier. What if Jake hadn't arrived? Would her feeble attempts have scared off the snake? She didn't really want to know the answer. She hugged her knees closer to her chest.

"Are you cold, Aunt Michelle?" Brooke asked. "I'll get you the afghan."

"No, thanks, honey. I'm fine." Michelle put her arm around Brooke and pulled her to her side just as she heard a firm knock on the front door. Jake was earlier than she'd expected. "That's your daddy."

Brooke jumped up to answer the door. Michelle followed a few steps behind her.

Jake stood in the doorway. The light from the lamp on the end table behind her glinted off his raven hair as he gave Brooke a hug then straightened to look at Michelle.

"How do you feel?" he asked. His voice was warm, as if he really cared how she had fared.

"Better." She tried to smile. "Would you like a cup of coffee?" It seemed she was always offering him something to drink. Maybe he had some news to tell her about the board meeting. She was sure that she'd been severely criticized.

"Not tonight, thanks. I'd better get Brooke home to bed. Tomorrow is a school day. Are you sure you'll be all right here by yourself?"

"Yes." She tilted her chin up, summoning as much courage as she could. She didn't want him to know how she really felt. That she longed to feel his arms around her again. She'd felt such strength when he'd held her. She wished she could ask him to stay for a while. "I'll be fine."

THE FOLLOWING TWO DAYS were pretty uneventful. Michelle had a little trouble sleeping, but not as much as she'd feared. She hadn't seen Jake since he'd picked up Brooke after the board meeting; he'd been on the river all day yesterday. As for her students—once they had gotten over their shock of the snake incident— they'd settled down to work. In fact, until a few minutes ago—when she'd had a small discipline problem with Antonio—there'd been no difficulties in her classroom since she'd restructured it.

Michelle breathed deeply and started to lean back in her chair when she saw Jake standing near the back of the room. In the after-school scramble, he must have wandered in while she was dealing with Antonio. "Hello, Jake. I didn't hear you."

"You were busy."

She tried not to notice how his snug, well-worn jeans molded his body as he walked toward her, nor how he thrust a hand in his back pocket before lazily propping one hip on the edge of her desk and stretching out a booted foot to rest only inches from her chair.

Michelle's mouth suddenly felt dry, and she swallowed a couple of times before she stood and faced him at eye level. She hoped he hadn't noticed her discomfort, although the look he gave her from under dark lashes hinted he wasn't immune to her, either. The large schoolroom was growing smaller and the air heavier with every passing second.

She tried, as she had before, to behave as if he were any other parent, but even to her own ears her voice lowered and became huskier than normal, quite unsuited to her words. "Antonio and I had a little problem, but it's been handled." She cleared her throat and spoke again. "Is there something I can do for you?"

"No, thanks. Brooke's waiting for me. I just thought I'd come in and see how she was doing in school." He removed his hand from his pocket and crossed his arms over his chest, creating a safe barrier between the two of them.

With the spell he'd cast on her broken, Michelle grinned in relief and ran a hand through her hair, brushing it away from her warm forehead. "That's as pitiful an excuse for checking up on me as I've ever heard. You know she's an excellent student, working considerably above her grade level."

"Yeah, I know. Genetics." Jake puffed out his chest.

"The Davis or the Evans genes?" Michelle countered.

A shadow passed over his face as his emotion changed. "I suspect both sets had a hand in a lot of what Brooke is today." He picked up a pencil from her desk, and rolled it around in his fingers. "How are you doing? Are things back to normal?"

Michelle didn't have to ask what he was talking about. She knew he meant the incident with the snake. "It was a one-day wonder. We had talked about it in detail when everyone got to school the next day." She shuddered at the thought. "We looked the Mojave up in the field guide. You'd mentioned how dangerous it was when Mike was bitten, but I didn't know what one looked like. Also, *Mr. Evans*—" Michelle crossed her arms over her chest "—the kids told me this is snake season. You didn't tell me there was a season for them. Why not?"

He shrugged. "I thought it would only scare you. But I should have warned you and told you how to kill them."

"I think I know what to do now. If my body will comply, that is." Michelle shivered at the thought.

"Other than the snake, how are things going?"

"You're checking up on me, aren't you?"

"I'm not spying on you, or I'd have come during the day."

Michelle appreciated that he hadn't, but wouldn't have been overly concerned had he come earlier to observe her interactions with the students. She was pleased with her management techniques, techniques she'd never had to use until she'd begun teaching in Sotol Junction.

She cocked her head, her small chin set in confidence. "The past two days have gone really well." She cast Jake a challenging eye. "Pablo came back yesterday."

"How's he doing?"

"Jake, he's so smart. If he were in school all the time, there's no telling what he could accomplish. Already, in math, he needs to be in algebra, and he's only a sixth-grader, although he is fourteen." She began to talk faster as her enthusiasm for her profession built. "I'm going to have to go home and brush up so I can teach him. I suspect within a year he'll be far past me. Although my grades were good, math was never my strong suit."

Jake smiled. "It was mine, but I almost failed English my freshman year in high school. I've never forgotten how angry my father was with me." He shrugged his shoulders in memory. "I thought he was going to whip me even though I was a head taller than he was by that time. He would've, too, if Mother hadn't stopped him."

Michelle wished she'd known the young Jake. She'd bet he was the cause of a lot of gray hairs. "Did you ever slack off again?"

"No way. My parents parked my car for the rest of the semester, and I needed my wheels. So I perked up and managed to get through school with a decent grade point."

Michelle grew thoughtful. "I wish Pablo had that support. It still bothers me that he lives first with Eduardo then with his parents. No one seems to really care for him."

"Lots of people care about Pablo, or he wouldn't be in school at all. It's just shown in a different way than what you're used to seeing," he told her. "The immediate family extends beyond parents and siblings. Aunts, uncles and cousins, they're all family. So, if you live with your grandmother, that's home, but so's your aunt's house. Pablo is as much at home with his uncle Eduardo as he is with his parents in Mexico." He must have seen the disapproval in her face because he added, "Before you get too judgmental, it's better than the boarding schools rich people often send their kids to."

Michelle nodded. "I agree. Even though I taught at one, I really felt sorry for the children. Regardless of the friendships they formed, they never lost that feeling of being alone, of being homesick."

"I'm sure that some kids here must feel it, but it doesn't seem to be a big problem."

"So you're saying that as far as Pablo is concerned, he's home here?"

"Sure. He's staying with an uncle, not a stranger." Jake put down the pencil and studied her face. "Did he give you any trouble today?"

"No. Why did you ask?"

"Uh . . . he and the last teacher didn't get along."

"I probably wouldn't have hit it off with him either, but I remembered what Paloma told me," she said. "I didn't tell Pablo what to do yesterday. Instead, I offered several things for him to choose from. He would have learned from any of them. Then, when I saw he was getting restless, I asked him if he'd mind helping the other children." Michelle smiled. "He took the job seriously."

"That's good."

"Today he came to me and said he wanted 'some harder stuff.'" She stopped and took a step closer to Jake. "You knew he was back, didn't you?"

Jake nodded.

"And that's one of the reasons you came in this afternoon, to see if I could handle him?"

"It's not the way you make it sound."

"Yes, it is." Michelle propped her hands on her hips. "I think I can deal with my class. In fact, today Antonio gave me the first discipline problem I've had in two weeks. What he did wasn't so bad. But when I reprimanded him, he wouldn't look me in the eyes."

Jake wasn't guilty of the same offense. His emerald eyes never left hers. "He didn't mean to be rude. It would have been disrespectful for him to have looked you in the face when you were getting on to him."

"Oh, no," Michelle groaned and dropped her hands back to her sides. "A cultural thing, right?"

"Yeah. His eyes were lowered in shame."

"Oh, how I wish I could stop making these mistakes. Is there a book I can study, so I won't keep making them?"

"I don't know. You could ask Paloma. She might be able to help. But if you hang around here long enough, you'll learn. There really aren't that many differences, and most people will cut you a little slack until you learn how to do things our way. In no time you'll fit right in."

"I thought you wanted me to fail at this job so you could get rid of me. Now you sound almost supportive."

He got off the desk and looked down at her. "Don't let it go to your head. I'm still not convinced this trip of yours to the border is purely altruistic, that you just want to help the poor, unfortunate kids of Sotol Junction."

"I never said that was all I wanted," she said in defense. "I've admitted I wanted to see Brooke, but I *do* want to help these children. Do you think it would be all right if I made visits to their homes? I don't want to offend anyone, but I think I could do more to help them if I worked with their parents. At least I'd know something about the students' backgrounds."

"That would be a good idea, but you'll have to speak Spanish because a lot of these kids' parents don't speak English." He jerked his head toward the door. "Antonio, there. His parents can't speak English."

"I know. I sent a note home with him written in Spanish, although it was probably ungrammatical."

"Won't matter. His folks can't read Spanish, either. Just speak it."

Michelle's growing spirits fell. "Great. And I thought I'd done something wonderful. I had a year of Spanish in college then switched to French. But I can still read a little, if I have enough time and a good dictionary," she said. "Paloma gave me a book about a 'magic way' to learn Spanish. I've worked on it every night, but the magic part hasn't shown up yet. Besides, I'm a little wary of saying much. I'd probably say something totally inappropriate like...I want a man when I mean I'm hungry."

"*Hombre. Hambre.* I see what you mean. A man could easily misunderstand that." He laughed.

His good humor was infectious, causing Michelle to join in his teasing. "Or easily *try* to misunderstand, right? I'll never speak Spanish to you, Jake Evans."

Almost imperceptibly, he leaned toward her so that only a few inches separated their bodies. She could feel the warmth radiating from him as he whispered, "That's a shame, since words of love are so much prettier in Spanish, more like music for the soul."

Michelle's heart seemed to be lodged somewhere in her throat because she couldn't voice a single comeback as he raised his hand to her hair. She felt his fingers as they slowly brushed a stray tendril away from her face. The simple gesture charged the atmosphere with an electricity that at any moment could erupt into lightning. Remembering how his arms had felt around her, Michelle knew she had to stop any chance of that happening again. She licked her lips and said, "I think it's safer when we fight."

"Safer? Are you afraid of me?" Jake asked, his hand still resting lightly against the side of her head. Funny, Michelle thought, when Brent touched her, she hardly noticed, but with Jake, the slight contact felt heavy and hot.

Afraid? Not of him, but of the feelings he caused every time she saw him. But she couldn't say that, so she said the only noncommittal thing she could think of. "Not really."

"Good." He stepped closer, his eyes burning into hers.

She made a feeble effort to back away, but his hand slid to her neck and restrained her. He stood still, giving her time to get used to the idea he was going to kiss her. And she knew he was going to do just that. He was going to lower his head and his lips were going to touch hers. Other men had done it before. Then why was she trembling? Because the other men didn't call their daughters Angel, didn't kill snakes as if they were houseflies or drop by school just so they could offer her support. And no other man made her forget to breathe.

She wanted Jake to kiss her. But if he did, she knew things would never be the same. *She* would never be the same. He wasn't someone a woman could get casually involved with. She had seen how committed he was to those he cared about—Brooke, Mike, Paloma and others. Any woman he loved was to be envied.

As if she were making the decision to jump off a cliff, Michelle took a deep breath, slowly closed her eyes and lifted her chin to meet Jake halfway. Their lips touched tentatively—exploring, searching for the unknown.

The taste of cinnamon gum lingered on his breath. His lips were warm and soft, demanding not because of force but the lack of it. He was disarming her with tenderness. The same tenderness she had seen him show toward Brooke and Paloma. She knew without a doubt that behind the dark pirate facade he was a vulnerable man. He was afraid of getting too close.

His failed marriage was to thank for that, Michelle suspected.

She felt his breathing become ragged and uneven as he drew her closer. Raising her arms, she slid them around his waist. Her fingers fanned across the taut muscles of his back as she pressed closer, urging him to deepen the kiss. She yielded to the mounting pressure of his lips and tilted her head to better accommodate him. Totally unprepared for the raw hunger that erupted, Michelle clung to him for support when his tongue probed the moist recesses of her mouth. She ceased to think.

Minutes? Hours? She wasn't sure how much time had passed when a loud sound registered in the far corner of her mind. The school clock was chiming the hour. The unexpected sound obviously penetrated Jake's consciousness too, and he slowly ended the kiss. He tilted his head back and took several deep breaths.

Surprised at the intensity of her own response, Michelle allowed him to cradle her face against his chest until they both could stand on their own.

Pulling away, Michelle stared up into eyes dark with emotion. Her voice was barely a whisper. "I..." was all she could manage. There weren't words to describe what had just occurred.

Jake drew back but didn't remove his hands entangled in her hair. He clasped her head firmly as he spoke. "I didn't plan for this to happen."

"I know." She believed him. Neither one of them could ever have planned the passion that had flared between them. "But we can't...it isn't right...if you weren't my sister's husband, I..."

"*Ex.* I'm your sister's ex-husband."

"Ex or not, Jake, it doesn't matter. The complication still exists. The fact remains that you're Brooke's father," she said. "We wouldn't be able to hide it from her, and how could we explain when I leave in a few weeks...?" Michelle's voice trailed off. Even to her own ears the excuse sounded feeble. But she knew pain would come from beginning a relationship with Jake only to abandon it to return to Boston. It wouldn't be right to do that to Jake or to Brooke.

Jake sighed and trailed his fingers along her neck until only his index finger rested lightly beneath her chin. Tilting her face upward, he stared deep into her eyes, then released his touch. "You're right. Brooke doesn't need to get her hopes up that you would be more than her aunt, then have them dashed. One woman she cared about has already walked out on her."

Michelle caught her breath. How could Jake be so warm one minute and so cold the next?

"It wasn't all DeeDee's fault, Jake. You changed your whole life without giving a moment's consideration about what was best for her."

"My decisions were made on what I thought was best for our family. The three of us. Her decision was based on what was best for her." Jake headed toward the door but stopped and glanced back toward Michelle. "I was right from the beginning. You are a lot like DeeDee. Afraid to take chances."

"I'm here, aren't I? That's taking a chance," Michelle said, stung. "And I didn't do a thing to warrant such ugly comments from you. I simply thought it best that we not start something we couldn't control."

Jake shook his head. "I'm not such a poor excuse for a man that I can't control myself around a woman—even you."

"No. You misunderstand everything I say."

"I didn't misunderstand a thing," he said, turning and striding away.

She busied herself with arranging pencils and pens in a jar on her desk and didn't look up until she heard the door close with a depressing thud. The room felt cold when Jake left, as though he'd taken all the warmth with him.

Michelle clenched and unclenched her fists until she felt the anger turning into hurt. Replaying the conversation in her mind, she realized that just when Jake had opened himself up to her, she'd shut him out. Leaning against the wall, she whispered, "I'm sorry, Jake. But you're still wrong. We don't have a future together, so we can't chance hurting Brooke."

JAKE HAD HARDLY STEPPED off the porch before he regretted his accusation. Still, he wondered how the hell he'd gotten himself into this mess? He'd vowed to stay away from this woman, fearing she was like her sister. In spite of his resolve, he'd begun to like—really like—Michelle Davis, but until today hadn't realized she shared his feelings. His mouth still burned from her kisses. The burgeoning feelings had forced him to say things he didn't really mean. Now he needed to make amends. But not yet, he thought, slamming the door to his pickup. Maybe later.

"Daddy, are you all right?"

For the first time, Jake noticed Brooke in the back seat. "Yes. Sorry to keep you waiting." The woman had made him forget his own daughter's welfare. Maybe that was her plan. Seduce him into being a negligent father. But even as he thought it, he realized he was grasping at anything, anything at all to keep from falling in love with Michelle Davis.

MICHELLE WAS ALMOST ready for bed when the phone rang. Expecting her mother, she let some of her displeasure show in the tone of her voice. "Hello."

"Michelle?" a deep baritone asked.

It was Jake. The very last person she expected, considering the way they had parted. There could only be one reason for him to call. "Jake, is something wrong with Brooke?"

"No. I just didn't think I could go to sleep until I called to apologize for being so rude to you this afternoon."

Michelle smiled. "I'll accept your apology, if you'll accept mine."

"Then it's a done deal. In fact, it makes my next offer easier."

"What do you have in mind?"

"I thought about what you'd said about getting to know the students better. That hasn't happened around here since Mrs. Escalante retired a few years back. I think it's a great idea. Anyway, if you can schedule those home visits when I have some time off, I'll go with you as translator. It might help you learn Spanish a little quicker."

Michelle couldn't speak for a minute, she was so moved by his thoughtfulness. "That would be wonderful, Jake. Thank you. It'll make the job much easier. I really think the parents will accept me more if you're there to introduce me and translate."

Michelle didn't try to conceal her excitement. Jake's assistance would make all the difference in the world. "I know you're busy, so I'll come by your office, and we can work out a schedule. I'd like to get started soon since I have so little time." Too bad she didn't have more time, she thought. If she had a whole year, she could really make a difference.

"I'm on the river tomorrow and Sunday, but I'll be in the office in the evenings if you want to come in."

"That sounds great." A thought crossed Michelle's mind, cooling some of her enthusiasm. "Jake, with Cynthia and Mike out, you don't have time to go with me. Besides, I'd feel guilty taking you away from your office work when I know you're so busy."

"We'll work it out. In exchange for my services as interpreter, maybe you can keep Brooke some nights so I can work late to catch back up."

"I'd like for Brooke to stay with me whether you help me or not. But I still think you're getting the short end of the stick."

"Can you type?"

"Sure. Why?"

"Because I can't, and Victoria's not much better. If you're interested, you can salve your conscience by typing a few letters for me. With Mike out of the hospital, Cynthia should be back in the office for a few hours a day next week, but these letters really need to be in the mail before then."

"I'd be happy to type them." Michelle liked the compromise. She'd help him and he'd help her. The thought struck her that for once they were acting like a family. She liked it. A lot.

CHAPTER ELEVEN

JAKE STRAINED against the oars as the raft—full of passengers—was blown upriver by the wind rushing into the canyon. The towering fifteen-hundred-foot cliffs loomed on either side of him, blocking all but a narrow ribbon of turquoise sky from view. This last few hundred feet were the toughest of the trip, but his body was in shape for the Herculean effort of forcing the raft to go against the strong current.

Tonight, he would feel few, if any, aftereffects—unlike the first couple of weeks he'd guided rafts down the Rio Grande. Four years ago the challenge had been backbreaking. Then, every muscle in his body had ached and rebelled against the enforced torture. Only the thought of sitting behind a desk staring at a computer monitor had given Jake the incentive to continue. Now his body was perfectly adapted to the physical work and the arid heat. Jake had no regrets about coming to the Big Bend.

The decision to turn his life around had been a private struggle for several months before he'd broached the topic with DeeDee. Considering her complaints about him being gone all the time, he'd naively thought she would've been more receptive. Instead, she'd lashed out at him about dragging them to the hinterlands, about being foolhardy and relinquishing his financial responsibility to his family.

At least, that had been her first response.

In an about-face after a visit to Boston, she'd begun to encourage him to make a new start. Excited, he forged ahead with his plans, thrilled to be getting a chance to follow his dream. Then he'd found out about Philip.

He gritted his teeth at the memory and pulled harder on the oars, the opening in the canyon looming before him. It had hurt losing his wife and his belief in "until death do us part." It had taken a long time for Jake to realize that it wasn't his fault. That his dissatisfaction and rejection of the daily urban grind hadn't caused their divorce. The breakup had been inevitable.

So he and Brooke had come out on their own. Jake had made a life for himself and his daughter. And now, DeeDee's sister was here opening old wounds and creating new dreams.

In only a couple of hours he would be back in Sotol Junction. He hoped Michelle would be waiting for him. She'd said last night she would come by so they could work out a schedule for home visits. He'd felt better after volunteering to help her. It wasn't her fault she was such an alluring woman. She was an angel in the devil's land. She wasn't purposely doing anything to make him want her, but want her, he did. More than he could remember wanting any woman, even DeeDee.

And it wasn't just her looks. It was the way she was trying to adapt in a different culture, and the way she was determined to learn Spanish, even though she wasn't going to stay in Sotol Junction long enough to use it. But her willingness to try showed a commitment to her students and a depth of character he hadn't expected.

AT THREE O'CLOCK, Michelle ran a bath and prepared to meet Jake. She knew from previous occasions that he would probably arrive back in Sotol soon after six, and she wanted to get to his office in enough time to do the typing he said he'd leave for her. She was anxious about seeing him and took longer to dress than usual. Finally, she decided on pale pink walking shorts with a matching T-shirt and sweater. She tied her hair up with a pink ribbon and slowly drove to Junction Outfitters.

When she arrived, Victoria greeted her and told her that Jake had left the letters on his desk. "I guess my two-finger peck on the typewriter didn't impress him," the teenager said.

"If you want me to, I'll teach you how to use the word processor," Michelle offered.

A wide grin spread across Victoria's face. "I'd like that."

"We'll start next week. After school." Seeing the pleasure on Victoria's face gave Michelle an idea. She could open the school at night to teach adults to use the computer, or speak English, or maybe to read. Shelving her sudden enthusiasm, she looked around the cramped quarters. If she used the computer at the receptionist's desk, Victoria would have to stand.

Becoming aware of Michelle's dilemma, Victoria said, "Why don't you use the computer in Jake's office? That's the only place that'll give you some privacy." Victoria nodded toward a couple of shoppers who were browsing through the merchandise.

Feeling like an intruder, Michelle edged her way into the office and placed her purse on the edge of the old leather sofa. A woodsy, masculine smell hung in the air almost within reach.

The large oak desk and the sofa took up almost the entire cubicle. Taking a seat in Jake's old office chair, she scanned the desk top which was covered with papers and what appeared to be junk. Opening the bright red folder Jake had left for her, Michelle went to work and typed the letters. Finished, she put the file back on his desk, accidentally knocking some letters to the floor. Bending down to retrieve them, Michelle didn't mean to read anything, but she couldn't help noticing the Past Due stamped on the first letter. It was from a liability insurance company and the amount owed was several thousand dollars.

Quickly, she straightened the pile of correspondence, trying to avoid reading the papers, although she could tell they were bills. Now she could see why Paloma had been concerned.

The hush-hush conversation she'd overheard at the fiesta sprang into her mind.

Was Jake in such dire financial straits that he would illegally harvest the protected *candelilla* plant? If he was, and her mother ever found out, she would use it to get custody of Brooke.

Michelle knew she didn't want Jake to lose Brooke. How could she help? she wondered. A loan? No, Jake would be insulted at the suggestion. Maybe she could run the business on the weekends so that he wouldn't have to pay Victoria.

Startled out of her reverie by loud, excited voices, she turned to face the doorway.

"What a trip!" said a tall, stocky young man. "Sure was a welcome break from the office. I hate to go back Monday."

"But," a young woman who Michelle guessed was his wife said, "you can go back and tell everyone you saw a peregrine falcon!"

"Put us down for another trip, same time next year," the husband said to Jake. "Okay?"

Michelle watched as Jake wrote the couple's name on the wall calendar. Then he unlocked the vault door so the river runners could retrieve their personal belongings.

A slow twenty minutes ticked away on the wall clock before Jake finally came into his office. "Hope you didn't have to wait long." He settled down in the chair behind the desk and leaned forward.

"Jake, you're too tired to bother with scheduling home visits right now."

"No, I'm not. Let me find my calendar and we'll see what we can work out. It's cool in here and I can relax a little."

Michelle said, "I thought one of my first visits should be to Eduardo, to talk to him about Pablo. He has a real future if he stays in school. I could make that visit without you since Eduardo speaks English."

"Why don't you wait until I can go with you? Let's see . . ." He held up a small pocket calendar. "How about Wednesday afternoon?"

"Okay. But I'd rather we schedule a couple of visits where I really need you to translate. I can go to Eduardo's Monday or Tuesday by myself."

"I . . . uh . . . don't think you should go without me."

"Why not?"

"It wouldn't be right for a single woman to visit a man in his house."

"But—" Michelle leaned forward "—I just want to talk about Pablo."

"But—" Jake, too, leaned forward and punctuated each word with a nod "—it just isn't done."

Michelle sighed. "All right. Wednesday at four?"

He smiled. "Okay. Now, what about Antonio?"

"Do you think we can do both visits the same afternoon?"

The time passed quickly as they agreed to make two visits Wednesday and two the following week. In fact, the atmosphere was so pleasant, Jake was reluctant to have the afternoon come to an end. Since Brooke was spending the night with Katy, he didn't have to get back home soon. "Why don't you let me buy you supper? There's a restaurant in the hotel that isn't half-bad."

After only a moment of consideration, Michelle agreed. "Thank you. I'd enjoy that."

"Let me freshen up." Then, without waiting for a reply, he disappeared through a doorway. A few minutes later, he returned, buttoning a fresh shirt, then tucking it into his jeans. His hair had been combed and a bead of moisture still clung to one eyebrow. He grinned and said, "Ready. I always keep a change of clothes here at the office in case of an emergency."

They walked along the boardwalk to the hotel. The Western-style dining room was about half-full when they arrived. Obviously, it had been decorated with tourists in mind. Red brocade Victorian paper covered the walls and imitation gaslight chandeliers hung from the ceiling.

They were met by a young woman who greeted Jake warmly and seated them several tables away from the other diners. A couple of large palm fronds shielded their table and gave it a feeling of intimacy, a feeling Michelle both welcomed and feared. The growing attraction she felt for Jake had to be tempered with reality, she told herself. She was leaving Texas in a little more than a month, Jake might be involved in something illegal, her mother hated him and he had been her sister's husband.

She remembered her father approving of Jake. He'd said the young man had a lot of sense. Her father was usually right. Her mother, on the other hand, had always resented the fact that Jake had taken DeeDee to live in Houston.

"Have you decided?" Jake's question interrupted Michelle's thoughts.

She'd been staring at the menu, without seeing it. Quickly, she made a selection. "I'll have the chicken quesadillas and a salad."

Jake placed their order, then gave his full attention to her. "What were you thinking about just now? You had an awful scowl on your face. This place isn't that bad, is it?"

Michelle grinned. "It has a charm of its own."

All through the delicious meal, Michelle couldn't help wondering whether DeeDee had ever regretted leaving Jake. She couldn't imagine any woman in her right mind not wanting him. He was a good father, everybody seemed to like him, he was considerate, and, she decided as she looked across the table at him through lowered lids, he certainly wasn't hard on the eyes. He had more than all the right attributes—he exuded that special something that set him apart from ordinary men.

After the meal, Jake settled back in the old-fashioned barrel chair and said, "Something's on your mind. You've been looking at me all night. Have I grown a wart or something?''

Michelle tried not to blush. "It's nothing."

"Out with it."

"I . . . was wondering what happened between you and DeeDee," Michelle said, wiping the moisture off the outside of her tea glass with a fingertip. "All I've ever heard is Mother's version, and it doesn't show you in a very good light."

"I'm sure it doesn't." Jake leaned forward and propped his elbows on the tabletop.

She realized that talking about something so personal made him uncomfortable and she wanted to reach over and take his hand to reassure him. "You don't have to tell me if you don't want to. I know it really isn't any of my business."

"In a way it is, or you wouldn't be here." Jake's eyes narrowed and darkened as he studied her across the table. "It's a long story."

"That's okay. I'm a good listener."

A wry smile crossed his face. "For today?"

"For today," she agreed.

Jake inhaled deeply and began. "After I graduated from college, I got a job with a big investment firm in Houston. That was back when things were really hot. The amount of money you could make was limited only by the hours you were willing to put in." He fell silent and rubbed his chin in reflection. "It was almost too easy."

He continued, "Then one weekend, when I was staying in Nantucket with a friend after a business trip, I met DeeDee. She was everything I thought I wanted in a woman. Beautiful, smart, fun...exactly what I had pictured for the perfect wife."

"What changed your mind?"

He leaned back and smiled. "Being married to DeeDee was an experience. You know how she was. She attacked life, almost afraid she would miss something unless she kept up that relentless pace of hers." He sighed. "After a while, I couldn't keep up. I worked sixteen-hour days trying to make the money we'd both become accustomed to. Then, when I'd get home, she would want to go out or have friends over." Again, he paused. "It's the same old story. I sound like I'm blaming DeeDee, but I'm not. I was as much or more at fault."

Michelle sat quietly, waiting for him to continue.

"DeeDee and I went for weeks without really seeing each other, though we lived in the same house. She gave up trying to include me in her plans at night. She was either gone or asleep when I came in after work, and I left in the mornings before she woke up."

He leaned forward, and spoke in a voice so low Michelle had to strain to hear. "One night, I came home, got a drink and went out to the patio. When I pulled a pack of cigarettes out of my pocket, I realized I'd smoked the whole pack that day. An hour later, I was well into the second pack and my third bourbon. That's what it took to relieve the knot that formed between my shoulders at work every day. Later, when I got up and went to the bedroom, DeeDee was already asleep on the far side of our king-size bed. I hadn't said three words to her in over a week, and it had been at least a month since we'd made love. And I didn't really care. There I was, only thirty-one years old. I smoked and drank too much, had put on twenty pounds and didn't care whether I made love to my wife. I knew then that I had to do something. I was killing myself and probably her, as well." He stopped and stared directly into Michelle's eyes. "But you know what the worst part was?"

She shook her head and whispered, "No."

"I had missed the first four years of Brooke's life. Oh, I saw her. She was usually up with her nanny when I left for work, and we spent some time together on the weekends. But it wasn't enough. I vowed then that whatever I did, it would be something where I could spend time with my daughter, that I wasn't going to miss the next fourteen years."

Michelle blinked away the tears beginning to form in her eyes.

Jake continued, "In the beginning, I was deluded enough to think DeeDee would be happy, that she would support my decision." His voice became harder. "But I soon realized that was unrealistic. There was no way she would fit in down here. At first, we just agreed to a separation. I came here to Sotol Junction to get the business started and she stayed in Houston. It wasn't long before she told me about Philip."

"Were you very upset?" Michelle asked.

"I was furious. Even though I wasn't sure I wanted the marriage to work, my ego was shot. No man wants to hear that his wife has found his replacement. For me, what made it bearable was Brooke. DeeDee agreed to give me custody since Philip's job required so much travel."

Michelle detected pain in his voice. "I'm sorry that things didn't work out."

He took a deep breath. "It was probably for the better. DeeDee loved traveling all over the world and staying in ritzy hotels, so she was happy. And Brooke and I have been happy here. I don't want that to change. She's been through enough. First, the divorce and moving here. Then her mother's death. I don't want anything else to upset her."

Michelle understood the implication of his words. "Jake, I don't want to hurt Brooke... or you." She placed her hand on his arm. It was the first time she had purposely touched him and his skin was warm under her hands that had become chilled from holding the tea glass. "Please believe me. All I want is for you and Brooke to be happy."

"Then don't mess with us."

ON SUNDAY the piercing morning light filtered between the shutters on Michelle's bedroom window, casting slits of brightness across her face. The warmth on her cheek teased her into full alertness and she remembered the previous evening. Jake's warning to leave him and Brooke alone still hurt.

She sat up in bed and looked at the clock. Today was Easter Sunday. Although she seldom went to church anymore, she didn't like to miss Easter or Christmas services.

Michelle could picture her mother sitting in the family pew at this minute, head held high, as she listened to the Episcopalian liturgy. She wondered what Elizabeth's prayers would be. Her granddaughter coming to live with her? A wave of guilt and homesickness swept over Michelle. After church, she'd call her mother.

An hour later, Michelle walked through the cars and pickups parked haphazardly around the small Catholic church, the only church in town. She paused briefly in the tiny vestibule, and, looking at the crowded rows of wooden pews, tiptoed forward and squeezed in next to Cynthia who had both Katy and Brooke with her. Hugging her niece, Michelle was ashamed that she hadn't called to invite Brooke to church, herself. Then she turned her attention to the service.

Homely images besieged her. Women with bowed, shawl-covered heads were praying silently, while a few people, including Eduardo, were lighting candles on a side table. For whom? Michelle wondered when she saw his face screwed up in anguish, clearly fighting back tears. His dead wife? He crossed himself, and, shoulders rounded and head down, shuffled back to his place among the parishioners. In a flash of sympathy, tears gathered in Michelle's eyes.

She raised her eyes to the altar, then to the image of the crucified Christ hanging in the center of the background. As the priest intoned the liturgy, a peacefulness settled over her.

Michelle watched as people filed forward for communion and asked for forgiveness, for blessings, for hope. She'd seen them enjoying life and laughter, and now, in the same earnestness, they sought refuge in God.

When the service was over, Brooke and Katy flew out of the building to participate in the Easter-egg hunt that was to be held in the side yard. Michelle walked slowly, speaking to the few people she knew, while others came up and hugged her, welcoming her to the service.

She and Cynthia stood beneath a tree and watched as the children waited for instructions before gathering the eggs, many of them filled with the traditional confetti.

Michelle thought Cynthia still looked drawn, although she'd been home for five days. She recalled the frustrations the woman had voiced at school earlier. "How are things going?"

Cynthia sighed and brushed her long, straight hair back over her shoulder. "I'm supposed to say fine, but that's not really true. Mike is so depressed."

"Well, I'd say that was normal. He was an active person and now he has to stay down. Just as soon as he can go back to work, he'll feel better."

"Oh, it's more than that. He has too much time to brood about money. I told him if he'd had a real job somewhere, he'd be getting workmen's compensation."

Cynthia was more depressed than Mike, Michelle decided. Cynthia needed to get out of the house and— and do what? Go to the drugstore for ice cream? Michelle tried to think of some advantage to owning Junction Outfitters. "Well, here, you're your own boss."

"No, we're not. Regulations and responsibilities are the boss. No regular work hours." Cynthia gave a funny-sounding laugh, "Oh, yes, actually there are. Twenty-four hours a day. I tell you, Michelle, I can't take it anymore. When school is out, I'm taking Katy and leaving. If Mike wants to come, he can. But if he doesn't, then I know what's more important to him."

Michelle felt an ache of sadness. She'd heard almost the same words from her sister. She hadn't known how to respond to DeeDee then.

And she didn't know how to comfort Cynthia now.

CHAPTER TWELVE

MICHELLE WAS UNDRESSING when the phone rang. Struggling to get out of her dress, she headed toward the living room to answer it.

"I hope you went to church," Elizabeth said as soon as Michelle said hello.

"Yes, I did, Mother. There's one small church in town that everyone goes to if they don't want to drive to Alpine or Presidio. Then, there was an Easter-egg hunt. Brooke found so many eggs, she'll have a stomachache for a month if she eats them."

"Surely Jacob will have the foresight to ration them. I must say, I'm relieved that you went to church, although I'm sure the service wasn't what you're used to."

"It was very nice, Mother. Very genuine."

There was a brief pause before Elizabeth again veered the conversation to her concerns. "I saw Brent with that Worthington girl. You know, the one that's just a teeny bit fat."

Katherine Worthington wasn't the least bit fat, in Michelle's opinion. "They'll make a good couple."

"That wasn't what I meant. If you don't want her to end up being Mrs. Paxton, you need to do something. Have you called him or written at all? I know he's written you because he told me he had.''

"No, I haven't, Mother. I don't want to do anything. Brent is a nice man, but neither of us is interested in marrying the other.''

"I think you are making a big mistake. His father owns—''

"I don't care what his father owns. I don't care what Brent owns. There are other reasons for marriage besides wealth.''

"I suppose you are talking about love.'' Elizabeth sniffed. "Love is entirely overrated. DeeDee thought the same thing, but thank goodness for Philip, she learned otherwise.''

Michelle wondered if DeeDee hadn't had some help from her mother. "Did you know Philip before he and DeeDee met?''

"I'd met him a couple of times at your uncle Ian's. They did business together.''

"When?''

"Oh, it must have been five or six years ago.''

"Mother, when DeeDee came home to visit while Jake—I mean Jacob—was down here, did you introduce Philip to your *married* daughter and suggest she was going through a bad time and could use a little consolation?'' Michelle could tell from the pregnant pause on the other end of the line that she was right.

"It wasn't quite like that. I introduced them because I hated for DeeDee to attend dinner parties alone. Philip was a gracious escort.''

"Who broke up a marriage. Didn't you even stop to consider Brooke or Jacob?"

"That marriage was already doomed. From day one! I only did what I thought was best."

"I'm sure you did." Michelle's voice was laced with sarcasm. She wondered if Jake knew what part her mother had played in the breakup of his marriage. He probably suspected Elizabeth had had something to do with it. No wonder he was so distrustful of the Davis women.

"Don't use that tone of voice with me. I *am* your mother."

"Yes, Mother, you are that."

"Well, I can see this conversation is getting us nowhere. When you get to know Jacob Evans better, you will understand why I did what I did. You can't trust that man, Michelle. Don't make that mistake."

Michelle said goodbye to her mother and sat on the edge of the sofa for a while. Easter Sunday, a day of peace and remembrance. Yet all she felt was turmoil. First from Cynthia and now from her mother. Then she thought of Jake standing at the river's edge, black hair glistening, and felt better.

THAT EVENING after he'd unloaded the van and stowed the rafting gear, Jake saw Eduardo and Ramon sitting on a bench on the boardwalk outside the hotel. They looked like extras from a movie in their worn-out baggy jeans, boots run down at the heels and black cowboy hats that looked as if they'd been through two stampedes and lost each time. They were leaning forward with their elbows propped on their knees, chewing on toothpicks. He knew what they wanted.

Jake walked up to the two men and greeted them. *"Buenas tardes."*

"Sí." Ramon leaned back and pushed his hat off his forehead. "I see you've been pretty busy, Jake. How was the trip today?"

"Good. Easter weekend is one of the busiest of the season. I've got a full house tomorrow and Tuesday, too." He rolled his shoulders to ease his overworked muscles and then rested against one of the cedar posts that held up the porch above the boardwalk. It was a beautiful evening. The desert air was beginning to cool and the cicadas were wound up.

Eduardo interrupted the tranquillity. "You find any good *candelilla?*"

"Yeah, I spotted some." Jake propped the sole of his sandal against the post and studied the two men. "Between Tapado Canyon and Rancherias Rapids."

"That's three miles of country, man."

"It's pretty much scattered over the entire area."

"Park side or Mexican?" Ramon asked.

"I don't answer that question. You know that." Jake wouldn't tell them whether the *candelilla* he had spotted grew within the protected domain of the National Park Service where plants, even flowers, couldn't be picked, or if it was on the Mexican side of the Rio Grande. He wanted to help the local people as much as he could because he knew they relied on the wax harvest for any extra money. "Extra" money meant they could buy clothes, shoes or take a trip into Mexico to see their families.

Because *candelilla* was a weed and in no danger of disappearing, the local people couldn't understand why the United States government wanted to protect it. *Candelilla* had been pulled in the Big Bend for hundreds of years and the people felt it was their birthright, so they tended to ignore the law. The problem was finding a large enough concentration of the plant to make the trip worthwhile. They'd go in at night, pull them up and get out without getting caught by the park rangers.

Jake didn't intend to know when any of this took place.

JAKE WAS WAITING for Michelle when school let out Wednesday afternoon. He'd spent most of the day catching up on paperwork and getting the gear ready for the coming weekend river runs. Wesley had worked out well on Easter break, so Jake planned to keep him on for weekends until Mike came back.

Taking his usual stance by the back door of the schoolhouse, Jake waited for the last student to leave. Brooke came by and gave him a hug on her way to the office to stay with Victoria while he and Michelle went on the home visits. Brooke refused to be driven, preferring to run with Katy down their special shortcut. Michelle had stopped objecting.

Michelle hugged the younger children and made sure they had all of their things before shepherding them out the door. Watching her now as she knelt and whispered to a little girl made Jake want to take her in his arms.

He wanted to feel her soft skin, to bury his fingers in her long blond hair, kiss her full pink lips . . . all the things he shouldn't do.

"Jake?"

He'd been so preoccupied, he hadn't realized she'd come to stand beside him. But now he could smell a lingering trace of perfume and feel the aura of warmth that seemed to surround her wherever she went. God! He was going crazy. On the one hand he knew he should avoid her, but on the other he couldn't stay away.

"Jake?" she repeated. "I'm ready."

"Great. Let's take my pickup. Antonio lives a little way out of town and the road may be too rough for your car." His words were rushed as he tried to cover for his lack of attention.

"Fine. I'll get my things and lock up." She pulled a purse out of a filing cabinet behind her desk and grabbed a leather-bound notebook. Together, the two items likely cost as much as some of the people here made in a month. Jake had to keep reminding himself that she didn't belong here.

Michelle stepped aside to allow Jake to go out the door, before closing and locking it. She was nervous about seeing him after the way they had parted at the restaurant. "I want to thank you again for coming with me," she said as they walked to his pickup.

"You're more than welcome. Besides, you typed those letters for me. That was thanks enough." He held the passenger door open for her as she struggled to climb into the cab gracefully.

She noticed Jake's eyes narrow when the front of her long skirt slid open, exposing her leg to above the knee. Not that much flesh showed. In fact, he'd seen her several times in shorts that revealed more of her legs. But that was before he'd kissed her, before he'd bared his soul about the breakup of his marriage and before he'd asked her to leave him alone. Those things made what was happening now even more confusing. He was interested in her, she could tell that, but he was fighting it because of who she was—just as she should be fighting her growing feelings for him. Carefully adjusting her skirt to cover her knee, she settled into the seat and looked at Jake. He stood with one hand on top of the open door and the other on the cab above her head.

"Jake, about the other night..." It was hard to talk when his body filled the narrow space, blocking out the sunlight. "I know you distrust me, but can't we still be friends?"

He gave a short laugh and said, "Most men consider that phrase an insult. And after the way you kissed me, do you honestly think we can be *friends?*"

"We've got to get along, for Brooke's sake."

"I'm getting along. I'm here helping you out, aren't I?"

"Yes, but I'm not sure you want to be."

"We'll talk about it later. We've got parent conferences to take care of now." With those words, he slammed the door shut, went around to the driver's side and climbed in. He turned the key in the ignition and the old truck roared to life.

Two hours later, after both visits were completed, Jake drove down a rutted path between the trees that lined the Rio Grande and stopped on a narrow stretch of gravelly bank a few feet from the water's edge. The sun had disappeared behind the limestone cliffs to the west, casting the river and its banks into cool shadows. He turned and looked at her, a smile pulling at the corners of his mouth. "Want to go for a walk?"

"Sure," she answered, getting out and joining him beside the truck. "I think the visits went well. Don't you?"

He knew she was stalling, putting off the conversation they were going to have, but a few minutes wouldn't matter. "Yeah. I was surprised Eduardo understood and agreed to talk to his brother about Pablo staying here and possibly going to junior high instead of dropping out."

"I think you're the one responsible for that. You saw how far I was getting with him until you intervened."

Jake nodded and took her elbow to guide her along the narrow path. It would be easier to talk if they were moving. "I warned you about the way women are perceived here. They are loved, but they're not expected to worry themselves over anything important. That's a man's job." He grinned and brushed a tree branch out of their way.

Michelle sighed. "It appears to me they are desired more than loved, and from what I've seen, they work as hard or harder than the men. Antonio's mother was making fresh tortillas for dinner because her husband doesn't like the ones left over from lunch that are only a few a hours old. I know it's just a different culture. But I don't like the way the women are treated."

"I don't either," he agreed. He knew he wanted to be important to the woman he chose to spend the rest of his life with, but he didn't want to be the only thing in her life. That would be suffocating, for her and for him.

He came to a halt when he realized that for the first time in four years he'd thought about the future with a woman in it. A woman he could love and cherish but also share his dreams and problems with. A helpmate with whom to bounce around ideas about his business and to share the joys of Brooke's childhood. Being a single parent was lonely.

Michelle had stopped also and was looking at him as if she hadn't heard correctly. "You agree?"

"Yes, I may not like all the things that are done here, but I don't have to pass judgment on them," he said. "In this place, the unspoken agreement is to live and let live. There's a loose social structure here, much less restrictive than what you're used to. A few of the Mexican families still practice many of the old customs, but they are gradually becoming more Americanized. The next generation probably won't make tortillas at all. They'll go to the store and buy them like I do. Which is unfortunate because store-bought tortillas aren't as good,'' he added to lighten their conversation. "Seriously, both cultures have a lot to give to each other.''

She hugged her arms to her side and looked across the murky water toward Mexico. "I don't know how long I'd have to live here before I'd believe that. Everybody's life seems so hard, so far removed from the twentieth century. Except for Paloma and Ramon Abalos.''

"You understand more than you think. Today you handled Eduardo pretty well—for an Anglo woman. And Antonio's mother thinks you are the best teacher Sotol Junction has ever had because you let her know what Antonio was doing.''

"And you, Jake, what do you think?''

"I think you are by far the prettiest teacher that's been here.'' As soon as he said it, he regretted the flippancy.

She frowned at him. "That's not what I mean. I know you didn't vote to hire me and I just—''

"How do you know that?'' What happened at a board meeting in executive session wasn't supposed to be public knowledge, even though the vote was in open forum. But, who would've been so cruel as to tell Michelle?

"Word gets around in a small town, even things that are supposed to be confidential," she told him.

"You heard right. I didn't have a problem with your credentials. I didn't vote for you because I figured you were coming to do Elizabeth's dirty work for her."

"And do you still think that?" Before he could answer, she turned to face him and the look she gave him was almost a plea for understanding. "I won't deny that my coming here was Mother's idea. She did ask me to check on Brooke, but I never—"

He put his hands on her shoulders and interrupted her confession. "Don't lie to me, Michelle, I know you've had your doubts about my ability to rear Brooke."

She gave a slight nod. "Yes, but my doubts have been more with this place than with you."

"Is that what you tell your mother?"

"I haven't told my mother anything that would hurt you."

"Then I'll bet her feathers are ruffled."

Michelle grinned at the thought. "You're right. She's not very happy with me. She's afraid I'm falling for you and am on the same path to ruin as DeeDee."

His fingers tightened on her shoulders as he took a step closer. "And are you . . . falling for me?"

She looked up at him and hesitated. His own longing was mirrored in her eyes. Finally she whispered, "No."

"No, huh?" he challenged. Her response lacked conviction, but he didn't contradict her. He'd never considered the possibility she might start loving him. Hell! He figured she'd have a wall of armor against him so thick even Cupid couldn't get to her heart. The thought of her love scared him to death, yet hope burst from the buried recesses of his soul.

"I'm not falling in love with you," she said, "but I don't think you're quite as bad as I'd thought at first. In fact, I think you're a good father."

"That's nice. I like being a good father." He wasn't paying much attention to her words, it was the melody of her voice that had him enthralled. The soft seductive music wove its magic around his heart.

He cupped her chin in one hand. When she started to pull away, he gently brushed the tender skin of her lower lip with his thumb. He felt her take a deep breath before unconsciously allowing her lips to part, and when he removed his hand she ran the tip of her tongue over her lips to moisten them. The innocent gesture almost brought him to his knees. His hands slid down her arms and pulled her closer until he felt the wind wrap the bottom of her skirt around his leg.

Michelle gave in to the gentle tug of the fabric as it formed a cocoon around their bodies, isolating them from the cooling breeze and the censure of the outside world.

Tonight—for just this one time—she was going to do what she wanted to do rather than what she should. And she wanted to feel Jake's hard lean body crushed against hers, she wanted to feel his warm lips over hers, she wanted to feel his long loose hair threaded through her fingers.

When she looked into his eyes, she knew he wanted the same thing. "Jake?"

"Yeah?"

"Friends can kiss, can't they?" she murmured.

"Oh, yes." His hands rose to the sides of her face and he tilted it to give him better access to her waiting lips. His mouth met hers in a melding of passion and need that was so stunning her knees almost buckled from the sheer masculine force that assailed her. She tugged at the leather strap holding his hair and released it.

There was nothing experimental or hesitant about his kisses. It was as if he knew exactly how to make her moan with pleasure and yearn for more. His hands roamed freely over her shoulders and her back, coaxing her closer until there was no doubt how much he wanted her. It was as if his hands had made that journey many times before, as if his lips had teased hers night after night, as if he knew how she would react to his every move. As if he were making love to his wife.

DeeDee!

As soon as her sister's name entered Michelle's foggy mind, she pulled back. An unpleasant thought

entered her mind. Could he be using her to replace
DeeDee? Was it her sister he really wanted?

"Michelle, what's wrong?" His voice was ragged.

She forced the words out in a breathless whisper.
"We shouldn't be doing this. We might be seen."

"We're miles from anywhere." He stepped back and
in a gesture of frustration, ran a hand through his hair.
"You don't have to explain what happened but I know
you wanted me just as much as I did you. And your
pulling back doesn't have a damn thing to do with being afraid someone will see us." He took her arm and
hauled her back toward the pickup. "Let's go."

CHAPTER THIRTEEN

MICHELLE DID HER BEST to avoid Jake for the next few days. His kiss had shaken her, forcing her to consider the possibility she was falling in love with him. But that was all it was—just a possibility. When she left Sotol Junction, she would soon forget about the way his hands had felt as they caressed her skin, the way his lips had coaxed hers into response, the way his body had pressed against hers.

Who was she trying to kid? She doubted she would ever forget the way emotions had washed over her as forcefully as the river had washed over the rocks only a short distance away. Like the water eroding the steadfastness of the rocks, Jake was slowly eroding her resistance. And that frightened her, for no matter how much he affected her, she didn't want to be a substitute for her sister.

Jake seemed to have no lingering feelings for DeeDee, but she'd been his wife, so surely, comparisons between the sisters was inevitable.

And what about her mother's warning that Jake would do whatever it took to win Michelle's sympathies? Would that include pretending he wanted more from her than a lustful interlude? Pretending that he wanted her to stay?

She was still debating the topic Saturday night, when she heard a vehicle pull up in front of her house. For a second, her heart skipped in anticipation. Jake was the only person she knew who might come to visit this late. But as quickly as her heart had filled with joy, she discounted the idea. If there was one thing she'd learned well in Sotol Junction, it was the sound of Jake's old pickup on the rutted driveway, and this wasn't it.

She wrapped a robe around her and was almost at the door when she heard the light knock. Michelle opened the door to Cynthia, who stood in the shaft of light pouring out from the living room, her eyes swollen and red.

"I...hate to bother...you." The woman was clearly distraught.

"What's the matter, Cynthia?" Michelle stepped back. "Come on inside."

"No...Katy's in the Jeep. I just came by to see if you would mind opening the school and letting me get her school things."

"Tonight?" Michelle tried not to sound as incredulous as she felt.

"Yes, please." Cynthia nodded as she clearly fought back more tears. "Mike and I had a fight and...I just can't take any more. I'm leaving. I'm going back to East Texas where there are theaters and trees and hospitals."

"Oh, Cynthia." Michelle put her arms around the weeping woman. "I'm so sorry. I'd hoped the two of you would work things out."

"There's no way. Tonight I finally realized that Mike doesn't love me. And now that he's walking again, he doesn't even need me."

"I'm sure that's not true."

"Would you mind opening the school?" Cynthia straightened her spine as she changed the subject. "Katy will want her own crayons and notebooks, and if you don't mind checking her out, I'll take her documents to the new school."

"I don't mind, but don't you think you're rushing things to leave tonight? Maybe you'll see things differently in the morning."

"No, I've made up my mind."

Michelle could see that nothing she could say would change Cynthia's mind. In any case, it wasn't really any of her business. "Okay. Let me get my keys and I'll follow you to school."

Cynthia smiled wanly, "Thanks. I'm sorry about this." She continued to talk while Michelle got her purse. "I really hate to move Katy to another school so close to the end of the year. Besides, she really liked having you for a teacher. All the students do. And you've impressed a lot of the families. Take Jake, for example, you're probably the best thing that's happened to him in a long time."

Michelle stopped in the process of closing the front door. "Why? What do you mean?"

"Before you got here, Jake just seemed to exist. He worked hard and all, but he didn't get excited about anything. Brooke was the only thing he cared about. He was a great guy, but I never saw him mad, or very happy, for that matter. But now, since I've gone back to work, I've seen him both ways. I don't know what's going on between you two, but it's put some life back in him." Cynthia walked toward the Jeep as she talked, then she stopped. "Be careful, Michelle. Learn from my mistake. Regardless of what you feel for Jake, whatever he promises you, don't stay here. You'll soon regret it." And with that, she opened the door and climbed in, leaving Michelle staring.

Michelle picked her way through the darkness to her car, thinking about Cynthia's mixed messages. If the first bit of information—that Jake had more than a passing interest in her—was wrong, then the warning meant nothing. After all, Cynthia and Mike's problems had nothing to do with her and Jake.

The possibility he was more than just physically attracted to her was exciting. Yet, that didn't change the fact he'd been her sister's husband.

Michelle pulled into the school yard seconds after Cynthia and Katy. As she unlocked the door, she noticed how uncharacteristically quiet Katy was. Michelle's heart went out to the little girl as she trailed behind the two adults into the building. Michelle flipped on the lights in the empty school and turned to Cynthia. "I'll get the things you need while Katy cleans out her desk."

MICHELLE WAS GLAD when Sunday morning finally came, bringing an end to a restless night. She'd awakened more than once worrying about Cynthia and Katy. The child had hugged Michelle, and with tears trickling down her cheeks, asked Michelle to tell Brooke that she was her best friend ever and to tell her goodbye.

Tears had rushed to Michelle's eyes and a knot had formed in her throat as she stood silently watching the Jeep speed away until its lights vanished in the darkness, taking a little girl from her father and a woman from the man she'd promised to love forever.

Sotol Junction had separated them.

And Cynthia had warned Michelle.

Once in the night, she'd awakened from a dream in which she and Jake had fought about . . . she couldn't remember what. But, in her frustration and in the dead of the night, she'd taken Brooke back to Boston with her. Even in sleep, she'd known she'd transferred Cynthia and Mike's problems to her and Jake. Yet, the anguish she'd felt had been so personal.

Michelle knew Brooke would experience that same anguish today when she learned Katy had gone. Determined to spend the day trying to comfort her niece, she glanced at the bedside clock.

Oh, Lord, she thought, scrambling to her feet and going to the phone. It was already seven o'clock. She'd be lucky if she caught Jake before he left for the day.

She was relieved to find him still at home and agreeable to leaving Brooke with her rather than Victoria's family. In fact, she had time for a quick bath before she went to the kitchen to make breakfast for the little girl.

Just as she slid a tin of bran muffins into the oven, she heard Jake's pickup arrive. Closing the oven door, she ran to the front door.

When Brooke yawned widely, Jake explained, "It was a rough night. She's still a little tired."

"Honey, would you like to rest for a while?" Michelle took her to the spare bedroom that she kept ready for Brooke and Katy's overnight stays. Something that wouldn't happen now.

With Brooke safely tucked in between the sheets, Jake and Michelle stepped out on the front porch.

Jake spoke first. "I guess you know Cynthia left Mike last night, don't you?"

"Yes. She came by here and wanted to collect Katy's things from school."

"I can't believe she kicked him when he was already down."

"That's not the way she viewed it."

"Oh, I guess she gave you the hard-luck story of how she'd sacrificed everything to move to Sotol Junction for Mike."

"Didn't she?"

Jake looked down at Michelle. There was no physical resemblance to DeeDee, but he suspected their reasoning was the same. He could tell by her face that she took Cynthia's side without even bothering to learn Mike's side of the story.

"I don't care what she said. Cynthia's never been able to cope when things go wrong. She finds a hole to crawl in during a thunderstorm, surfacing only when the sun's shining. She was that way in Houston and she's that way here."

"Paloma did say something about Cynthia's not being very strong."

"Perhaps I shouldn't have criticized Cynthia, but don't make any harsh judgments against Mike. He's the salt of the earth."

"You told Brooke, didn't you?"

"Yeah, I told her. She was a little too sleepy for it to sink in. Besides, I didn't give her both barrels. I decided I'd go into more detail tonight when I get back in." His green eyes clouded at the thought. "You won't take sides, will you?"

She shook her head. "No, I won't," she whispered in understanding. "I really can appreciate both points of view."

As a feeling of trust overtook him, Jake lowered his head at the same time Michelle lifted hers slightly.

She was so lovely with the morning light reflecting the rosiness of her cheeks, Jake had to swallow. He slid his tongue over suddenly parched lips. She licked her lips in response. He couldn't move. If he did, he wasn't sure he would stop this time—not if she was willing. Then, as if by mutual agreement, they moved apart.

"I guess I'd better go." Jake said.

"And I guess I'd better check the muffins," she said. But neither made an effort to leave.

A small plane buzzed overhead, breaking the tension.

"That's probably my group for the day." Jake was grateful for the interruption. He wasn't sure how much longer he'd have been able to resist pulling her into his arms to taste.

Not much longer, he thought.

CHAPTER FOURTEEN

WORRY ABOUT the busy day ahead nagged at Jake as he headed toward Junction Outfitters early Monday morning. Fifteen people would arrive in a couple of hours, eager to float down the Rio Grande, and he had a lot of work to do. Just as he wheeled around the corner in front of the row of shops, Jake noticed lights from the outer office spilling out onto the boardwalk. Who the hell . . . ?

He was certain he'd switched off the lights the night before. With a wry thought, he decided it'd be his luck if he was the victim of the only break-in in town in the four years he'd lived here. He was sure it wasn't Greg who thought being on time was being ten minutes late. Cynthia had a key, but she was gone.

That left Mike.

"Damn! I thought he knew better," Jake mumbled to himself before slamming the pickup door and taking the wooden steps to the boardwalk in a single bound. He was right. "What in the deuce are you doing here?"

Mike, sitting behind the reception counter shuffling papers, raised his palm, ready to deflect any criticism. "Hell's bells, Jake. You know what I'm doing here."

"Yeah, committing suicide."

"Look, I can't just sit at home today, staring at my toes and feeling sorry for myself. Besides, you need me. I may not be able to guide a raft yet, but I can damn sure answer the phone and fill out papers the same as Victoria or Cynthia." His voice seemed to catch at his wife's name, but he continued, "And I can type as good as any man can with these." He wiggled his index fingers.

"You know I should send you packing, *pronto*." Jake tried to hide a grin as he poured himself a cup of coffee from the half-drained pot. He'd really missed Mike's irreverence.

"I *ain't* movin'." Mike leaned back in his chair and, in defiance, crossed his arms over his chest. "You need me today." Nodding his head toward the calendar posted on the wall, Mike defended his reasoning. "I see you have two rafts going out this morning. So you gotta have me."

"You're a grown man and make your own choices. I just don't want to hear any moaning and groaning from you at the end of the day." Jake really could use Mike's help since Victoria had gone to visit relatives and wouldn't be able to fill in for the absentee Cynthia.

Mike said, "I reckon I've earned the right to moan and groan if I want to."

Jake chuckled. "Yeah, you have. Actually, I'm rather glad to see your ornery ole carcass propped up in that chair. I was beginning to think you were on permanent disability." He slapped his partner on the shoulder. "Good to have you back."

"Thanks."

"Just take it easy, okay?"

"I'm not plannin' on having a footrace with anyone. I'm just gonna sit here on my tail, answer the telephone and maybe schedule some trips. I see here—" he waved a letter "—your old company in Houston is interested in working out some corporate 'bonding' excursions. If this comes to pass, it oughta put us in the black."

Jake nodded. "It's a fact it won't hurt the ledger any. If Lance Bradford happens to call while I'm gone today, tell him the middle of next month looks like a good time for me. He and another guy named Gary want to come and scout things out. Sort of a dry run before they sign a contract."

"Sure thing, and if a tourist comes in, maybe I can palm off a couple of those caps you thought was such a hotshot idea."

"I'd be eternally grateful." Jake had only been half listening to the salesman the day he'd ordered the caps. He'd still swear he'd agreed to buy two dozen rather than two gross. Oh, well. Water under the bridge.

"And who knows, maybe someone will drop by for a friendly game of dominoes. Worrying about them cheatin' me rather than 'bout myself sounds pretty good about now.'' He looked like a dejected puppy hunkering outside on a porch during a thunderstorm. Jake decided that it was probably the best thing for Mike to be at the office. ''You gonna be okay, here by yourself today?''

''Yeah.'' Mike picked up a stack of papers and began thumbing through them, effectively dismissing Jake.

Jake sympathized with Mike's feelings. As the saying went: He'd been there and done that. If it hadn't been for the long hours he'd put in getting Junction Outfitters started, he'd have gone crazy. Were all women as fickle as DeeDee and Cynthia? Or had he and Mike just fallen in love with the wrong kind of women?

He couldn't see Paloma dumping a man she loved. How about Michelle? Now, where did that thought come from? he wondered. The question was irrelevant because he was never going to put himself in the position to find out.

His thoughts were interrupted by a sharp knock on the front door. Through the front glass, he could make out an older man and his wife huddled in windbreakers against the morning chill. The first of his guests had arrived. Time to get to work.

In less than an hour, all fifteen of the day's river runners came in, some had been before and others were apprehensive novices. With Mike's help, Jake processed them and had them on their way to the launching spot in short order.

THE NEXT COUPLE OF DAYS at Junction Outfitters passed in a blur. It was as though Mike's presence was a lucky talisman, because each trip was filled with people who decided at the last minute to do something exciting to tell the folks back home about. A rafting excursion fit their bill. Mike seemed to thrive despite the extra workload. His complexion developed a healthy glow, even though there was a sadness in his eyes that showed how much he missed his wife and daughter. Greg had even begun to come in a few minutes early, and Jake had talked Wesley into coming down to Sotol Junction Wednesdays and Fridays, and, after a little haggling, any other days he didn't have classes at Sul Ross.

Jake particularly wanted Wesley to come in this Wednesday because Michelle was coming by after school. They were going to make the last home visit. The prospect of being with Michelle was something Jake was really looking forward to, so he was happy to take one of the short half-day Wednesday trips and clean up as soon as he arrived back at the office. He was on the phone when he heard her voice in the front office.

"Hello, Mike. You're looking more fit every day," Michelle said.

"Of course I am. Can't keep a good man down, you know."

"That's what Jake says. Is he here yet?"

"Be just a minute," Jake called from his office. He cursed himself for having placed the call to Lance in

Houston and now being tied up waiting to finalize the plans for the weekend excursion in May.

"Take your time." Michelle peeked into his office looking as fresh as she did early in the morning. How did anyone look that good after a whole day with children? "I've got to go by the post office to pick up my mail, anyway. Be right back."

Jake was waiting outside on the boardwalk when she emerged from the post office, tucking her mail into a canvas bag.

"Ready?" he asked, leading her toward the pickup.

"Ready."

Fifteen minutes later, Jake pulled up outside a shed covered with tar paper, some asbestos shingles, a few sheets of tin and linoleum. Michelle gasped. "Is this where Javier lives?"

"Yeah."

"You've got to be kidding. I can't believe anyone in the United States lives in these conditions."

Jake motioned toward the rude shelter. "We're in the States and so is that hovel. It's bad, but I can tell you that I've been across the border and seen some places that don't have four walls, much less a floor."

Michelle said nothing.

"I know it's hard to hide your reaction, but I should warn you the place is probably worse inside than outside. Try not to show your feelings."

Before they got to the door, three toddlers, all clad in wet, dirty diapers, gathered in the opening. Javier peeked out from behind them and called out, *"Mamá, Mamá. Mi maestra."*

A woman who looked to be no more than twenty came to the door. She pushed her way through the children as she tucked her straight, black hair behind her ears and smoothed the front of her shapeless dress with her hands. *"Hola."*

"Hola, Señora Salinas. Como está?" Michelle listened intently as Jake asked the woman how she was and told her the purpose of their visit.

After a few exchanges Michelle didn't quite understand, Jake translated for her. "She said she was just fixin' to feed the kids supper, but for us to come on in and then she'll be happy to talk with us in a few minutes."

The odor was the first thing Michelle noticed as she entered the house. She didn't know if it came from the soiled clothes that were piled in a corner of the room or from the chickens that were strutting around the kitchen. A small, black skillet of refried beans and a stack of tortillas that had been spread with something resembling scrambled eggs sat on the surface of an old Formica-topped table.

The odor was overwhelming, and despite her best intentions, Michelle had to turn her head to keep the family from seeing how badly she was affected. "Just a minute, please," she said. "I left something in the pickup." She stepped outside and sucked in a deep breath of fresh air. As an excuse for her rapid departure, she rummaged through her canvas bag and retrieved a picture book to give to the children.

Satisfied she could go into the house without offending the Salinas family, Michelle took one more deep breath. When she stepped back in, she saw Señora Salinas hand each child a rolled tortilla which they immediately shared with the chickens. She offered Jake and Michelle a filled tortilla, but they declined.

In a corner of the front room, a bare mattress was heaped with rumpled blankets, and Michelle assumed that was where the four children slept. At the other end of the room, Michelle glimpsed a metal-framed bed through an open doorway that led to a lean-to room.

Señora Salinas pointed to an old chair that looked as if it had been made from sotol and strung with some type of sisal. Michelle sat down carefully. She uttered a few words about Javier's limited progress in school, which Jake translated. Señora Salinas couldn't help much because she'd never been to school. Neither had her husband, so they could not read a word in English or Spanish. In fact, Señora Salinas said one of the reasons they had moved to the United States was so their children could get a few years of free education, something that would have been unattainable on a remote Mexican ranch.

Michelle had never felt so helpless. How had other teachers coped? She listened as Jake made their goodbyes, then politely said, *"Adiós."*

When they got back to the pickup, Michelle closed her eyes and in an effort to gain control, raised her chin and took a deep breath, blowing it out from between pursed lips. She didn't want to cry in front of Jake.

"Are you going to be all right?" he asked, his voice full of concern as he put his hand on her shoulder and gave it a squeeze.

"My heart goes out to Javier... he's such an adorable little boy and look how he lives. It just isn't fair."

"Yeah. I didn't know it was quite this bad, either." Jake leaned over and opened the door of the truck. "Come on. Let's get outta here."

"What does Javier's father do for a living?" Michelle climbed in and laid her head against the seat. Her heart ached for Javier with his thick curly hair and his bright eyes that she could imagine growing wary and hopeless.

"Nothing, as far as I know."

"No job?"

Jake shook his head. "Since he can't read or write, that only leaves manual work. And according to Paloma, he's not been well and hasn't been able to get a job on one of the local ranches."

"The situation seems so hopeless." Michelle sighed. "And the mother, poor woman, needs help. too. Then there are the little children. God, I wish there was something I could do."

After he pulled onto the dirt road that led back into Sotol Junction, Jake reached over and covered her hand that lay clenched in the seat between them. He didn't say a word, but the simple gesture let her know that he understood her frustration.

She turned and gave him a halfhearted smile. "Thanks for being there for me again. I couldn't have done it alone."

"This time I can't say I enjoyed it. But you're welcome." His mouth turned up in an easy grin but his eyes didn't flicker with any humor.

"Isn't there some kind of government program that can help them?" When Jake shrugged, Michelle said, "There must be something we can do."

"I don't know if there's a county program or not, but I'll bet Paloma can tell us who to contact. We'll do what we can."

Michelle smiled her thanks. Jake really was a good man. DeeDee and her mother just hadn't given him a chance.

When he pulled up in front of the boardwalk, he turned to her. "I'll buy you a drink. I know I could sure use one about now."

Michelle didn't want to be alone with her thoughts. She knew she would have a hard time sleeping tonight. While she wouldn't be in Sotol Junction very long, she silently vowed to help the Salinas family as much as she could. Now, she just wanted to block the afternoon from her mind, so she nodded at Jake's suggestion. "I'd like that."

He let go of her hand only long enough for her to get out of the pickup, then he took it again to help her up the wooden steps—a move that was unnecessary but that made Michelle feel protected in a world she was quickly learning could be very harsh. She threaded her fingers through his and walked by his side to the restaurant in the hotel. She needed his support and strength. "Thanks again for everything, Jake."

"You know, I didn't tell you this before, but I was really glad when you stopped calling me Jacob," he said. "Jacob was the ass I left in Houston."

"Jake suits you so much better." She smiled at him.

FRIDAY, when Jake arrived back from the river, he noticed a dust-covered pale blue truck pulling off the main highway. He recognized Eduardo and Pablo sitting in the cab, but not the four men sitting in the truck bed.

He figured they were headed for the mountains to begin the *candelilla* harvest. Eduardo usually hired illegal aliens to do the backbreaking job of pulling up the *candelilla* by the roots. The plant was nearly as stubborn about being pulled up as the burros were about carrying the harvest down from the rocky terrain to vehicles waiting to cart the crop to the pilas.

Once the men were across the border in Mexico, the work started full force. They would inspect the fifty-gallon barrels and replace any that had rusted through since last summer. Holes would be dug and filled with mesquite for a fire. The plants would be cooked in a cauldron of boiling water and acid until a foam rose to the top. Using whatever tools were available, the men would skim off the foam and allow it to cool into a wax. Finally, they would smuggle the wax back across the river to market it for a higher price in the U.S.

In a primitive way, Jake admired the people who risked their lives working with the volatile acid to provide money for their families. On the one hand, he envied the men who would be going into the rugged limestone mountains to camp for several days while they worked, and on the other, he was glad he was staying at home.

Michelle would disapprove of the illegality of the act, but would sympathize with the need of the people. Hell, she'd probably get in contact with someone at the agricultural extension office to teach the locals to plant the stuff. He grinned at the thought of her trying to persuade some bureaucrat to plant a weed that would cost ten times over what it could be sold for.

With growing anticipation, he drove to Michelle's. He knew he should do everything in his power to avoid her until she left Sotol Junction, but he'd been pleased when she'd asked Brooke to stay with her this afternoon after school. That meant he'd get the opportunity to see her. As he strolled to the front door, he felt like a teenager picking up a date.

He tapped on the door and nudged it open when he didn't get a response. "Michelle?"

"In here," she softly called from the kitchen doorway. "I'm finishing the dishes. Brooke lay down on my bed a few minutes ago to rest. She really missed Katy today.''

''Yeah. She's been pretty upset all week.'' He followed Michelle into the kitchen. ''Katy called a couple of nights ago, said they were living with Cynthia's parents and that Cynthia was crying all the time. I'm glad she's not having an easy go of it.'' Jake leaned against the counter and watched Michelle reach to put away a platter. She was wearing a short romper that left much of her slender legs exposed. Fighting the urge to stroke their silken curves, he crammed his hands into his pocket.

Michelle shut the cabinet door with a little more force than necessary, then winced at the loud noise it made.

He knew she was reacting to his words. He asked, ''You don't think Cynthia brought it on herself?''

She turned to face him. Only the faint color in her cheeks belied her outward calm. ''Look at it through her eyes. She almost lost the man she loved to an accident that wouldn't have happened if they'd stayed in the city.''

''In the city, he could have been shot by an AK-47.''

She sighed. ''We've been over this before. I don't think either one of us is going to change our minds.''

''Not likely.'' He watched her carefully fold the dish towel on the counter. ''You're wrong, you know. This place is not more dangerous than the city. And if Cynthia really loved Mike, she'd want to be with him no matter where he lived.''

"That works two ways, you know." Her point made, she didn't want to get into an argument. "Do you think she'll come back?"

He shrugged. "Don't know. She's never liked it here. Thought it was too far from just about everything."

Michelle leaned against the counter beside Jake. "She's *about* right. But I hope she comes back for Mike and Katy's sake."

He crossed his arms. "I talked to Paloma again today. She and Father Alvarez went out to Javier's yesterday. I think the two of them can help the Salinas family."

Michelle flashed him a smile that did something deep in the pit of his stomach. He discovered he enjoyed making her happy.

"Yes, Paloma and Father Alvarez will make a big difference." She stepped closer, until only a foot or so separated them. "I don't suppose you know anything about a tall man with a ponytail who was nice enough to deliver some food and diapers to Señora Salinas yesterday evening, would you?"

Jake, uncomfortable with praise, looked away and made a grunting noncommittal sound. Then he asked, "How'd you find out, anyway?"

"Javier told me." Michelle lightly touched his arm, her voice was soft and caressing as she whispered, "Considering how busy you are, you're more than thoughtful, Jake."

"Aw, it wasn't much, and, besides, I had to go out that direction for something, anyway."

"I see." Her voice reflected indulgent disbelief.

"You're a fine one to point a finger. Paloma said you were arranging parenting and adult education classes and had asked her about getting Señora Salinas to come." In fact, Paloma hadn't missed the chance to let him know how he'd misjudged Michelle. The thing was, even if he had been wrong about his ex-sister-in-law, it was now too late to do anything about it. She was leaving in a few weeks.

Suddenly, he was acutely aware of her fingers resting on his bare flesh. He uncrossed his arms, trying to gain control of the situation by taking her fingers off his arm, but as soon as his hand closed over hers, and she swayed toward him, his resolve faltered.

As he drew her to him, her lips parted, inviting him to taste their sweetness. He pulled her against him in one desperate motion and covered her mouth with his own.

He reveled in feeling her hands caressing his neck, holding him closer as if she, too, couldn't get enough. When the tip of her tongue snaked between his lips, he felt as though he would burst with the need to make love to her, to make her his. The overwhelming need to be one with another person rocked him.

Moaning her own pleasure and frustration, Michelle threaded her fingers through his hair and with catlike grace rubbed her body against his.

With one hand he cradled her head, preventing her from ending the kiss, and with his other hand he explored the treasures she so passionately offered. Her skin was as soft as it looked. Even the dry desert wind hadn't affected its silkiness. When his hand brushed her breast, she gasped against his mouth. Her breath mingled with his as he pulled away only far enough to unbutton the front of her romper. His callused fingers fumbled with the tiny buttons until her own fingers came to his aid. He stepped back to watch as she slowly revealed the white lace of her bra and the swell of perfectly formed breasts.

Her eyes raised to meet his as if seeking his approval. "You're wonderful," he whispered. Putting his hands under her arms, he lifted her onto the counter. When he brushed her long blond hair off her shoulder and lowered his head to nuzzle her neck and trail kisses downward, she arched her back and rested her head against the cabinet doors. The simple gesture was one of complete trust.

Somewhere in the far recesses of his brain he heard the noise a split second before he felt Michelle stiffen. She leaned forward and rested her head on the top of his. Gasping for breath, she whispered as she fumbled with her buttons, "Brooke. Brooke's up."

He turned to shield Michelle as she slid down from the counter behind him and straightened her clothes. He was running his hands through his hair trying to give it some semblance of order when Brooke appeared in the kitchen doorway, yawning.

Her eyes heavy with sleep and her voice low, she said, "I didn't know you were here, Daddy. I guess I went to sleep." She went over and hugged Jake.

"You were all tired out, Angel. Did you have a good day?"

Brooke nodded and yawned again. "Aunt Michelle told me that Katy might come back this summer to see her daddy. Do you think she might?"

Jake regained control of his breathing while Brooke talked. "Maybe, Angel. Are you about ready to go home?" He felt Michelle slide from behind him and come to stand by his side.

"Yes, I'm awake now. Do you think I could come back tomorrow for a while. I'm going to teach Aunt Michelle how to make brownies. She can't cook much of anything."

Michelle explained, her voice sounding unnaturally hoarse, "From a mix and for a school party."

"Sounds fine to me." At the moment he'd agree to anything because nothing made sense. His brain hadn't adjusted to the sudden change of events. He turned to Michelle. Her hair was disheveled, her lips swollen from his kisses and her eyes almost navy with longing, though she was doing her best to cover the signs of their aborted lovemaking. "I guess so." Fighting the urge to give her one last good-night kiss, he cupped her chin and said, "Brooke and I will be going now. I'll talk to you tomorrow."

Michelle stood in the kitchen for several minutes after she heard the front door shut. Not once, she realized, had she thought of DeeDee while Jake was kissing her.

In bed, rest eluded her as she lay awake for hours fighting the demons that plagued her. What would Brooke think? Michelle knew what her mother would think. Elizabeth Davis would have a hissy fit if she knew Michelle was falling in love with Jake Evans.

Jake.

She said his name over and over, marveling at its beauty and strength, so appropriate for the man it represented. But she was leaving Sotol Junction in less than four weeks.

Jake belonged here.

She belonged in Boston.

CHAPTER FIFTEEN

"DO YOU LIKE Aunt Michelle, Daddy?" Brooke asked when they arrived home.

"Yeah, I do. Why do you ask?" Jake opened the front door and turned to his daughter. He'd been expecting the question. Brooke was a bright kid, and God knows, he and Michelle had probably looked embarrassed when Brooke had walked in.

"You aren't as grumpy around her as you were when she first came here."

"I wasn't grumpy."

"Yes, you were."

"I wasn't. Now, scoot on into your room, Angel, and go to bed." He watched until Brooke was in her room before flipping off the living-room light and turning to go to his own room.

"I'm glad you like her, Daddy," Brooke called out. "I like her a lot, too."

Jake smiled at his daughter's approval. At least that was one obstacle he and Michelle wouldn't have to overcome. Tossing his clothes into a pile by the closet, he crossed to the bathroom and turned on the shower. He doubted that a cold shower would really put out the fire that still burned within him. Besides, he didn't see any point in inflicting more pain on an already aching body, so he turned the tap to warm and climbed into the stall.

Half an hour later he stretched out on the cool sheets, crossed his hands behind his head and stared at the ceiling. Had he really gone and fallen in love with Michelle Davis? He thought so and he also thought it was the absolute stupidest thing he could possibly have done.

History was repeating itself. She wasn't going to stay in Sotol Junction, and he wasn't going to leave. Even if they could work out some type of compromise, the thought of having Elizabeth Davis for his mother-in-law again made his head hurt.

At half-past three, he was still staring at the ceiling—when he wasn't checking the clock on the nightstand. The emotions ignited by Michelle's passionate response refused to go away. Maybe the cold shower would have helped. The memory of the faint scent of flowers in the valley between her breasts haunted him until he sat up, punched the pillow into shape and made another futile attempt at sleep.

He'd just drifted into a fitful sleep when he heard a loud pounding on the front door. Who the hell could it be? Had something happened to Michelle? Mike? Paloma? He rolled from bed and pulled on his jeans as he hobbled barefoot through the living room.

He managed to finish zipping his pants at the same time he opened the door. Pablo stood on the front porch shuffling from foot to foot, a frightened look on his face.

Though Jake's Spanish was good, he had a hard time following the youngster as he haltingly explained what had brought him to Jake's door at this time of night. Finally, Jake understood that the *candelilla* harvesters were in trouble. They were stranded in the park because their truck wouldn't start. If they were caught, they would be fined, and it was only about three hours until sunrise.

"Please, *señor,* you'll go get them," Pablo pleaded.

Jake ran his fingers through his hair and nodded. "Sure. Give me a minute to get dressed." He hurried back to the bedroom and pulled on his boots, then tugged a khaki shirt from a hanger and returned to the living room. While he dressed, he considered what to do about Brooke. He couldn't leave her alone, and he didn't want to wake her up and take her to Paloma's, or, God forbid, Michelle's.

"Pablo, you better stay here with Brooke just in case she wakes up and is scared." Jake shoved his shirt in his pants and rezipped them.

"But, *señor,* how will you find Tío and the others?"

"Tell me where they are, and I'll find them. How long did it take you to walk here?"

"What time is it?"

"Four."

Pablo thought a minute. "It was a little after midnight when Tio Eduardo drove the truck off the road, so—"

"Which road?" Jake interrupted.

"The one just south of the mesa," Pablo answered.

"Okay, Pablo. I'd better go find them before they rack up so much in fines that even Donald Trump couldn't get their butts out of jail. You lie down on the sofa and rest. I'll have your uncle back here in a couple of hours."

An hour later, Jake was beginning to doubt his promise. There were no signs of the *candelilla* harvesters near the road Pablo had described. After backtracking a second time and driving slowly with his pickup door open so he could see the side of the road, Jake spotted two faint tracks that led off into the brush and rock. He flipped the headlights off to avoid detection and veered from the main road.

Swerving to miss *lechuguilla* spines that would puncture a tire, Jake bounced through the desert in the cool early-morning air. Finally, he saw headlights flash on and off in the distance. Eduardo was taking a calculated risk signaling.

When Jake pulled up beside the stranded truck and got out, he grinned at Eduardo's obvious relief. "Trouble?"

"*Sí.* This ole jalopy is one sorry son-of-a-bitch, eh, Señor Jake. That Alpine dealer cheated me. Burros are much better," Eduardo explained.

"If you've gotta bellyache about a twenty-year-old pickup that you've wrecked twice since I've lived here, save it for later. Right now, we've got to get out of here before we're spotted. What's the problem?" A large sliver of orange sun was sneaking over the distant mountains casting long, eerie shadows among the men.

"The battery. She's dead."

Jake had pulled his pickup into position and Juan was already hooking up the battery cables to Eduardo's truck when Jake noticed a cloud of dust coming toward them. "Looks like we got company."

Eduardo mumbled a string of curse words in Spanish as they watched the official white Blazer come to a halt a few yards away. A ranger got out and surveyed the group before deciding it was safe to approach.

There was nothing Jake could do, so he leaned against the truck, crossed his arms and waited while the man strolled up to Eduardo.

"Kinda out a little early this morning, aren't you, boys? Get lost or something?" The ranger who'd replaced Dale Blevins a few weeks ago was a scrawny kid who, from the way he shoved out his chest, was obviously proud of his badge. Jake wished one of the veteran officers had found them, someone who'd mellowed a little.

"*Qué?*" Eduardo looked as innocent as a newborn babe.

The officer repeated his question. Eduardo again acted as though he didn't understand English.

"Damn. *No habla inglés,* my ass," the ranger said, peering at the *candelilla* in the back of Eduardo's pickup. "You boys smuggling drugs?"

The ranger searched the mute faces. Then he spotted Jake. "You understand English. Right?"

The others were planning to play dumb to the language, but Jake didn't have that luxury. He'd taken an instant dislike to the disrespectful man, but he tried to control the disdain in his voice. "Yeah."

"I'm Ranger Terrell. You want to tell me what you're doing here?"

Hoping he could talk his way out of trouble, Jake straightened and nodded toward the five men who were lined up by the other truck. "Their pickup broke down. I know it's a problem with them being off the road, but they apparently got lost in the dark. I was just going to give them a boost."

"You don't expect me to believe that crock of bull, do you?" Without waiting for an answer, the young ranger grinned and shook his head, obviously relishing the situation. Just a few weeks into the job, and he was already earning his pay. "Even if I did, it seems to me that being off the road's not the only trouble you boys got yourselves into."

One of the harvesters mumbled in Spanish that he wasn't a boy. Jake shot him a quelling look to get him to shut up. He didn't want anyone to further antagonize the ranger.

With pursed lips, Ranger Terrell walked around the pickup studying every detail before striding back to his vehicle with a sense of purpose.

Jake knew they were in for trouble as he watched the ranger mumble into his radio. Eduardo and Juan came to stand by his side.

His voice low enough not to carry in the still air, Jake told the two men, "This doesn't look good."

"Oh, but Señor Jake," Eduardo whispered, his back turned to the ranger's Blazer, "you can handle him. He's just a—"

He stopped in midsentence when the ranger started back toward them, a big pad in his hand. "You gentlemen are lucky today. I'd like to haul your butts in because you've earned serious citations for illegal harvesting, expired tags on the pickup and driving off the road."

Jake answered, "We're sorry, Ranger Terrell. I'll explain it to these guys, and they won't ever do it again."

"Good deal. Good deal. Now, if I can just see your license and . . . the license of whoever was driving that pickup." Jake and Eduardo pulled out their licenses simultaneously.

The ranger's eyebrows lifted at Eduardo's mistake. "You understand English, now?"

Eduardo smiled but didn't say a word.

As Terrell was writing up the citations, a second park-service vehicle pulled up beside the first, and two rangers got out. "Jake, what are you doing out here?" one of the men asked.

"Morning, Sam." Jake wished Sam had found them, to begin with. He'd been with the Big Bend park service for several years and was highly respected by the locals. "I reckon I'm getting myself a *serious* citation."

Terrell's eyes hardened. "I wouldn't take this lightly, Mr. Evans. For your information, stealing local flora and breaking vehicular and park regulations *are* serious offenses. Signs are posted everywhere. I suspect driving at night with your lights off kept you from seeing those signs. That, and—" nodding toward Eduardo and the other men "—not being able to read."

Jake stiffened when he saw rage cross the face of one of the young Mexicans a split second before the kid burst into English, "Damn *Gringo*. I can read!"

Eduardo reached out and caught the young man's arm. "Easy, Miguel," he warned.

Terrell spun around at the same time. "Don't cuss me, you—"

In the blink of an eye, Miguel jerked away from Eduardo and charged the ranger, fists swinging, while Jake lunged toward Miguel, trying to intercept the attack.

Miguel ducked and Jake caught the ranger in the chest, sending them both sprawling to the ground. While dust covered the three men in a fog that made breathing and seeing difficult, Jake felt a sharp punch to his lower jaw and tried to fend off a second attack. The next thing he knew, he was in the dirt, intertwined with Miguel and Park Ranger Terrell, fists flailing.

He felt strong hands on his shoulders separating him from the other two men. Sam hauled him against a pickup. "You've done it now. Terrell will insist we arrest you."

Jake tried to brush off some of the dust. He knew an excuse was pointless. He was going to make a trip to Alpine and the county jail.

IN THE WORLD of being neither fully awake nor fully asleep, Michelle was dreaming about Jake and his kisses when the phone rang, piercing the tranquillity of her fantasy. She groaned and got the slippers she still kept on top of the bed out of reach of scorpions, then she padded into the living room.

Eyes closed in a futile effort to deny the day, she picked up the receiver and mumbled, "Hello."

"Michelle. Did I wake you?" Mike sounded apologetic.

She started to say no because she knew everyone in Sotol Junction got up with the roosters, but her sleepy voice would belie any denial. "Yes, but it's okay."

"Hey, I'm sorry, but there's a problem."

Michelle was jarred awake. Visions of disaster flashed through her mind. "What is it, Mike?"

"It's Jake." The line became silent.

"What about Jake?" Her stomach knotted in fear waiting for his answer.

"It's not serious. I mean, he's okay. It's just that he's in jail."

"In jail?" Michelle's voice rose more in exclamation than question. How could he be in jail? He'd been in her arms less than fourteen hours ago. "For what?"

"Ah, I believe he said something about some trouble in the park and then assaulting a ranger."

Michelle went numb. "Assaulting a park ranger," she repeated as she sank down on the sofa, her legs too weak to hold her. "Jake wouldn't assault someone."

"It appears he did. Anyway, he needs one of us to go to Alpine and bail him out. He doesn't have his wallet or checkbook with him."

Michelle let Mike's words soak in, her initial shock and disbelief turning to uncertainty. Was this the shadowy side of Jake her mother warned her about?

"Michelle, are you still there?" Mike asked.

"Yes. I'm just a little stunned," she answered.

"Yeah, I figured you would be. I called Prof to go get Jake, but couldn't find him. I'd go myself, but I still can't drive because of my bum leg. Do you think you could get him?"

"Yes, of course I'll go. Give me a minute to get dressed. Uh, Mike, where's Brooke?"

"With Paloma."

"Does she know Jake's in jail?"

"I don't know, but you know this town. She'll find out soon enough."

ON THE DRIVE to Alpine, Michelle thought about Jake and how close they'd come to making love. In only a matter of weeks, what had once seemed so awkward now seemed so right. She'd grown to trust him, both for Brooke and herself, yet, only a few hours after leaving her arms, he'd gone to the national park and gotten into some kind of trouble. How?

Now she had to deal with the fact that Elizabeth may have been right all along. Maybe Jake wasn't the right person to raise Brooke. He'd been arrested—for assault, no less. The closer she got to Alpine the less worried and the more angry she became. The anger was directed at herself for having been taken in by a handsome, sensual man. Jake had know what she was doing in Sotol Junction, and he'd been on his best behavior. Until last night.

JAKE SAT on the wooden bench outside the sheriff's office. His pickup had been impounded, he didn't have a checkbook and he sure as hell hated for Brooke to find out he'd been arrested. Or Michelle. His stomach knotted when he thought about Elizabeth Davis's reaction. Maybe she wouldn't find out. If she did, she'd give him hell, making the cost of his bond seem like fourth-class postage.

At least he wasn't in a jail cell. He listened to the snoring coming from the arrest tank already full of weekend drunks. Miguel had been locked up since he was the one who'd begun the assault, and Eduardo and Juan and the other two men were locked up for harvesting *candelilla* and smuggling illegal aliens. But because they'd all sworn that Jake hadn't been involved, and had just come to their assistance, he'd been allowed to wait in the poorly lit hallway.

He walked inside the sheriff's office and filled a disposable cup with muddy coffee. It was already ten o'clock, so he figured Prof would show up to get him anytime. He'd just taken a seat again, when he noticed a tall blonde standing at the end of the hallway. She looked uncomfortable in the austere surroundings as she searched for someone to help her. When an officer pointed toward him, and the woman turned, Jake recognized Michelle.

Hell, of all the people to send to bail him out, she was the last person he would have chosen! What had possessed Mike? Jake would rather have had the priest. Someone he wasn't so determined not to let down. Then he felt a little guilty for assuming Michelle wouldn't understand.

As she strode down the corridor toward him, he couldn't make out her reaction until she stood in front of him. He got up to take her in his arms and explain, but her face was inscrutable, showing none of the emotion she'd displayed in his arms only hours earlier. He hesitated before offering a wry smile. "Thanks for coming to my rescue."

She ignored his overture. Her eyes and voice cool, she asked, "What do I do, Jake? I've never had to bail someone out of jail before."

He noted she'd reverted to calling him Jake. Swallowing his explanation of the night's events, he nodded toward the doorway leading into the sheriff's office. "I guess they'll tell you."

She stepped inside the small room, her body language leaving no room for doubt. She was angry. He followed her and waited impatiently by her side while she paid the bond. "Thanks. I'll repay you as soon as we get to Sotol Junction," he said as they walked out together, her back as ramrod-straight and stiff as he remembered her mother's.

"Hey, look. I said I'd repay you." Jake fought to keep his voice cool and matter-of-fact.

"The money's not a problem." Michelle's fingernails tapped at the steering wheel while she seemed to search for the correct question. "What happened last night after you left me?"

"Do you care?" He turned to face her, his eyes mirroring his disappointment and hurt. "Isn't this what you expected—wanted—to discover when you came out here? That I was really a criminal."

He noticed the slight flinch before she answered. "No, that isn't what I wanted." She tilted her head upward and splayed her hands. "Look, I guess I was embarrassed and uncomfortable in there. Okay? And, yes, I do care." She looked over at him. "Mike told me this had something to do with *candelilla* harvesting."

Jake leaned back against the headrest of the seat and explained as succinctly as possible what had happened the previous night.

The anger in Michelle's eyes turned to sympathy as she listened to him. "I read about the commercial value of the *candelilla* in the book you lent me. But why would Eduardo and the others risk getting fined or arrested to harvest it? Is it really that lucrative?"

"That depends on what you call lucrative. You wouldn't think so, but it provides pocket money for the folks around here. In fact," he said, "I get about as much profit out of it as anyone."

Michelle's eyes narrowed at what he'd said. She studied him, bidding him to continue.

"I get a six-pack of beer and get to listen to them bragging about how hard they worked."

She ignored the irony in his comment. "How about the others? How long will they be in jail?"

"Depends on if they're citizens or illegals. Eduardo's sister'll be coming later to see what she can do."

She shifted uneasily, then tentatively touched his arm. "Jake, I'm sorry I ever doubted you. I don't have a good excuse. It's just that this situation is something I've never had to deal with. I guess I always thought if someone got arrested they deserved it. I was wrong."

"I understand. It's your sheltered life." He covered her hand with his.

She smiled, her eyes as warm as they were yesterday in the kitchen. "It's late. How about getting something to eat? I'm starved.'' She withdrew her hand reluctantly and started the car.

Jake closed his eyes and sniffed at imaginary aromas. "I can smell it now. Ham, three eggs over easy, a steaming cup of decent coffee. There's a restaurant up here past the college that serves breakfast all day."

BY THE TIME they had finished eating and started back down the mountain toward Sotol Junction, Michelle had relaxed completely and was enjoying Jake's company. They seldom had a chance to be alone together and talk. There were so many things she wanted to know. "Why did you rescue them when you knew you might get caught?"

"They're my friends. Besides—" he began chuckling "—it was worth it to have seen the wide-eyed look on Terrell's face when he realized Miguel was going to hit him."

Michelle joined his laughter as she visualized the three men rolling around in the dirt. "I think I've seen something very similar in the playground."

"Little boys never grow up, right?" He leaned over the console and nuzzled her neck. "Despite my attempt at sophistication and maturity, I'm still a kid at heart."

The rough texture of his beard and musky smell of his body so close momentarily took her mind off her driving. "You better not do that, or we'll never get home."

"Would that be so bad?" He ran his hand from her knee to rest on her thigh.

"No...yes...I don't know. I can't think with you touching me."

Jake laughed a low contented growl and leaned back in his seat. "Good. At least I know you aren't immune to my advances."

Michelle immediately wished he hadn't moved to his side of the car, but she could drive safer with distance between them. "I'll bet you did your fair share of fighting in the playground."

"A little. It's hard to grow up with older brothers and not learn to stand up for yourself."

Michelle didn't know much about Jake's family. She'd met them at DeeDee's wedding and she knew they lived in Del Rio. "What's your family like?"

"My parents are good people. They've been married for forty-five years, now. Mom helped Dad grub part of the land to clear it for row crops as well as make pasture for cattle. They run a few cattle still, but they've been retired for several years. You'd like them. They floated the river with me once and Mom instructed me the entire trip."

"She doesn't think you've grown up, huh?"

"Nope. She says my ponytail and earring prove it. She seems to think it has something to do with adolescent defiance."

"Does it?"

"No. It just saves time getting haircuts."

It also made her heart beat at a faster pace, Michelle thought, admiring his bad-boy looks. In his hurry to rescue his friends, he hadn't taken the time to tie back his hair and it hung to his shoulders in a black mane. His cheeks and chin were covered by a dark shadow that would have given him a sinister appearance if it hadn't been for his warm smile. Brushing aside her awareness of him, she said, "Tell me about your brothers."

"One works for the Border Patrol down at Harlingen, and one is a cattle buyer."

"Maybe I'll meet them someday." The minute the words were out of her mouth, she regretted them. Of course she wouldn't meet his family. She'd be back in Boston and back in her old life.

The rest of the trip back to Sotol passed in silence.

"AUNT MICHELLE, Grandmother called," Brooke said when Jake and Michelle stopped by Paloma's to pick her up.

"She called several times," Paloma warned, her eyes filled with foreboding. "Since Brooke mentioned her father's little adventure, Mrs. Davis is primed for you."

Brooke was hopping from one foot to the other. "Were you really in jail?"

"Yeah, but Michelle got me out," Jake explained.

Paloma inserted, "It's the main topic down at the drugstore. Both tables are filled with domino players discussing you right now. You might need to go defend yourself."

"I suppose I should go home and call Mother," Michelle said. "Maybe I can do some damage control." Michelle hugged Brooke and looked up at Jake. His eyes were filled with concern and what looked like love. "Good luck dealing with the gossip."

"Good luck to you." Jake, apparently no longer caring what others thought, gave her a quick kiss. "If you can handle Elizabeth, I'll handle the rest of the town." As he walked out, he added, "And you've got the hardest job."

"No, MOTHER, it wasn't like that at all." Michelle listened to Elizabeth repeat her litany for the third time.

"Michelle, stop making excuses for that man. I knew he was unsavory when I sent you down there. Now he's proved it and so help me, if it's the last thing I do, I plan to wrestle Brooke from his control."

"Mother, you haven't listened to a word I've said. Jake was trying to help out some friends. He wasn't doing anything wrong."

Elizabeth sighed as though her daughter were slow-witted. "Michelle. People are not arrested in the United States for doing nothing wrong. Now, you listen to me. The first thing Monday morning, I'm calling my attorney. In the meantime, I want you to have a copy of Jacob's arrest record faxed to Frederick's law office."

"No."

Elizabeth gasped. "Michelle, you've never defied me this way. Now, you do as I say."

"No, Mother. Jake is a decent man, and I will not hurt him."

"Michelle, I said..."

Michelle held the receiver away from her ear, stared at it for a moment and then gently laid it in the cradle, a smile on her face.

"YOU'RE DOING ME DIRTY, Paloma, honey." Prof eyed the string of dominoes laid out on the board, studied his hand a moment longer, then selected his play. "Downright dirty."

"You've always said everything's fair in love and war, Prof. So quit complaining." Paloma chided him. "Besides, I've beaten you fair and square."

"So you have."

Hobbled footsteps interrupted their thoughts. The screen door slammed shut behind Mike. "Mind if I join you?" He pulled up a chair and dropped his cane on the floor. Without waiting for an answer, he cleared his throat and knocked on the table with his fist. "Deal me in."

"Looks like you're improving—" Prof motioned toward Mike's extended leg "—and just carrying that cane around for sympathy."

"Yeah, and defense against wiseacres."

As she shuffled the dominoes, Paloma decided to broach the topic that was on everyone's mind. "Mike, have you heard from Cynthia and Katy?"

Mike nodded. "Talked to Cynthia a couple of nights ago, and haven't slept a wink since. But I made a decision this morning. As soon as I can, I'm moving to East Texas."

"Have you told Cynthia?" Paloma asked.

"No. I didn't want to let her know until I'd worked out something with Jake. Don't know how I'm going to break it to him, either. He's all hepped up about a couple of friends from Houston coming in for a rafting trip. It's a big deal that could turn into some permanent business. If he can keep his mind on the trip, that is."

"Considering all that Jake's been through," Paloma said, "I've never known him not to keep his mind on business. What would keep him from it now?"

"He's invited Michelle to go with them," Mike explained.

"Well, well." Prof broke into a smile. "It's about time. Neither of them think anyone's noticed the way they look at each other. It's obvious they're sweet on each other. Michelle doesn't look as anxious to go back to Boston—and Jake . . ."

"Struts around like a stallion with a new mare," Mike finished for him. "Won't even let me stay in the same room alone with her."

"Tsk, tsk." The professor shook his head. "That boy's a goner. Mark my words, might as well just be the two of them going on this trip because those two other men are going to be ignored. Hope they don't fall out of the raft, because they'd surefire never be missed.''

"Sure would hurt my chances of unloading my part of the business if that was to happen." Mike screwed up his face as though he was deep in thought. "If I was any kind of man, I'd warn 'em they better not look at Michelle 'cause Jake'll have their hide." He leaned back and crossed his arms, an ornery expression on his face. "But I never was much of a man, so I'm just gonna let them take their chances. Be kind of fun to see if Jake ends back up in Alpine at the 'county facilities.'''

Prof laughed, absolutely gloating. "I didn't think I'd live to see our brand-spanking-new criminal fall in love." He glanced at Paloma. "I was of the opinion that this place was too dry and barren to foster any of that kind of stuff."

"Can you believe Jake's gone bonkers over our schoolmarm?" Mike said, pouring himself another glass of tea.

"I have no trouble believing it."

Mike grunted. "I'd say he'd better look before he leaps into a heap of trouble. Michelle wouldn't like living here anymore'n Cynthia did. She's got too many Boston ties, friends, family and all."

"She's already cut one tie," Paloma said. When Mike flashed her a quizzical look, she explained.

"Michelle told me that she'd encouraged the man she'd been dating in Boston to find another interest."

Mike nodded in understanding.

They played a few more hands of dominoes, with Prof winning the last round. Mike slapped the rest of his dominoes down, then propped his elbows on the table. "How's your business doing, anyway?"

"For a man of such limited memory," Prof answered, "I think I'm safe to say fair to middling. Just perfect for a guy who likes to piddle."

"Want to piddle in a little more business?" Mike asked.

"What do you mean?" Prof asked, straightening up.

"It'll be a lot easier to break my news to Jake if I had a potential partner available for him to consider. I thought you might be interested."

"Lord, I don't know. I'll have to think about it."

Paloma looked at her watch and got up. "Well, you boys can discuss this without me. The afternoon's almost gone, and I need to open the gallery before the river runners return."

Prof looked up in feigned disbelief. "I should've known. Let me win a round and you turn tail and run."

CHAPTER SIXTEEN

As soon as the students stormed out of the school the following Friday at one-thirty for the *Cinco de Mayo* holiday, Michelle locked the doors and hurried toward Junction Outfitters. She'd spent last night packing and repacking for the upcoming weekend river float until she'd finally called Jake for advice. While she was excited about the trip, the prospect of spending two whole days in Jake's company had her feeling like a child on Christmas Eve.

She pulled up in front of the boardwalk, and seeing Jake was busy, disappeared into the propped-open door of the tiny post office. Mike was standing with his back to her, pulling mail from his wall box, unaware she had entered. She opened her box and half-heartedly thumbed through the stack of sale circulars while, from under long lashes, she watched Mike doing the same thing.

Mike was gazing so intently at a small white rectangle that Michelle hesitated to interrupt him. Finally, he turned the envelope over, gave it a couple of hard shakes and held it up to the afternoon sunlight pouring through the window before tearing off one end.

Michelle watched emotions flood across his face, from ones of despair to one of pure joy. "Hot dog, Cynthia and Katy are coming home," he announced to the room, slapping the opened letter against his leg. He whirled around and saw Michelle, the mixture of joy and relief reflecting from his eyes unaffected by her presence.

"Oh, Mike. That's wonderful." Michelle stepped forward to hug him. "When?"

"Cynthia said she'd wait on my call to see if I wanted her to come back." He rolled his eyes in disbelief. "As if there was any doubt. So if I call right now, she could be on her way tomorrow. Be here by late Sunday."

The postmistress who had been listening to the conversation leaned up against the bars that separated the foyer from the back and put in her two cents' worth. "It's about time that girl came to her senses and got back here where she belongs."

"Two of us came to our senses," Mike said. "Well, folks, I gotta go make a phone call." He left his cane on the floor where he'd dropped it.

Happy for Mike, Michelle rifled through the rest of her mail and came to a stop at the sight of her mother's stationery. Apprehensively, she tore open the envelope and pulled out a cream-colored vellum note card. Michelle doubted the tasteful gold initials in its center signaled a courtesy note.

They didn't.

Michelle,

I'm glad you've come to see things my way. Fred got his own copy of Jacob's arrest record yesterday. He thinks with your testimony and other circumstantial evidence, I have a chance of gaining custody of Brooke. I know this has been difficult for you, but I knew you would reach the only possible decision. After all, we Davises must stick together to protect our own. I'm truly proud to call you daughter. I look forward to seeing you soon.

Love,
Mother

Michelle frowned in bewilderment. She hadn't sent her mother's attorney anything, and she hadn't agreed to testify. Frederick Latham could have obtained the information from several sources. Her mother's underhanded maneuvering made her angry. Should she warn Jake that Elizabeth was coming after him with her guns blazing?

Stepping into the sunshine warmed the coolness Elizabeth's letter had caused, and when Michelle looked down the boardwalk to where Jake and two other men were loading the van, she shelved the idea of warning him until after the trip. She didn't want him to worry about anything except this river run. He needed this excursion to be successful in order to get the corporate contract he'd been counting on.

Satisfied with her reasoning, Michelle listened to the music of Jake's footsteps on the wooden planks as he strolled toward her. His face was alive with a smile, and his eyes embraced her with their warmth. It was the exact opposite of the look he'd given her when he'd first met her at this same place nearly two months ago. No, she wasn't about to mention her mother and ruin the first time he'd been this relaxed with her.

She started guiltily when she remembered the offending note she still clutched in her hand. Quickly, she tucked it into the wildflower field guide she was carrying.

"Good afternoon. Are you ready to rough it?" His voice was teasing and held a hint of challenge. "Lance and Gary are waiting in the van."

So he didn't think she was up to this. Well, she had a thing or two to show him. In the six weeks she had been in Sotol Junction, she'd changed. She no longer shuddered at the mere mention of a scorpion, though the thought of a snake or a *niña de la tierra* still sent cold chills down her spine. She could cook a few basic meals, eat a jalapeño pepper, handle a classroom full of mismatched kids, deal with Pablo's marauding burro and she could bail a man out of jail.

She felt in control of her life. She doubted Elizabeth would be proud of any of her daughter's accomplishments.

"You bet." With a flick of her head, Michelle tossed her ponytail over her shoulder and grinned. "I'm more than ready. I've been waiting for a month to do this. Do you think the weather will hold?''

Jake chuckled as he cocked his head toward the sun. "I hope not." The temperature had already reached 102 degrees, ten degrees shy of what it would be in July. "I'd rather it cool down a little."

"I guess that was a foolish question. It hasn't rained since I got here," she said. "Jake, I feel a little guilty about leaving Brooke with Paloma this weekend. She wanted to come so badly."

"Brooke won't miss us a minute. Paloma will see to it. You sound as if you don't want to be alone with me." Jake stepped in front of her, stopping her in her tracks, and gazed down at her, their eyes exchanging a current of attraction broken only when Michelle swallowed.

"Having two other guys with us isn't exactly being alone with you." Her voice nearly failed her. "But it might have been safer if Brooke were with us."

"You'll be safe with me."

She knew he wasn't talking about floating down the river or the rapids, and it wasn't her physical body she felt was in danger. It was her heart.

"We won't do anything you don't want to," he promised.

That was the problem. She wanted to.

The spell was broken when a man called down the boardwalk, "Come on, you two. We've got a river to ride."

"That's Gary," Jake explained, taking Michelle's satchel. "This thing weighs a ton. Did you bring everything you own?"

"No, but I was afraid I'd forget something I needed."

Jake laughed as they walked toward the van. "You sound a little nervous. I'm sure you packed enough. You had excellent advice."

"I'm sorry I called you twice last night, but I didn't know what kind of clothes to bring."

"I wasn't sorry you called. But I bet you didn't take my advice."

Michelle lowered her voice to barely a whisper as they neared the van. "Oh, but I did."

Jake slowed the pace and looked at her, his eyes blazing with emotion. "You did?"

She grinned. "Yes, I didn't bring anything to sleep in."

CHAPTER SEVENTEEN

MICHELLE SMILED AT the two men who were leaning up against the van waiting for her and Jake. She was a bit nervous about meeting Lance and Gary, both of whom had known Jake in Houston, which meant they had also known DeeDee.

"Lance, Gary," Jake said, firmly clutching her elbow in support, "this is Michelle."

"Hello." She shook Lance's hand.

A walking advertisement for Eddie Bauer, Lance was a tall, good-looking man with an even tan and expensively trimmed blond hair. His perfect smile, whether a testament to the wonders of genetics or orthodontics, was warm as he shook her hand. "Nice to meet you," Lance said in a slow drawl that placed him as a Texan.

Short and a little pudgy, Gary was the opposite of his companion. It was hard to decide if he was letting his hair grow or if he needed a haircut. Jake had told her that although Gary was the youngest of the three men, he was the one who would make the final decision whether or not to book excursions with Junction

Outfitters. She couldn't help noticing the stained T-shirt he was wearing over his loose tan shorts.

Gary extended one hand while pushing his glasses up the bridge of his nose with the other. "Glad to meet you, Michelle. Saw you admiring my shirt. This isn't blood." He gestured to the red-orange stains. "This is my spaghetti-eating shirt."

At Michelle's frown, he explained. "This is what I wear every time I eat spaghetti. That way, I don't ruin more than one. Jake said not to bring anything I was very proud of. Might end up in the river."

Jake glanced over his shoulder at Gary and teased, "But I didn't know you were going to bring your dirty clothes."

"Hey, man, I ran them through the dryer first. Warmed 'em up and killed most of the insects."

For a split second, Michelle believed him and let her expression show before she caught herself. By the time Jake pulled the van up to the putting-in site, Michelle felt a little like the only girl at a boys' camp. She would have to be tough or the three men were going to make dog meat of her. In the span of fifteen minutes, she knew that every chance Gary got, he was going to tell her some big lie, and he had two willing accomplices. She was seeing a new side to Jake.

A blast of dry desert wind hit her when she hopped out of the air-conditioned van. She adjusted her sunglasses and the bill of her visor to shield herself from the sun, which was still high overhead and relentlessly baking everything in sight. She doubted her double-duty sunscreen would keep her from becoming one of its victims.

The men wrestled the unwieldy raft from the trailer and shoved it half into the water. Then she helped load it with everything they would need for the two-day trip. Michelle searched around the raft trying to decide where to stow her duffel bag.

Jake pointed toward a container. "You'll probably want to store your camera in that box over there. It's waterproof." He gave her a devil-may-care grin. "In case we take on water or capsize."

"Don't tempt fate by saying such things, Jake Evans." She swatted him, missing when he dodged sideways.

By the time they were ready to push off, all four of them were hot and sweaty.

Gary swiped his arm across his forehead. "Hell couldn't be much hotter than here."

"I believe that's what you used to say every August in Houston," Jake reminded him.

"But that was August, and this is May," Lance joined in the complaint.

"Dip your shirt in the water and put it back on," Jake instructed. "It'll help keep you cool."

A slightly horrified expression marred Lance's face when he looked at the brown water and then at his new camp shirt. "You're kidding."

Gary peeled off his T-shirt and grinned in satisfaction. "Told you," he said.

Michelle was a little nervous at the prospect of pulling off her T-shirt even though she was wearing a bathing suit underneath. She wasn't sure whether she was daunted by being the only woman present and knowing the men would watch, or because Jake had turned his attention toward her. It didn't really matter how much of her skin actually showed—he could just look at her and she felt exposed. She turned her back to the men and tentatively pulled off her shirt, dipped it in the water and, when she'd finished putting it back on, turned around.

Jake had his hands thrust in his pockets and his straw hat pulled down low over his eyes. He'd watched her, but he'd positioned his body between her and the other two men so they couldn't have seen much. His obvious maneuvering to protect her sent simultaneous chills and sparks through her veins. They were in for a long trip if he kept this up.

As if he'd done nothing out of the ordinary, Jake tossed his hat in the raft, stripped his shirt above his head, then dipped it into the opaque water as the others had. Michelle crossed her arms and openly admired him as he fought to get his arms back through the wet, clinging sleeves. His body was awesome, and she fought the urge to put her arms around him. Yes, it was going to be a long, wonderful trip, she thought as she took the life jacket he offered.

"Keep it close. You don't really need to put it on until we get to some rapids. The water isn't over five feet deep in most places." He helped her into the front of the raft after Lance and Gary had climbed into the back, then untied the mooring line and shoved off.

Jake checked the ten-foot oars in the their locks for a final time and gently guided the raft toward the middle of the river before settling into a slow, easy rhythm. The only sound was the splash of the oars in water and their own breathing as they floated between the seep willows and carizo reed lining the banks of the Rio Grande.

Michelle listened intently as Jake began explaining the geological formations and history of the area to the two men in the rear. "The right side of the river is Mexico and the left side is Big Bend National Park in the U.S."

"My God, Jake. You oughta be a history professor somewhere with knowledge like that." A robust laugh burst from Lance at Gary's comment.

"I just don't want to tax you boys' intelligence too much and I want to see that you get your money's worth. That includes the whole spiel."

Michelle chuckled. She'd enjoyed every word Jake had said. Whether it was his vast knowledge or the sound of his deep resonant voice, she wasn't sure, but she wanted to keep him talking, so she pointed to a band of sorrels grazing a short distance away. "Look at the horses."

"Ah, yes, I was getting to that. Because there's no barrier between the two countries other than the river, people and livestock come and go. Fact is, a lot of the animals get a little encouragement from their owners to cross the river during the day and graze in the park where there's more food."

"I didn't think the rangers allowed interlopers." Michelle's voice held a hint of mischief.

His eyes, sparkling with warning cloaked in humor, shifted slightly. "Animals aren't threats unless they become nuisances or hang around too long. Then they're rounded up and taken to Alpine where the owners have to pay a fine to get them back."

Michelle interjected in a low voice, "Like some people we know."

Jake pretended he hadn't heard her. "But all in all, there are no hard feelings between the park rangers and the Mexican ranchers."

Content, they continued down the muddy water that gently flowed over a limestone rock bed. Tenacious reeds and flimsy trees clung to the sides of the white sandy beaches where two Mexican women and several children were washing their clothes.

Just as the pace of the water picked up, a faint roar and splashing could be heard ahead. Jake wasn't having to row nearly as hard as he had earlier. "We're approaching the first set of rapids," he explained. "We might get a little wet."

The thought of a cooling spray sounded great, Michelle thought as she clutched the rope along the top edge of the raft and watched the waves getting closer.

Moments later, Gary told them what he thought of their first white-water experience. "Hell, I've gotten more action on the log plume at Six Flags. Michelle, you ever been so bored in your life?"

"I'm not a bit bored, Gary. The river, the cliffs, the mesas... they're..." She searched for words to describe the stark beauty, but came up empty. She and Jake exchanged a look of understanding.

Jake broke his gaze away from hers. "Just wait a little while, Gary, and we'll get to the good stuff. According to information from the park service, the Mexicans have let a little water out of the Rio Concho Dam, so the Rio Grande's been rising all day. Depending on how fast the water reaches us, we should be in for a pretty good ride."

"That's what we came for," Gary said.

"Just be patient." Jake maneuvered the raft sideways and into the shade that was beginning to form a narrow ribbon of cool darkness along the western cliffs.

"What are those barrels up there?" Lance asked.

"That's a *candelilla* camp with *pilas*." He gave Michelle a pointed look.

She turned to face him, their knees only a few inches apart in the cramped raft. "What's a *pila?*" she asked in a syrupy voice.

"It's the split barrels piled up there." He lowered his voice so only she could hear him. "Are you wanting to start something?" he teased.

She shrugged and whispered, "I just thought your friends would like to hear the whole story about your recent exploits."

Gary asked, "What are you two whispering about? What story?"

"Nothing," said Jake, pulling hard on the oars. "Just lean back awhile and admire the scenery."

After five hours on the river, Jake guided them to the sandy beach on the Mexican side of the river. "We're stopping here for the night."

He helped Michelle out of the raft where she joined Lance and Gary to stare in awe at the opening of a fern-filled arroyo splitting the majestic gray cliffs on both sides of the canyon. No one said a word for several seconds, then Gary voiced Michelle's concern. "Where's that portable potty you were so insistent on bringing?"

Chuckling, Jake dug it out and handed it to Gary. Then he pointed down the beach to a clump of palo-verde trees on a rock ledge. "You can set it there away from camp and the river. Everyone can have a little privacy."

As Michelle helped unload the raft, she marveled at Jake's efficiency in stowing the tents, sleeping bags and cooler, along with her own canvas satchel containing everything she'd packed for the trip. She'd tucked the book Jake had loaned her in it since this might be the last chance she'd have to study the flowers of the region. The thought of never seeing the Rio Grande, Big Bend or the people who had become her friends made her sad.

Maybe she could come back to see Brooke in the fall, even if it was only for a few days. And she would see Jake, too. The realization that she didn't have to leave Sotol Junction forever cheered her up.

Lance took one handle of the heavy cooler she was trying to drag up the beach. "So, you're DeeDee's sister?"

"Yes, I am." Michelle had nervously anticipated the question for the last five hours. "Did you know her?"

"Yeah, we met at the office and I saw her at a few parties. You don't remind me of her at all." He took the cooler and put it near the area Jake had set up to prepare the food.

"I'm not sure whether to take that as a compliment to me or to DeeDee."

"I didn't mean it either way. It's just that you're different. I can't see DeeDee going on this kind of trip or helping unload when there are three men to do it."

Jake looked up when they finished piling the gear at the campsite. "Thanks. Now, if you want to, you've got plenty of time to take a walk and get the kinks out of your legs while I start dinner."

Whistling a show tune, Gary strolled up to the group in time to hear the last part of the conversation. "When do we eat?"

"In about an hour." Jake laid a fire pan in the sand. "If you can find me some dry driftwood for a fire, I might be able to cut the time to fifty-eight minutes."

"I thought you said the guests didn't have to do anything on these trips except take it easy."

"That's right, but you *ain't* a guest."

Gary looked wounded. "If I go get the driftwood, will the food be worthwhile?"

"How about some spaghetti?" Michelle said, laying her hand on Jake's shoulder.

"Oh, hell." Gary frowned and wiped his hands down his chest and over his belly. "My spaghetti-eating shirt is sorta dirty, and I didn't bring my backup."

Lance groaned, "Let's go get that wood for the fire."

"While they find wood, may I help with dinner?" At the surprised look Jake gave her, she explained, "I've learned to do a few things since I moved here, and," she added seductively, "I'm good at following directions."

His eyes showed he'd caught her mood. "Mmm, I've got some pretty good suggestions for later. In the meantime, though, I've got fifty-six minutes left to turn out a meal. If you want to wash up, there's some soap in that duffel bag.''

"I thought you said we couldn't contaminate the river." Michelle remembered Jake's warning about having to carry *everything* out of the canyon, even the toilet tissue.

"It's biodegradable."

"I should have known." And she should have. Jake loved this canyon and would do nothing to harm it. Or Brooke. Or her.

The more she learned about him, the more impressed she was by him, she thought as she watched more than she helped him prepare a gourmet meal. He carefully layered Cornish game hens, asparagus wrapped in red peppers and biscuits in a cast iron Dutch oven half buried in the coals. While that cooked, they set up a folding table, covered it with a tablecloth, and in this wilderness, used ceramic dishes and stainless flatware. Michelle did make herself useful by tossing the prepared salad with avocados and orange sections. As a finishing touch, Jake uncorked a bottle of an award-winning Texas wine.

"My wife doesn't set a table this good when the preacher comes to eat," Gary said as he sat on the cooler.

After dinner, Jake opened a tin of homemade candy. "It's *camote,* a sweet-potato candy Paloma made for *Cinco de Mayo.* Since we're missing the official celebration, I thought you might like to taste the candy everyone back in Sotol will be eating tonight and tomorrow."

By the time they were through, twilight was falling and the canyon had taken on an eerie glow. As a breeze wafted from the water, they sipped the last of the wine, reluctant to break the ambience. But when the brightest stars Michelle had ever seen appeared like glitter in the sky, they all rose and cleaned the area, storing everything away for the night.

Bidding the other two men goodnight, Jake grabbed a flashlight and a sleeping bag, then offered his hand to Michelle. "Come with me. There's something I want to show you."

Seeing the promise in his eyes, she took his hand, acutely aware she was willing to follow him anywhere. A full moon was rising over the distant cliff, bathing the canyon in a silver glow that illuminated the way through the brush and small trees. As the arroyo widened, Michelle spotted a spring-fed pool nestled in the limestone rocks. Momentarily, she was afraid to speak, afraid words would mar the beauty.

Jake stood quietly while Michelle surveyed the fairy-tale scene. Amid large, white boulders, moonlight danced on the water. Ferns hung from the cliffs overhead creating an Eden in the desert. "Why didn't you tell the others about this place?" she whispered in awe.

"I didn't want the others to come with us. I've been wanting to bring you here for a long time." He dropped the sleeping bag on a narrow beach and turned her to face him.

The hastening dusk prevented her from reading all the nuances of Jake's emotions, but the pent-up passion he'd controlled all day shone clearly from his eyes. Since the evening they'd kissed in her kitchen, she'd known she was going to make love to Jake Evans despite the fact it was probably a bad idea.

As if he'd read her mind, he said, "I know we shouldn't be doing this, but I can't just let you walk out of my life without telling you how I feel. Even if these few days are all—"

She interrupted him with a fingertip against his lips. "Shh . . . shh. It won't be. I can come back to visit."

His hands on her arms tightened, digging into the soft flesh. "That won't be enough. I know it won't be for me, and I don't think it will for you."

He was right. A long-distance romance wasn't what she wanted. She wanted to wake up beside him every morning. If she stayed in Sotol Junction with Jake, her mother would never forgive her, but if she left . . . The thought brought tears to her eyes. "I don't know . . ." She shook her head in the faint light as if the movement would suddenly clear her mind and provide a solution.

He dropped his hands to his sides and turned away. His voice was raw when he finally spoke. "Despite my better judgment, I've fallen in love with you, Michelle. And all you can say is you don't know."

"That's not fair, Jake." She wanted to tell him she loved him, too, but that would make the parting harder. "It's just...the past," she whispered, suddenly feeling the three feet separating them could just as well have been a thousand miles. Somehow, this wasn't the way she'd pictured being in love.

"I know. So what do we do?" He ran his fingers through his hair, causing it to come loose, framing his face in a stark darkness that made her knees weak.

"I haven't come up with a good answer." She couldn't ask him to go back to Boston with her, and she knew he wasn't going to ask her to stay with him. Neither could ask that of the other.

Abruptly turning toward the pool, Jake tugged his shirt over his head. "Let's go for a swim. We'll both feel better even if it doesn't solve any of our problems."

She watched him strip to a brief pair of trunks that hugged his body so closely he might as well be wearing nothing. She'd seen parts of his body bare before, but nothing had prepared her for the total picture of his maleness. Standing on the white limestone boulder, his legs spread apart, his raven hair loose around his shoulders and the moonlight caressing his powerful muscles, he looked like an Aztec god.

Before morning she would feel those arms around her, those lips on hers, that skin against hers. The anticipation was almost more than she could bear. She wanted Jake. They'd waited for days for this moment, and though the water looked inviting, what she wanted wasn't a swim.

She stood still as he stepped toward her and took the edge of her T-shirt and slowly, tantalizingly, pulled it over her head. Then he unbuttoned and slipped her shorts down her legs, his fingers brushing the warm flesh of her thighs. Her nerves tingling, she stepped out of the shorts and nudged off her running shoes. Jake tugged the ribbon out of her hair, allowing her blond curls to tumble onto her shoulders.

He ran his fingers through her hair and kissed the tip of her nose. "Come on," he whispered, pulling her up on a higher rock. "We've got all night." He turned from her, letting the desert air fill the void where he'd stood. "The water's deep enough here we can dive safely." Without another word, he plunged into the water below.

Seconds later, Michelle followed, never considering whether it was wise, whether there were eddies or snakes hiding in the dark depths. The truth was, she trusted Jake completely. The blessed coolness of the spring-fed pool washed over her before she rose to the surface and brushed the water from her face. She searched for Jake amid the shadows and rocks, feeling his presence before she saw him. As they lazily circled the small pool, their bodies hovered like two parentheses with the water between them.

Finally, he gestured with one hand toward the rock strewn with their clothes and sleeping bag. She followed his lead into the shallower water where they could stand up. The water reached to her thighs, offering little protection against the cooling air or Jake's sizzling gaze. Waves of longing washed over her.

Jake watched her pull her hair away from her face, twist the water out of it, then shake the strands down her back. The graceful actions tugged at his heart. For weeks, he'd imagined her just this way every time he'd rowed past the arroyo. He'd never felt such a need before, to possess, to protect and cherish. The knowledge she would never be his completely was brushed to the far recesses of his mind.

Her body shimmered in the moonlight as she turned to face him, causing him to groan. As he stepped forward, she looked up at him through damp lashes. "Jake?" Her voice was low and soft, but he heard the desire in her question.

"Mmm?"

"Jake, I don't know what we're doing to do." Nervously, she moistened her lips with the tip of her tongue. "I—"

He silenced her with his lips. "No talking," he murmured against her mouth. The kiss quickly became one of total abandonment. Whether it was the primeval surroundings or the passions long denied, he didn't know, but despite his intention to take things slowly and easily, he buried his hands in her hair and crushed her to him. His mouth twisted on hers searching for fulfillment, for something that would put out the fire inside him.

With a whimper, her lips parted, while her hands came up to tangle in his hair. Matching his own hunger, she moved against his aching body as if pleading with him to release her from the torment he was causing.

Holding her mouth firmly against his with one hand cradled to the back of her head, he allowed his other hand to slide down her neck, her shoulders. Her flesh burned under his exploring fingertips as he gently edged first one bathing-suit strap down, then the other.

Slowly he ended the kiss, wanting to feast his eyes on her high, rounded breasts exposed in the moonlight. Unable to deny himself the pleasure of finally touching the silky globes, he rubbed the backs of his fingers against the soft skin. She was beautiful, better than his fantasies. He felt her tremble when he brushed across her hardening nipples.

She moaned and involuntarily arched her back in a movement so sensual that Jake's knees almost buckled. He was throbbing with the need to make love to her, but he wanted to make the moment last for as long as possible. He was making memories. Memories to get him through the long empty days without her.

Taking her hand, he said, *"Vamos hacer el amor."*

Michelle didn't need a translation. She wanted to make love, too. Stumbling out of the water, her legs too weak to support her weight, she climbed the rocks with his help. When they reached the top, he let go of her hand and spread the sleeping bag on the boulder. Then he turned and pulled her back into his arms. This time his kiss was gentler, more coaxing, as if he were pleading with her to give him everything, her body, her heart and her soul.

What he didn't know was he already possessed them.

HOURS LATER, exhausted and satiated, Michelle lay snuggled against Jake's side. "Won't Lance and Gary be worried when we don't come back?" The question was rhetorical; she really didn't care.

Jake propped up on one elbow and smiled. "Michelle, I left with a bedroll and a beautiful woman. Those two aren't stupid enough to come after me, and I hope they don't think I'm stupid enough to return soon."

She smiled and slid her arm over his shoulder as he rolled to his back and pulled her on top of him. They forgot about Lance and Gary. They forgot about DeeDee and Elizabeth. Only this isolated world composed of Jake and Michelle was real.

WITH DAWN READY to break, the smell of coffee wafted up the rocks to greet Michelle and Jake as they strolled into camp, hand in hand. Lance and Gary grunted a good-morning and resumed drinking.

They didn't seem in the least interested in how Jake and Michelle had spent the night.

"We saved you some cereal." Lance stood up. "But we couldn't find the bananas you said you brought," he said, pouring another couple of cups of coffee and handing one to Michelle while Jake went to find the fruit. "It sure is pretty out here in the morning, isn't it?"

Michelle was grateful for the way he was trying to put her at ease. No wonder Jake claimed him as a friend. "It really is beautiful. I like the desert, too, but this is so different."

Unlike the heat of the desert, the air was cool in the dark canyon. Above them, the tops of the cliffs glowed with the rising sunlight, and swallows darted back and forth in a frenzy to feed their hatchlings. She'd never realized how much life there was in this raw edge of Texas. Even the purple wildflower Gary had sticking out of his T-shirt pocket seemed as lovely as any orchid she'd ever seen.

"Is this a formal breakfast?" she asked, nodding toward the flower.

"Oh, this boutonniere?" He pulled the flower from his pocket and rolled it between his fingers. "Nope. I was just wondering what kind of flower it was. There's a big patch of them down by the bank. Do you know what it is?"

Michelle shook her head. "If they're not roses or daisies, I'm pretty much lost at identifying flowers. Jake may know, and if he doesn't, his field guide is in my canvas bag." She looked at the pile of supplies Jake was rummaging through a short distance away. "Have him get it out for you."

Still clutching his mysterious flower, Gary strolled over to join Jake while Michelle poured herself a bowl of cereal and sat down against a log to eat.

The wonder of the night before still seemed unreal, like a dream, one from which she hoped she would never awaken. Jake's confession of love thrilled her. She knew with a certainty born of love that she was paramount in Jake's life. And he was paramount in hers.

Michelle knew she'd allowed her mother to control her life for too long. For twenty-eight years. Well, it was over. A pang of conscience pierced Michelle as she thought of her mother's lonely existence. She had to keep her mother in her life, but it would be by Michelle's rules now. She and Jake would work something out.

They had to.

When a tanned leg appeared in her peripheral vision, Michelle looked up to see Jake. The welcoming smile died on her face when she saw the cold expression on his face.

"What the hell is this?" His voice laced with anger, he tossed a vellum note card into the sand beside her.

CHAPTER EIGHTEEN

MICHELLE'S HEART plunged to her stomach as she struggled to get up. "It's not what you think. I—"

"I think it's pretty obvious." He lowered his voice so the others couldn't detect the venom. "You double-crossing, two-faced…" He struggled to keep from calling her what she knew he wanted to. "You even stooped to sleeping with me. How low can you get?" He wheeled around and started to leave without waiting for an answer.

"No, Jake." She grabbed at his arm, but he shrugged it off. "Listen. I didn't send Mother's attorney anything. She asked me to, but I refused, so when I got the note yesterday I was just as surprised as you are."

He didn't look at her but stared off across the murky water to the opposite bank. "Elizabeth seems pretty sure you'll testify against me. Someone must have told her you would." He turned his head and glared at her. "I don't think it was a little birdie."

One look at his face told Michelle there was no point arguing with him.

Seconds passed before Jake spoke again in a voice filled with bitterness. "You used me, Michelle. You used me to get to Brooke."

"I didn't. Jake, please, you've got to believe me. I've done nothing wrong."

"Believing you is what got me to this point. I swore I wouldn't fall in love with another woman who cared more about herself and her own agenda than about me. I should have known you were just like your sister."

Michelle flinched at his angry words, but refusing to wilt and play the poor hapless victim, she stared up into his blazing eyes. "I'd love to oblige you and leave Sotol Junction, but I'm not going to desert the kids. However, you're going to eat every word you've said when you realize I've told you the truth." She took a deep breath. "When it sinks through that thick skull of yours, you're going to regret what we could have had."

"Yeah, and what was that? Were you expecting me to come visit you in Boston every couple of weeks? Because you sure as hell weren't planning on staying here."

Michelle bristled at what would have been true only a week ago. "You don't know what I would have done if you'd asked me to stay."

He responded with a dry, disbelieving chuckle. "Are you saying you would have stayed with me if I'd asked?"

She considered not answering the question, but she was growing angrier by the moment, and she wanted to give him something to think about in his lonely bed at night after she was gone. "Yes, Jake. I would have stayed."

"Yeah, sure." She could hear regret in his voice. "I thought I really knew you and I almost believed we had something."

"We did. We do," she whispered.

He shook his head as if trying to deny it to himself. "Get your things. We need to get packed and on the river. I've got clients waiting, and a living to make." With those words, he turned and strolled back up the beach.

With a heavy heart, Michelle watched him walk away from her. Aware there had likely been witnesses to the argument, she looked around for Gary and Lance, but they had discreetly disappeared.

While she went through the motions of packing up the breakfast things, she tried to sort through what had just happened. What hurt the most was that he could think she would make love with him as a ploy to get Brooke.

Jake was trying not to think as he repacked the gear. He was so hurt and angry, he felt disembodied. He could have been a robot tying the coolers into the raft. Gary and Lance must have sensed his mood, because they didn't say a word as they helped him finish loading.

Jake noticed Michelle wouldn't look at him as she climbed over the side of the inflatable raft and settled as far away from him as she could get. She looked so sad. Could she really be acting? Maybe he'd been too hasty. Maybe he should have given her a chance to explain.

Back on the river, he felt the emotional tension seep from his muscles as physical tension took over. He was comfortable here.

It wasn't long before the entrance to Santa Elena Canyon appeared like a slit in a rock wall. A natural cathedral, it towered above them as a testament to the wonders of nature.

Jake watched Michelle turn her face toward the cool air rushing out of the canyon to greet them. The wind teasing her hair exalted her beauty. Could she really be so duplicitous?

The pain caused from the discovery of Elizabeth's note had made him physically ill. When he'd pulled the field guide out of the bag, the paper had fallen to the ground. If he hadn't seen his name when he picked up the note, he wouldn't have read it. He exhaled deeply at the memory and took a big bite of water with the oars. At least he could work off some of his frustrations rowing. Jake figured they might get through the canyon in record time, the way he felt right now.

To Michelle, the morning seemed interminable until finally Jake steered the raft onto one of the few narrow beaches in the canyon. The atmosphere at lunch was a little easier thanks to Lance and Gary. At one point, the three men discussed plans for the company, which gave Michelle time to study her surroundings.

Looking around, she shivered at the realization of the true isolation of this narrow corridor in the earth's crust. Neither helicopters nor radios could intrude in the primeval setting. Despite her anguish, or perhaps because of it, Michelle's eyes misted at the serene beauty.

When they resumed the ride, Jake told them more about the canyon. The ever-deepening chasm would soon tower fifteen hundred feet on either side of them. He also explained that they would experience an optical illusion and think they were floating uphill.

"How much farther is it to the Rock Slide?" Lance asked. "That's what I came for."

"Ten minutes or so," Jake replied. "You should be able to hear it soon."

Michelle had heard about the Rock Slide ever since she'd arrived in Sotol Junction. That people were supposed to have died in the Class IV rapid made it the stuff of legends. Its difficult white-water created by constricted passages required precise maneuvering. Open canoes couldn't pass through, and if anyone got in trouble, rescue was difficult. Michelle had read all that in the brochure earlier. Now, as the faint roar of the rapids could be heard up ahead, those words began to mean something. She was excited and anxious.

If only she could concentrate and relegate her personal problems to another place in her mind, this would be the thrill of a lifetime.

"Make sure your life jackets are strapped on tight," Jake said from his position in the middle of the raft. "And keep your hands and feet in the raft."

Minutes later they reached the spot where tons of rock had sheered off the canyon walls and tumbled into the river restricting the gorge. The Rio Grande wove its way around boulders, some as large as houses.

Jake landed the raft on the Mexican side above the rapids and sized up the situation. "It looks like we can make it, although it's going to be a rough ride. The water from the opened dam has hit, and a four-inch rise in open country can mean a one-foot rise in the Slide, creating suck holes," he explained, coming back to the raft. "We'll see some of those holes. When it's dangerous like this, park rangers often sit on the Texas side and watch for accidents."

The three passengers craned their necks looking up.

"In fact," Jake continued, "in the early 1850s, a survey team scouted the river by sending an empty boat through the Slide to see if the water was navigable. All that came out was planks and splinters."

Michelle wasn't sure how much of what Jake was telling was just hype to get their blood pumping as fast as the rapids, or whether he was preparing them for a treacherous ride.

The sound of the rapids had gotten so loud that Jake had to raise his voice as he explained their route. They would go through the Mexican gate because the Texas gate was clogged with logs and rocks from a previous flash flood, making navigation impossible.

Michelle wrapped her fingers tighter around the ropes to hold on as Jake maneuvered the raft through the first rocks. The roar had become deafening. Conversation was out of the question. At first she was aware of Jake straining at the oars, his face a mask of concentration, but soon she was conscious only of the power of the rapids and the whirlpools that created suck holes.

Despite Jake's efforts, as they passed through the series of gates and falls, the raft was tossed up and down and spun sideways. Sprays of water doused them all from head to toe, splashing their faces until it was hard to see. For a brief moment, the raft leveled out, but just as Michelle relaxed, the front end shot up, then fell into a bottomless chasm. She thought she saw Gary and Lance launched over her head, and just as she was sucked under, she saw gear and supplies whirl around her.

She felt a sharp pain, then nothing until she realized she couldn't breathe. Her chest burned from lack of oxygen. In a moment of sheer panic, she clawed at the watery tomb engulfing her, but despite her life jacket, the current holding her under was too strong for her to surface. She didn't want to die this way, she thought as a wave of unconsciousness washed over her. She hadn't told Jake how much she loved him. She had to live to tell him.

With the last of her energy, she tried once more to surface, then, when she'd almost given up, she felt an arm around her neck and realized someone was struggling to get her above the water. Resisting the urge to fight, she relaxed. The next thing she knew, she was lying on a large flat boulder gasping for breath. She lay still for several seconds until she could breathe regularly. Pushing up on her elbow, she saw Jake stretched out beside her, but Lance and Gary were nowhere to be seen.

Ignoring the dull throb in her head, she crawled over to Jake. "Jake, are you all right?"

"Mmm," he moaned.

She struggled to sit up, then she turned back to him. His skin looked pale. "What's wrong? Where are you hurt?" When she saw his left ankle, she knew.

It was already beginning to swell over his shoe. She reached for the knife at his waist. Jake had explained the first time she'd seen it that all the guides carried one in order to cut people free if they got tangled in the ropes of a capsized raft.

When she unsnapped the sheath, Jake struggled to prop himself up on his elbows. "I'm going to cut off your shoe before your ankle is so swollen we can't," she explained. "Does it hurt very much?"

Through gritted teeth, Jake said, "Like the devil."

Michelle carefully cut the shoe and removed it, then slipped off his sock. When she started to touch his ankle, he stopped her. "Don't," he said. "No need to check. I can tell it's broken."

Michelle knew he was right. "Your ankle needs to be elevated." She looked around for something that would be the right height. "How about my life jacket?"

"Use mine. Just help me get it off."

Afraid she'd jar him, Michelle gingerly helped him shrug out of the jacket, then propped his foot on it. With his ankle in place, she asked, "What happened to Gary and Lance? Did you see them?"

"Yeah. They made it past the suck holes. I saw them floating toward the mouth of the canyon. There's a phone there, and they'll call Greg. He'll send someone in after us. But it'll probably be morning before anyone gets here. So I guess we're stuck."

"That doesn't worry me much, but I'm worried about your injury."

"There's not much else we can do but wait." He lay back down as if the exertion of sitting up had sapped his strength.

Michelle knew he was in a lot of pain. If they had to stay here for fifteen hours they were going to need water. Though she'd already swallowed a cupful of water when the raft capsized, the thought of purposely drinking from the polluted Rio Grande wasn't appealing. "I'm going to look and see if any of our supplies washed up on the rocks."

"Be careful," Jake mumbled. "Those wet rocks are awfully slippery, and if you fall back in..." He didn't finish his sentence.

"I'll be careful," she assured him. "I'll keep my life jacket on." When she was sure Jake was as comfortable as she could possibly make him, she set out to look for their supplies.

White water roared and swirled below her as she climbed over the boulders that littered the canyon floor. Her search was fruitful. She found the cooler wedged between two rocks, and though she couldn't dislodge it, she could get food and water out of it, as needed. She located two ripped and soggy sleeping bags, dragged them up on the rocks and spread them out to dry. Last night, Jake's arms had shielded her from the desert's chill, but tonight, if he went into shock, he'd need more warmth than she could give him. Maybe in the remaining hours of sunlight, the bags would dry out.

Farther down the canyon, Michelle found the old, waterproof ammo box Jake stored the camera and first-aid supplies in. Using a stick, she managed to fish the box over close enough that she could get it. She saw other supplies caught on the other side of the river, but there was no way she could reach them.

Pleased with her success, she hurried back to Jake. "Look what I found," she said, setting the ammo box on the rock and opening it. "Here's some painkillers. Would you like one?"

"I'd like to take the whole damn bottle." He grimaced when he moved to gulp down the two pills she offered him.

Twilight came early, and as the shadows slowly covered the canyon, Michelle lay on the rock beside Jake. She nestled as closely to him as she could without making him uncomfortable. She needed to keep him warm since the sleeping bags were still slightly damp. But when she felt his body convulse in shivers, she knew she had to do more. Taking matches from the ammo box, she built a campfire from the driftwood she'd managed to scrounge earlier.

Soon the fire was licking the darkness with tongues of flame. Above them, starlight flickered through pinpricks in the narrow black ribbon of sky. Transfixed by the surrounding light and the roar of the rapids, Michelle wished she could share her feelings with Jake. Now, finally, her soul understood the hold this land had on him.

With her head propped on her knees, Michelle studied Jake, who seemed to have gotten some relief from the medication and had fallen into a fitful rest. His mouth was set hard. Not even in sleep was he able to relax. She reached over and touched his forehead for the tenth time, checking to see if he was going into shock. His skin was smooth, not clammy. She brushed the hair away from his temple and, noticing how the tiny gold loop in his ear glinted in the firelight, she traced her finger over it.

She remembered how much like a pirate Jake had looked when she'd first seen him. Cold and foreboding. Dangerous. Until he'd seen Brooke. Never would Michelle have imagined that one day he might look at her with that same warmth, or how much she would grow to love him. Or how messed up their lives could get.

Though she didn't think he could hear her, she explained what her mother had wanted her to do and how she'd resisted. She told him how much she loved this place and how she wanted to stay with him.

When she had said all there was to say, she got up to check the sleeping bags. The fire had almost completed the job the sun and wind had begun. One of the bags was dry enough to use. She had carried it to Jake and knelt down to spread it across his bare legs when she saw a slight movement to his right. Rising up on her knees to see what it was, she looked down at the shadowed triangle formed by Jake's body and the rock. Bile rose in her throat.

"Oh my God," she moaned.

She tried to move but couldn't. Only her thoughts and heart raced as a snake slithered to rest along the warmth of Jake's side. She didn't know what kind of snake it was. What if it was poisonous? Like the one that bit Mike? What if the reptile bit Jake? He'd die before help got here. But she couldn't force herself to move. She was paralyzed.

IT LOOKED as if the entire adult population and half the children of Sotol Junction were gathered in front of Junction Outfitters at midnight when Cynthia pulled into the caliche parking lot.

Paloma watched her climb stiffly from the Jeep and look around for her husband. Mike was spearheading the loading of a raft on the trailer as Greg, Wesley and Eduardo hustled together other equipment. "What's going on?" Cynthia asked no one in particular.

Hearing her voice, Mike whirled and swung her into his arms. "Damn, woman, but it's good to see you!" He gave her a big kiss. "I didn't think you were going to be here until tomorrow."

"I left as soon as you called. Oh, honey, I'm sorry..."

Paloma didn't hear the rest of the conversation amid all the commotion, but she watched Mike go over to the Jeep and give his sleeping daughter a kiss. It was good to see that little family back together, yet she wondered how Cynthia would react when she heard about Jake and Michelle.

She didn't have to wonder long because Cynthia and Mike returned arm in arm. After hugging Paloma, Cynthia, her voice full of tears said, "I'm sorry to hear about the accident."

"Jake told us it would be a hell of a ride," Gary told them, still sounding a little shaky from the harrowing experience. "I don't think he anticipated just how hard it would be."

"You never know what the Slide will be like from one time to the next," Mike explained. "But Jake's the best guide around." He turned to Greg and Wesley as they walked up. "The park rangers will be waiting for you at the river." His voice was filled with frustration and regret. "I'll bring the van around to the mouth of the canyon and wait."

Paloma knew the rangers were joining the search because their help might be needed. Lance and Gary had seen Jake but they hadn't seen Michelle before they were swept away.

Cynthia clutched Mike's arm. "You've got to go, too, Mike."

Mike visibly relaxed. "Honey, are you sure?"

"Yes. They're our friends." She kissed him on the cheek. "I'll be waiting when you get back."

As they watched, the team scrambled into the van, Paloma felt Prof drape his arm over her shoulder and pull her close in comfort.

"My daddy will be okay, won't he?" Brooke asked. She'd remained quiet during all the preparations and chaos.

"Of course he will." Paloma assured her. "He's a resourceful man."

"Um, I know. Besides, Aunt Michelle will protect him," the little girl said, then yawned.

"Yes. Now, why don't you lie down in the back for a while. It's after midnight."

After Brooke was tucked in on the sofa in the crowded office, Paloma went back out front where Prof was waiting with a cup of hot coffee. "I figured you were planning on staying here for the night," he said.

Paloma nodded. "I think Brooke will feel safer and I want to be here if there's any word."

Prof slipped his hands on either side of her face and held her cheeks with loving tenderness. "You're some woman, Paloma Tarango."

Smiling, she took his face in her hands. At this late stage of her life, Paloma was glad to have a soul mate, someone who was making her days—and nights—warmer. "And you're some man, Professor Broselow. For an Anglo."

STILL ON HER KNEES, Michelle watched the snake for what seemed like hours. Never taking her eyes off the shadowy reptile, she willed Jake not to move. "Oh, God," she prayed, "let the snake crawl away."

When Jake started moaning, Michelle snapped out of her trance. She couldn't let him get bitten. "Jake, don't move," she whispered above the roar of the water. She didn't know if she believed the kids about snakes being deaf, but she wasn't going to take a chance.

"Don't move," she whispered again. "There's a snake against your other side. Don't move. Please, don't move." After she repeated it three times, he seemed to understand.

He focused his eyes on Michelle. "What kind?"

"I don't know, but I think it's brown with lighter stripes."

Jake breathed slowly as if trying not to move. "Does it have rattlers?"

Keeping her body rigid, Michelle stretched her neck trying to get a better view. "I can't see it that well."

"Where exactly is it?" Jake's voice echoed Michelle's in its control.

"If you stretched out your fingers, you could touch it." The thought sent a wave of adrenaline through her body. "What can I do? How can I kill it?"

"Can you reach a good-size rock?"

Finally daring to turn her head a little, Michelle glanced around the area. "There's one a few feet to my right."

"Back up slowly and pick it up."

With every ounce of determination she could muster, Michelle inched toward the rock and picked it up.

Jake licked his lips. "When I say three, I'm going to roll toward you as fast as I can. You get the snake." His eyes searched hers for agreement.

She hoisted the rock above her head and nodded.

The moment Jake moved, Michelle lunged, smashing the rock down on the snake's head. She grabbed another boulder and struck the writhing body again and again.

Finally, she collapsed in a heap on Jake's chest. His arms came up to encircle her and he gently stroked her back and her hair as she sobbed. He said, "There. There. You did it. You got him."

"I...thought...it was going to...kill you," she said through her tears. "And I wasn't going to...be able to stop him."

"Shh...shh. It's all right." As her sobs subsided, his arms tightened and became more demanding. "You were brave." He clutched her to him as if he would never let her go.

After several minutes, she drew back and wiped her eyes with the back of her hand. "I was afraid I was going to lose you, and you would never know how I really felt about you. *Te amo.*"

He pulled her back to him and kissed her. "Say it again," he whispered against her mouth. "Tell me you love me again."

"*Te amo. Te amo,*" she repeated over and over.

"I thought you were never going to speak to me in Spanish."

"That was the second phrase I practiced to say to you."

"What was the first?"

"Let's just say I heard it on the playground at school, and it seemed appropriate. Especially about seven this morning."

"About that." Jake struggled to sit up. "I think I knew down deep you hadn't lied to me, but it was there in black and white." He kissed her again. *"Te amo."*

"But we still have a problem. Mother will try to get custody of Brooke."

"She'll have a hard time when you and I are married. Did you mean it when you said you would stay in Sotol?"

"Yes, I meant it. I've grown to love it here." She looked around them. In the growing dawn, the limestone looked pink. "Well, maybe not this rock exactly."

He chuckled weakly, "Wesley and Greg better get here soon. I've been macho for about as long as I can stand. What I want to do is scream."

"I wish there was something I could do."

"You've done it. I'm the happiest man alive right now, and I've got a broken ankle."

They lay wrapped in each other's arms thinking and planning for the future. "Do you think it will bother you that I was married to DeeDee?" Jake asked after a while.

"I don't think so," she said. "There may be times when I feel awkward, but I think I can work through it. Take this trip, for instance. At first it bothered me that Gary and Lance had known you and DeeDee as a couple. I felt like they were comparing us and that maybe I didn't measure up.''

''Honey, please don't ever think that. No one compares to you.''

Michelle relaxed. He'd said the words she wanted to hear. She'd never felt quite pretty enough, vivacious enough, daring enough. But would DeeDee have been able to save Jake? She knew the answer, just as she knew she would never again wonder whether she was good enough.

''Our problem,'' Jake said, ''is that we were both afraid of being vulnerable, so we kept our feelings inside.''

''Communicating is hard, though,'' Michelle agreed. ''Take Cynthia and Mike. They really didn't talk to each other, and look what a mess they got in.''

''Let's make a pact not to let that happen to us in the future,'' he said. ''Promise me you will always talk to me about the way you feel.''

''I promise.'' She squeezed Jake's hand, leaned back against the rock and looked at the narrow band of dawn forming above them. She was filled with peace and a sense of belonging. And she knew, with stunning clarity, that she belonged here in this awesome country with Jake Evans.

CHAPTER NINETEEN

LATE THE NEXT afternoon, Michelle, exhausted, walked into her house. She'd left Jake in the hospital at Alpine with a new pin holding his ankle together. Dozens of people had either called or driven the sixty miles from Sotol Junction to see him. Prof and Paloma had brought Brooke to visit but didn't stay long. Prof had joked about needing to get back to a domino game. Already the group was trying to come up with a new name for Junction Outfitters. Something more appropriate like the Crutch Club, or Joint Outfitters.

Jake had laughed and offered a few suggestions of his own. Despite the accident, Lance and Gary signed the contract to bring their clients and employees river rafting. They, too, had joked about the great story they had to tell when they got back to Houston.

Michelle still shivered at the thought of the snake and how close she had come to losing the man she loved. Nothing was going to separate them again, she thought, as she flung a toothbrush and underwear into an overnight bag. She wanted to get back to the hospital as soon as she could. But first, Michelle had to do something she was not looking forward to. She had to call her mother.

She straightened her back and walked over to the phone to deliver the speech she'd rehearsed during the drive from Alpine. On the eighth ring, Michelle wilted just a little, afraid that any delay would sap her courage. Then, just as she started to hang up the phone, she heard her mother say, "Hello."

Her own tone confident and sure, Michelle began, "Hello, Mother. I..."

"Michelle, it's about time you called. I talked to Brooke earlier and she told me there'd been an accident and that she's staying the night with some friend called Katy because Jacob is in the hospital. That is what I've been..."

Twisting the phone cord around her finger, Michelle interrupted her mother. "Yes, it's true, Mother, but..."

"Michelle, I want you *away* from that man. Any man who would..."

Michelle held the phone out in front of her face and stared at the receiver. She didn't need to put it to her ear. She could hear everything Elizabeth Davis was loudly proclaiming from over two thousand miles away.

With each passing second Michelle grew angrier. Finally, she closed her eyes, took a deep breath and said, "Mother, just be quiet and listen to me. *Please,*" She hadn't rehearsed the *please.*

"I beg your pardon," Elizabeth said, her voice sounding stunned.

"I mean it, Mother. I have something important to tell you. If you interrupt me, even one time, I'll hang up the phone and write you a letter. Do you understand?"

"Michelle, you have lost your mind. You've never been rude to me before."

"I'm not being rude, Mother. I'm just not going to allow you to tell me what to do with my life anymore. Although I do want to thank you for suggesting I come to Sotol Junction. Now, are you ready to listen?"

"It doesn't seem that I have much of a choice, does it?" Elizabeth sniffed.

"No, you don't." Michelle, buoyed by her own words and Elizabeth's acquiescence, continued. "Mother, never again are you to criticize Jake Evans to me. Not as a man and not as a father. Brooke idolizes her father and with good reason. He takes time for her. She knows what he does, and he knows what she does—every day. They're a family, Mother. So I want you to call off your lawyer!"

The next part of the conversation was harder. Michelle didn't want to hurt her mother. Elizabeth hadn't recovered from losing DeeDee and Michelle didn't want her to think she was losing a second daughter. "Mother, I'll be sending my resignation to Ms. Delmonico in the next few days because I plan to teach in Sotol Junction next year. These children need me. Really need me.'' Michelle thought of Pablo who'd come with his uncle to see Jake in the hospital. Pablo had told her he'd moved in with Eduardo and wouldn't miss another day—if she'd help him with algebra. ''But the best part, Mother, is that Jake has asked me to marry him. I said yes.''

Other than a short gasp, the line was quiet.

Michelle continued, ''We haven't set a date, but it will be a June wedding. I'll want you to come help plan the wedding. That will give you some time to really get to know Jake. Then you'll understand why I love him.''

With all my heart, body and soul.

EPILOGUE

Sotol Junction
August 8

THE PADDLE FAN whirring above the heads of the domino players hardly budged the hot mid-August air. Prof clenched his pipe between his teeth while Paloma stared unrelentingly at his mouth. "I've made a big concession, Paloma. It's not lit." He tipped the pipe bowl to reveal tamped-down, dry tobacco. "You're going to have to get used to this thing if you want to date me." He winked and flashed her a knowing smile.

"That's because it's too hot to light it." She bantered back, knowing it was useless to scold Prof for smoking. Besides, time was on her side. Paloma turned her attention to Mike. She was glad he'd taken the afternoon off to relax. He and Jake had been so busy with new business that even Michelle had pitched in. Cynthia had helped until it had gotten so hot. Thinking of Cynthia, Paloma's voice filled with concern. "Is this heat giving Cynthia any problems with her pregnancy?"

"Not a one," Mike answered, leaning forward in the chair and pulling a neatly folded handkerchief out of his hip pocket. "Katy's the problem—she's an impatient little cuss. Wants her brother or sister *tomorrow*."

Paloma laughed in acknowledgment. "Yesterday, when she and Brooke were in the shop, they were figuring out a way to badger Jake and Michelle into having a baby."

"Wouldn't be a bad idea at all." Wiping the sweat beads off his brow, he finally played a domino. Pouring himself another glass of iced tea, Mike downed half of it. "The Good Lord knows it's too hot to work, and it's damn near too hot to play dominoes. Katy says it's too hot to start school Monday, too."

"I know. We've got to get a larger cooling unit for school." Paloma scanned the group. "I think that needs to be an agenda item next week."

"Well, I don't think school should start in the middle of August, but chalk it up to our legislators," Bill Wiley said. "Those idiots don't have as much sense as my dumbest ole heifer cow." His head punctuated his words while he pulled a wadded-up handkerchief from his hip pocket to wipe his own forehead.

"Why don't you run for the legislature, Bill? You'd fit right in." Prof flashed Paloma an amused look over his wire-framed glasses. "You could get a law passed so Texas schools don't start until after Labor Day."

"Having someone in Austin with a little common sense wouldn't hurt 'em none," Bill said.

Paloma held her fist to her mouth and coughed, trying to smother the laughter she felt erupting.

Oblivious, Bill flipped a domino over and over on its sides while he screwed up his mouth in thought. "You know, seeing as how Jake had the sense to marry us a schoolteacher, I *don't* have any pressing concerns to take care of this year. I just might investigate that possibility."

Paloma kicked Prof under the table and gave him a see-the-monster-you've-created look until he held up both palms in submission.

Prof cleared his throat. "But, Bill, what if Michelle gets pregnant and decides to stay home next year? We'd be back to square one—needing a teacher."

"Ah, hell. I didn't think of that. That means—"

"That it's time to play dominoes." Paloma pointed to the board.

COMING NEXT MONTH

#706 DANIEL • Tracy Hughes
Return to Calloway Corners
Daniel Calloway's father is getting out of jail. And Daniel's
come back home to set the record straight. The last time he
was in Calloway Corners—with Becca Harris, the only
woman he's ever loved—a man was killed. That man was
Becca's father, the town preacher, and Daniel's father was
found guilty. Can Daniel and Becca rise above the past and
build a future for themselves?

#707 TEXAS STANDOFF • Ruth Alana Smith
Home on the Ranch
E. Z. Winston has one love—the land her father left her.
Then city slicker Colin Majors washes into her life on the
tide of a flash flood. They share a night of passion that leads
to a bond neither anticipated, and E.Z. soon finds herself in
over her head. In more ways than one....

#708 THE MAN NEXT DOOR • Ellen James
The man next door has problems. He's an ex-cop, turned
P.I., pretending to be a writer. He has a partner who's pretending she's pregnant. His son isn't pretending anything,
but then, the boy's barely talking to him. And to top it off,
he's becoming dangerously attracted to the woman next
door, a woman he's been paid to investigate, a woman who
just might be pretending that she *hasn't* murdered her husband.

#709 A SUITABLE BODYGUARD • Kathryn Shay
Family Man
Cord McKay has quit the New York police force and come
home to raise his little girl in the small town where he was
born. He needs a job, but the last thing he wants to do is act
as bodyguard to Stacey Webb, daughter of the one man who
knows why Cord fled town as a teenager. The problem is
that Stacey's in real danger. And even though she doesn't
remember what happened eighteen years ago, Cord does—
and he owes her big time.

REBECCA

43 LIGHT STREET

YORK

FACE TO FACE

Bestselling author Rebecca York returns to "43 Light Street" for an original story of past secrets, deadly deceptions—and the most intimate betrayal.

She woke in a hospital—with amnesia...and with child. According to her rescuer, whose striking face is the last image she remembers, she's Justine Hollingsworth. But nothing about her life seems to fit, except for the baby inside her and Mike Lancer's arms around her. Consumed by forbidden passion and racked by nameless fear, she must discover if she is Justine...or the victim of some mind game. Her life—and her unborn child's—depends on it....

Don't miss *Face To Face*—Available in October, wherever Harlequin books are sold.

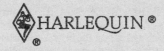

HARLEQUIN ®

®

43FTF

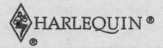

HARLEQUIN SUPERROMANCE®

If you've always felt there's something special about a
man raising a family on his own...you won't want to
miss Harlequin Superromance's touching series

**He's sexy, he's single...and he's a father!
Can any woman resist?**

A SUITABLE BODYGUARD
by Kathryn Shay

Cord McKay has quit the New York Police force and come
home to raise his little girl in the small town where he was
born. He needs a job but the last thing he wants to do is act
as bodyguard to Stacey Webb, daughter of the one man
who knows why Cord fled town as a teenager. The problem
is that Stacey's in real danger. And even though she
doesn't remember what happened eighteen years ago,
Cord does...and he owes her big time.

Available in September

Be sure to watch for this and upcoming FAMILY MAN
titles. Fall in love with our sexy fathers, each determined
to do the best he can for his kids.

Look for them wherever Harlequin books are sold.

HARLEQUIN SUPERROMANCE®

Come West with us!

In Superromance's series of Western romances, you can visit a ranch—and fall in love with a man of the West!

In September, watch for

Texas Standoff
by Ruth Alana Smith

Let us take you to Cheyenne Moon Ranch, in the Texas Hill Country

Rancher Elise (E.Z.) Winston, who runs the most successful spread in the county, knows how to stand up for herself, her rights and her ranch. But when she rescues Dallas lawyer Colin Majors from a flash flood, she soon finds herself in over her head—in more ways than one.... *A story full of Texas spunk and Texas speak!*

Look for upcoming HOME ON THE RANCH titles wherever Harlequin books are sold.

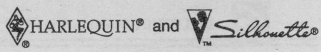

are proud to present...

HERE COME THE
GROOMS™

Four marriage-minded stories written by top
Harlequin and Silhouette authors!

Next month, you'll find:

A Practical Marriage	by Dallas Schulze
Marry Sunshine	by Anne McAllister
The Cowboy and the Chauffeur	by Elizabeth August
McConnell's Bride	by Naomi Horton

ADDED BONUS! In every edition of
Here Come the Grooms you'll find $5.00 worth
of coupons good for Harlequin and Silhouette
products.

On sale at your favorite Harlequin and Silhouette
retail outlet.

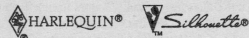